DEADLY VALENTINE

By Carolyn G. Hart

DEADLY VALENTINE

CAROLYN G. HART

A CRIME CLUB BOOK
DOUBLEDAY
New York *London* *Toronto* *Sydney* *Auckland*

A Crime Club Book
PUBLISHED BY DOUBLEDAY

a division of Bantam Doubleday Dell Publishing Group, Inc.
666 Fifth Avenue, New York, New York 10103

DOUBLEDAY and the portrayal of a man
with a gun are trademarks of Doubleday,
a division of Bantam Doubleday Dell
Publishing Group, Inc.

ISBN 0-385-26518-2

To all Sisters in Crime:
Wishing you
Good books
Good luck
God's blessing.

DEADLY VALENTINE

ONE

The face might have been sculpted in stone. It wasn't simply from absorption in a delicate, tedious task. Oh no. It was more than that. Much more. The taut muscles reflected icy determination, ruthless decision, implacable resolve.

The gloved hand worked patiently, skillfully, with the cut-out letters, plucking them from their separate piles, applying glue with a toothpick, placing them neatly against the heart, scissored from scarlet construction paper.

Finally, it was done. A derisive, merciless smile touched the artist's mouth.

TWO

Sydney Cahill was determined not to cry.

Crying made your eyes red and swollen.

And it never helped.

Despite her resolution, more hot tears welled. She grabbed a tissue and carefully patted her eyes dry. Swallowing jerkily, she leaned anxiously toward the mirror. Did she look dreadful? Soft black hair framed a face as delicate and translucent as porcelain. When Howard fell in love with her, he had told her she had skin as smooth as a gardenia. "Your hair, your eyes . . ." In her memory, his voice was soft, tender, loving.

Now he was cold and aloof. Now his eyes didn't follow her when she crossed the room. Now there were no more presents, no more surprises. Now he didn't come to her.

Frantically, she reached across her dresser for her jewel case. Opening it, her eyes darted from memento to memento. That jade pin, from Carl. The little intaglio ring of onyx, from Bruce. She smiled tremulously. Oh, that lovely butterfly pin, a golden filigree inset with crystals, from Bobby.

Her breathing quieted. She picked up one piece, then another, remembering the giver and the love.

Without warning, tears brimmed again, hiding the bright glitter of the stones, the glisten of the gold.

Sydney snapped shut the jewel case and stumbled to her feet. She ran to her bath and splashed water on her face. Her reflection was blurred in the mirror. Gently, Sydney caressed her skin with the soft face towel and remembered the night that Howard had dried her body, wet from the hot tub, in a luxurious beach towel and . . .

Love.

Her heart cried out for love.

THREE

Joel Graham typed slowly, clumsily. His dad had made him take typing last year instead of study hall. As usual, he had put forth as little effort as possible. Still, it had almost been worth the boring time it took, because his dad got him an Apple computer and Jesus, it did make school easier. Old hag-face Thompson, the typing teacher, was right about that. And all those neat games! Joel finished typing the title of the essay. The stupid required essay.

AN EMBARRASSMENT OF ROCHES.

He snickered and spaced back to make the correction.

AN EMBARRASSMENT OF RICHES.

Mrs. Borelli made them write one goddam essay after another. And she picked the topics. So what was he going to write about? What did he have too much of?

Then he thought what he had that probably not one other stud in the senior class had! Goddam, wouldn't he love to write it all down. Women lusting for him. Older women. He could have them whenever he wanted. At least he could have until yesterday afternoon. That had been a hell of a deal. He still felt half mad, sending him home like he was a kid, his pants unzipped. But it had its funny side, too. He'd never forget the look on their faces. Two of them. Hot for his body! Be a hoot to write it all down. Mrs. Borelli would have a seizure.

Joel moused the cursor backward, wrote:

AN EMBARRASSMENT OF BITCHES

He moved uncomfortably in his chair. Shit, it made him horny. He glanced at the clock. Maybe he could get some later tonight.

FOUR

Annie Laurance Darling was in a snit, which she thought she'd successfully concealed from her husband.

It didn't help her mood when Max grinned at her, that devil-may-care, damnably *attractive* grin, as they parted on the fog-shrouded boardwalk, each destined for his own establishment of business, and said cheerily, "Hope you feel better soon."

"I feel fine," she'd retorted furiously.

A benevolent smile, this time, which almost prompted her to explode, but she contained her outrage until she'd slammed shut the front door of Death on Demand, which rustled the line of decorative lace-edged red valentines strung above the center aisle.

"Fine!" she said aloud. Her voice echoed down the central corridor of her beloved mystery bookstore. She flicked on the front lights.

Tiny claws clicked against the polished heart pine floor and the new feline, Dorothy L., frolicked into view. She was already purring.

Annie reached down to pick up the kitten, then paused as an awesome growl reverberated, competitive on a sound scale with a Peterbilt truck in fourth gear and straining.

"Oh, Agatha," Annie said sadly.

Agatha crouched atop the bookcase devoted to Agatha Christie, for whom she was named. Amber eyes glowing with fury and heartbreak, the sleek, elegant black cat revved her growl another notch.

Annie stepped toward the bookcase, hand outstretched. "Agatha, love, please don't be so angry. Please. I still love you. You're the Number One cat, the best cat, the prettiest black cat in the whole world!"

A whip-quick paw, claws extended, snaked through the air, a livid scratch welled blood on the back of Annie's hand, and a flash of ebony signaled Agatha's abrupt departure into the darkness of the American Cozy area, between the south wall and a row of diagonal bookcases.

Dorothy L. twined around Annie's ankles, her good humor undiminished by the older cat's rage.

Annie grabbed a Kleenex from the box behind the cash desk and pressed it against the bleeding scratch, then sighed, scooped up the kitten, and started down the central aisle to the back of Death on Demand. Her goal was the coffee bar, which also, most importantly to felines, was the feeding area.

"Agatha doesn't mean to be ugly, Dorothy L. But she's heartbroken. You see, she was the *only* cat. She's dreadfully jealous of you."

Dorothy L., her purr a paean of happiness, wiggled from Annie's hand and wobbled up her arm to poke a tiny pink nose in her ear.

Putting the kitten down behind the coffee bar, Annie opened a can most succulently labeled CHOICE CUTS AND CHEESE, which she apportioned into two bowls. "Agatha, come here. Breakfast time."

Agatha, of course, didn't come. As Cleveland Amory explains so clearly in his delightful book, cats don't "come."

"You don't want to cut off your nose to spite your face," Annie called as she measured water and coffee.

No Agatha.

"Agatha, it's childish and silly to be jealous."

No Agatha. Dorothy L. finished her bowl and stepped to the second.

"And you're going to be rotund. You can't eat for two cats." Scooping up the fluffy white kitten, Annie carried her back up the center aisle, tucked her on an afghan behind the checkout counter, and went in search of Agatha.

She found her finally, hunkered beneath the delicate fronds of a Whitmanii fern.

Agatha would not be cajoled, entreated, or enticed, ignoring even a fresh offering of salmon. The look in her burning eyes would have daunted even Nero Wolfe.

Defeated, Annie walked morosely to the coffee bar. She studied the shelves filled with mugs. Upon each mug was inscribed the title of a famous mystery. Annie picked up NO HERO, in honor of John P. Marquand's first Mr. Moto book, because Annie clearly was no hero to a certain enraged cat. She poured a cup of Kahlúa Fudge. But not even the sinfully delicious brew could lift her spirits. Annie felt like a criminal, a betrayer, a heartbreaker. And anybody who didn't think a cat could be jealous, unforgivingly, furiously, pitiably jealous, just didn't know much about cats.

Or people, came the insidious thought.

She was *not* jealous.

Of course not.

She was too mature, too certain of her relationship with Max ever to harbor the *faintest* inkling of jealousy.

Agatha stalked into view, her eyes seeking the hated kitten. Reaching the bowls, she sniffed, growled again, low in her throat, then bit into her food.

"Don't growl and eat," Annie warned. "It will ruin your digestion."

Agatha ate, growled, ate, growled.

Annie sipped her coffee.

"It isn't the same thing at all," she told Agatha conversationally. But Annie's innate honesty wouldn't let that pass. "All right," she added irritably. "Maybe you have a point, Agatha."

The parallels were too clear.

Agatha had been secure in her world until the abrupt, heart-stopping advent of a competitor for Annie's affection and attention. Annie's soothing explanations that Dorothy L. was a foundling, an abandoned waif, helpless in the alley behind Death on Demand meant absolutely nothing to Agatha.

There *were* substantial differences in the two situations.

"I mean, I *know* Max isn't interested. I mean, it isn't his fault that witch lives next door. And I'm *not* a jealous person."

Even as she spoke, however, she felt hot all over, reliving the blaze of anger that had swept over her that morning.

It was so *outrageous*. There she and Max were, enjoying an early breakfast outside on their patio, taking delight in the changing landscape as the fog rolled in. It was a very private patio, so they'd felt quite comfortable to be outdoors in their nightclothes, she in a shorty cotton gown, Max in his boxer shorts and a T-shirt. Luscious in his boxer shorts. And up sauntered their next-door neighbor, Sydney Cahill, in a damn peach negligee just millimeters shy of sheer. At seven o'clock in the morning! Annie's mood was not improved by the fact that Sydney, whose mammillary endowment was spectacular, had to be the best-looking woman on Broward's Rock Island. On the island, hell! On the entire coast of South Carolina! And she'd had the temerity not only to join them, but to *drape* herself in the chair next to Max and lean close as she talked to him, revealing magnificent cleavage. Deliberately. Provocatively. With Annie sitting there!

"Outrageous!" Annie snapped aloud. "As far as she was concerned, I might as well have been a damn palm tree!"

Agatha's shoulders tensed.

"But I'm not jealous!" Annie insisted to glittery-eyed Agatha.

She reached down, tried to rub behind Agatha's ears. A truly horrendous growl erupted. Annie yanked back her hand to avoid bared teeth.

What a mess—an inconsolable cat and an irresistible husband who thought the wiles of a predatory female were *funny!* And a commitment to go to a party—tonight—where that witch could fling herself at Max again. Sydney was, after all, going to be their hostess and one could not ignore one's hostess.

Funny! What was funny about a gorgeous woman in a see-through negligee taking a dead set at someone's husband at the veritable crack of dawn? And Annie couldn't deny Sydney's beauty. Sydney was hauntingly lovely: enormous, soulful emerald-green eyes, hair so richly black it glistened like a moonlight-silvered midnight sea, a striking face remarkable for deep-set eyes, hollow cheeks, and tremulous, vulnerable mouth.

Annie didn't have to look in a mirror to tot up her own attributes—

sandy hair, serious gray eyes, a nice-enough nose sprinkled with freckles, a stubborn jaw. Fresh and wholesome, sure.

But not glamorous, by any means.

The phone rang.

Annie wondered if she would always give a slight start at Ma Bell's peal. Would she forever associate the telephone with her mother-in-law? Not that she didn't adore Laurel. But there was always the possibility—even Max had to admit it—that a call from his mother presaged difficulties, of one sort or another. Not that Laurel ever intended to cause trouble. Oh no. Laurel *meant* well.

Annie pondered the ringing phone. *Three, four.* Ingrid, her wonderful assistant, wouldn't be in until after lunch. Actually, the work load didn't require two of them, but Annie insisted that Ingrid come. February afternoons were too quiet and she and Ingrid could plan special events for summer when the tourists would be there in force. The island didn't exactly teem with visitors in February, despite the Chamber of Commerce's optimistic christening of the winter doldrums as the Adventure Season. However, it truly was the best time of year for shell seekers, and Max assured her that February was a fisherman's delight, flounder and spottail bass plentiful in the salt marsh creeks, plus lots of cobia and black and red drum. Thirty-five miles offshore at the Snapper Banks, fishing was good for black sea bass. And sixty-five miles out in the Atlantic was the Gulf Stream with plenty of fighting game fish—marlin, sailfish, wahoo, dolphin, and barracuda. This year the world's weather pattern was screwy and it had been uncommonly warm, which accounted for this morning's fog. Amber billows of fog normally wreathed the island in March. *Seven, eight.*

Annie lifted the receiver. "Death on Demand." Annie considered Death on Demand to be quite the most perfect name for a mystery bookstore. Admittedly, there were many mystery bookstores around the country with marvelous names: Grounds for Murder in San Diego, The Scene of the Crime in Los Angeles, The Footprints of a Gigantic Hound in Tucson, The Raven in Lawrence, Scotland Yard in Winnetka, Criminal Proceedings in Milwaukee, Once Upon a Crime in Minneapolis, Whodunit in Philadelphia, Booked for Murder in Madison, The Butler Did It in Baltimore, Murder Undercover in Cambridge, and the original Murder Ink in New York.

But nothing topped Death on Demand.

"Annie, my sweet, I do sometimes feel that we are *led.*"

Annie's hand tightened spasmodically on the receiver. God. Was she turning psychic? No. Absolutely not. She didn't believe in that nonsense. She'd merely thought about Laurel when the phone rang because Max's mother called a lot. So why shouldn't it be Laurel?

The husky, unforgettable voice—a mixture of Lauren Bacall, Marlene

Dietrich, and wood nymph—gamboled over the line. "Providential, I have no *doubt*. Do you know what I think?"

Annie might predict the next president, prognosticate about Edgar and Agatha awards, even foretell the gyrations of the stock market, but she would never, ever presume to hazard a guess at the dizzy twists and turns of her mother-in-law's mind.

Despite the little quiver of apprehension always present in any dealings with Laurel, Annie began to smile. "No, Laurel, what do you think?"

"The work of Saint Valentine, of course."

Had she missed something? Annie shook her head a little, but it didn't help. She was reduced, as was often the case, to helpless repetition. "Saint Valentine?"

"Of course. Can there be any doubt? After all, it *is* Saint Valentine's Day. I did think it was quite unkind that he was dropped from the Calendar of Saints. Along with Saint Christopher. *Such* a disappointment for travelers. But we all know about Saint Valentine. And I, for one, shall *always* believe in him. And today has only reaffirmed my faith. Oh my dear, to have one's heart *sing!* Even I, experienced in love as I am . . ."

As the husky voice flowed on, Annie raised a jaundiced brow. She met Agatha's dark gaze and held up five fingers, for Laurel's five marriages. Experienced, indeed. Of course, she had to be careful in her comments to Max. He always smiled fondly: "Mother," he would muse, "is so romantic."

Yeah.

". . . the handsomest man—well, perhaps not the very handsomest. There was that darling young man on Crete. But," and Laurel's tone was brisk, "the past is *past*. But today, when he walked out of the fog—"

A presentiment, so beloved of gothic heroines from Wilkie Collin's Rachel Verinder to Victoria Holt's Martha Leigh, electrified Annie. Fog. Fog? Grasping at the faintest of hopes, she asked, "Is it foggy in Connecticut, too?"

A trill of cheery laughter. "Connecticut? Annie, I'm not in Connecticut. I'm *here.*" Her tone was so open, so pleased, so certain of imparting pleasure.

"Here? On Broward's Rock?"

"Yes. Oh, I know it's unexpected. But yesterday I had the most compelling *feeling*. At first I didn't know what it might be."

"Indigestion?" Annie muttered.

But Laurel was too swept up in her account to hear. "And before I knew it, I was in the trunk room—and then I understood. A journey. I was to take a journey."

"I thought you always visited Deirdre in February." Max's youngest sister lived in San Diego. Everyone liked to visit her in February.

"Annie, how *clever* of you. That's what I first thought, too. But when I reached the airport, Chicago was snowed in. So, it became obvious. I was not meant to go to San Diego."

"Perhaps tomorrow—" Annie began feebly.

"Oh no, the portents were so clear. I opened my purse and do you know what fell out?"

Nothing would have surprised Annie. Burglar tools. The Watergate tapes. A wallaby.

And, of course, Annie did want to know. Laurel always had that effect upon her listeners. She made the Pied Piper look like a piker.

"What did you have in your purse?" Annie asked good-humoredly.

"A paperback of *Home Sweet Homicide.* I picked it up and then I knew. It was meant that I should come to you."

Annie wasn't sure just how to take this.

"Because it's a mystery?"

"Oh, my dear." The silvery voice betrayed just the slightest hint of disappointment. "No, no, no. Because you and dear Max have just moved into your new home—and I always think of you and homicide. Such an *automatic* association." The tiniest of sighs. "Of course, I wouldn't dream of *staying* with you. Newlyweds in their first true home, the construction just completed, for the very first week. That would be an *imposition.*" A pause. "Of course, it's turned out to be a little difficult. Several of the hotels are renovating. The smell of *paint.* And, I can scarcely believe it, but the Palmetto Inn—always my favorite—those dear ceiling fans—a whirr so familiar to Sadie Thompson, I'm sure—but no air conditioning then—the *dear* Palmetto Inn is full, booked for a computer conference, all those bytes and microchips, so I did drive out to your new home and, of course, that's when it happened. Definitely foreordained, the fog, the winding road"—the husky voice dipped lower —"almost a haunting landscape, really, diaphanous gray mist clinging to the low-spreading limbs of the live oaks . . ."

Annie, mesmerized, was nodding in cadence.

". . . fog swirling, curling, obscuring, revealing. The gate came as a *complete* surprise. So," she said brightly, "I ran off the road!"

Confused by the abrupt switch from travelogue to action, Annie latched on to the most concrete statement. "Laurel, are you all right?"

"Annie, the most exhilarating experience! I have been rescued! So like the stories of old, a gallant arriving in the nick of time. Though there were no dragons, merely inconvenience. But to have such a handsome man sweep to my rescue—a Bentley, not a horse—and open the gate and bring me here and even arrange for the rental car to be retrieved from the ditch and brought here. I can only report that I am swept to the heights. I am giddy with anticipation. I, my dear, AM IN LOVE."

If there was an appropriate reply, Annie didn't know it.

But Laurel swept on, saving Annie from an awkward pause. "So, you see, it was meant to be—Saint Valentine's Day, the fog, the unfamiliar lane, the gate. Annie, you and Max hadn't told me about the gate. Electronic. Just like a car wash, punching in the right sequence of numbers. So advanced for a remote island. Perhaps more privacy than one should need! However, I'm here—at your house—so clever to put the key beneath the ceramic cat, but I know I must find lodging, and I thought perhaps you—"

Annie knew her duty. She didn't even hesitate. At least, not for more than a single, wrenching second. "Oh, Laurel, of course, you'll stay with us. We even have a suite just for you—"

"The lovely pink and gold one?"

A little longer pause on Annie's part. "Uh, yes. Yes. That's the one."

"Oh, if you're sure . . ."

Their duet continued a moment longer, ending in Laurel's rapturous acceptance, Annie's determinedly pleasant protestations of pleasure.

"I'll call Max," Annie concluded.

"Is he at his office?" Laurel cried. "Don't bother. I'll do it. I know it will be *such* a surprise."

Truer words were never spoken, Annie decided as she replaced the receiver, torn between irritation and amusement. Life never seemed quite the rational, orderly process Annie believed it to be when Laurel was on the scene.

But Laurel did mean well.

The phone rang again.

Annie eyed it warily. Surely it wasn't Laurel again.

"Death on Demand."

"You won't believe what I bought in Hong Kong!"

This voice, too, was immediately recognizable to Annie, the clear enunciation that proclaimed an accomplished actress, the crisp tone of authority, and the note of triumph that could only mean a book collector's coup.

"Hi, Henny. What did you buy?" Annie asked with more than passing interest. Henny Brawley was not only her best customer, she was as knowledgeable about mysteries as H. R. F. Keating, the author of the Inspector Ghote books, who is equally well known as a critic and historian of the mystery.

"In a bookstall on the street, Annie. It was like finding a pot of gold at the grocery store!"

"Possibly," Annie said dryly, "you were led to the discovery."

"Led?"

"Saint Valentine at work, no doubt."

A soft chuckle. "I saw Laurel in a rental car ahead of me on the ferry. Did Saint Valentine lead her to you?"

"In a roundabout way."

"Well, maybe that's what happened to me, if old Val is the patron saint of book lovers, too. But, Annie, hold on to your hat—I found Arthur Upfield's *The Barrakee Mystery,* first edition, original wrapper."

"Oh, my God!" Upfield's second novel and first book featuring Detective Inspector Napoleon Bonaparte (Bony).

"Mint!" Henny continued dramatically.

Mint was a book dealer's designation meaning the book looks brand new.

Wow. A coup, indeed.

Annie ventured tentatively, "I saw that title listed in a catalog recently. The asking price was fifteen hundred dollars."

Henny cleared her throat. A drumroll it wasn't, but the effect was the same. Annie waited breathlessly.

"A dollar and a half."

"Saint Somebody must have been riding on your shoulder," Annie moaned. She'd never hear the end of this from Henny.

"My turn for luck, sweetie. Well, I guess I'd better see about my mail and do a little housecleaning. I just walked in the door, but I had to call you first thing." An infinitesimal pause, then, as if an afterthought, "Oh, Annie, who won the contest last month?"

Henny's voice was still triumphant over the Upfield book, but a tiny edge lurked beneath the good humor. Annie understood at once. Henny had departed from Broward's Rock just after Christmas on a round-the-world trip. Annie's refusal to let her enter the Death on Demand January mystery paintings contest by long distance obviously still rankled. Every month a local artist painted a scene from five famous mysteries. The first person to correctly identify author and title represented by each painting received a free book and coffee for a month. Henny, of course, was the all-time high winner, coming up with the right identifications in five of the last fifteen months. It was a three-way tie in November, but she had swept the field in December, coming up with the correct titles the day the five were hung! (Christmas titles, of course: *The Twelve Deaths of Christmas* by Marian Babson, *Tied Up in Tinsel* by Ngaio Marsh, *The Corpse in the Snowman* by Nicholas Blake, *A Holiday for Murder* by Agatha Christie, and *The Convivial Codfish* by Charlotte MacLeod. Next time Annie would pick some less familiar titles. She'd like to see Henny identify *The Santa Klaus Murder* by M. Doriel Hay, *The Murders Near Mapleton* by Brian Flynn, *Crime at Christmas* by C. H. B. Kitchin, *The Gooseberry Fool* by James McClure, and *Catt Out of the Bag* by Clifford Witting.)

Henny, of course, saw nothing wrong with her stranglehold on the contest. Annie, however, wanted to share the spoils among her other customers.

"Now, Henny, it really wouldn't have been fair of me to photograph the paintings and send them to you. Contestants have to come to the store and look for themselves."

"I don't recall seeing that rule."

"It never came up before."

An unimpressed sniff. "Well, who won? And what were the books?"

"I know you don't think it's fair to let her compete—" Annie began defensively.

"Emma Clyde!" It was a bleat.

Emma Clyde was Broward's Rock's claim to literary fame, creator of Marigold Rembrandt, a fictional little old lady sleuth second only in readers' affections to Miss Marple. Sixtyish and plump, three-time Edgar and double Anthony Award winner, Emma was partial to brilliant-hued caftans and improbable hair colors. Last month, her hair had verged on magenta.

"They were tough paintings," Annie countered vigorously.

"Why not let Ingrid compete? Or see if the latest Agatha and Anthony winners would like to take a shot."

"Now Henny," Annie soothed. "Just because people write mysteries doesn't mean they know everything about them—"

"Oh no. Just like surgeons hardly know any more than Joe Blow off the street about sutures and clamps."

Annie had a feeling she was losing this battle. Time for a diversion. "Now Henny, even you will have to admit that Emma's never written a mystery with an art background."

"That's right," came the grudging reply.

"The titles represented in last month's paintings were *The Rembrandt Panel*—"

"Oliver Banks."

"The Down East Murders—" She paused.

"Don't know it." An unhappy mumble.

"J. S. Borthwick." Annie tried to be a good sport and not crow. *"The Other David—"*

No hesitation this time. "Carolyn Coker."

"The Gold Frame—"

"Herbert Resnicow, of course. I do enjoy Norma and Alexander Gold even if *he* does take all the credit. But Alexander would be nowhere without Norma."

"—and *The Fourth Stage of Gainsborough Brown*—"

"Clarissa Watson. There's an author who knows what she's writing about. Did you know she has her own art gallery on Long Island? And I like Persis Willum. I get so tired of pretty young things as sleuths. I know Persis is attractive but she's in her thirties and a widow. And the way she uses her sketch pad!"

By the time Henny rang off, she was in fine form again, though she still felt Emma Clyde had an unfair advantage.

"But it's another month, isn't it. Has anyone cracked the February paintings yet?"

"Not yet."

"See you soon." The challenge was clear.

Annie sighed and turned away from the phone. At the coffee bar, she poured another mug of Kahlúa Fudge and looked up at the watercolors on the east wall.

She smiled.

Well, heck, they were terrific, if she did think so herself. Of course, Henny was so knowledgeable she would probably win at first sight.

Still, she wasn't unhappy at her choices. February might be dull, but it was the Valentine month and these sleuths were romantic duos who celebrated love as well as mystery.

The room pictured in the first painting was unprepossessing to an extreme—a sagging bed, dirt, dust, disrepair. Its well-dressed occupants, reflecting the taste of the twenties, surely looked out of place—an older man who radiated power, but whose countenance twisted with anger as two young men gripped him by either arm. Watching in shocked surprise were two young women, one truly beautiful with masses of auburn hair, the other striking with her bobbed black hair, piquant face, and elfin charm. The latter shot a look of triumph at one of the older man's captors, a young man with a pleasantly ugly face, exquisitely slicked-back red hair, and an aura of dogged, unconquerable Britishness.

She was especially fond of the book represented in the second painting. It was this excellent author's work at her best. This scene had no overtones of death. White clouds billowed across a blue sky above a strip of beach that curved to form a bay. The water surged against a spectacular rock, triangular in shape. Two bathers clambered about the rock, investigating the top and sides with much more intensity than casual beachgoers. The slightly tanned, dark-haired woman in her late twenties was not at all pretty but her intelligent, sensitive face was memorable. Her companion was fair and slim, but athletic. His confident bearing, perhaps just this side of arrogant, marked him as a man comfortable in any situation.

Annie had some misgivings about her choice for the third painting. It was most assuredly *not* that famous author's best work. Or even near it. But the pair depicted was among the most famous couples in mystery fiction even though only the one book was devoted to them. Hollywood made them famous. The hotel room was luxurious in the manner of the thirties, but its decorators assuredly never envisioned the derby-hatted thug in the doorway firing a black .38 automatic at the couple in bed. The ruggedly handsome man slammed his wife to one side as he rolled up and out of the bed toward their attacker.

The empty apartment in the fourth painting evoked a memory of the Greenwich Village of fifty years ago. Then as now bright young couples lived in apartments converted from family houses built in the 1890s. This apartment was empty and a little dusty. Nothing remarkable about it except for the look of horror on the faces of the couple peering into a bathroom by the flickering flame from a cigarette lighter. Normally, his pleasant face would have worn a mildly puzzled look when dealing with his vivacious, talkative wife. Their horror was easy to understand. A man's dead body lay in the bathtub, the head so battered that it flattened against the sloping end of the tub.

The last picture was cheerful. Annie grinned at these lovers. The darkly handsome man examined a marble-framed looking glass with a pocket magnifier as a petite young woman with long, fine brown hair watched curiously. They stood in the entry way of an old house, a summer place in New England. This author knew how to entertain her readers.

Annie gave the paintings a little salute. "Happy Valentine's Day," she said aloud.

Others than Annie, of course, were engaged that morning in the cheery contemplation of Saint Valentine and all that he represented. Max Darling, Annie's husband, tried again to make a huge bow with the red satin ribbon which persisted in slipping from the shiny, slick-surfaced, red-paper-wrapped box on his desk. The ribbon scooted from his fingers as if possessed. It was not only in Stephen King's world that inanimate material could actively thwart human design. He tried again and almost had it when the door to his office opened and his secretary, Barb, bounded inside, flashing a huge grin. She was tugging a wobbling mass of violently red heart-shaped balloons variously inscribed KISS ME SWEET, LOVE YOU, TOO, and BE MINE TONIGHT.

"Look what Annie's sent!"

The phone rang. Barb thrust the balloons at him and bolted back to the reception area to answer. Max lost control entirely of the ribbon as he made a futile grab for the string to the balloons. The ribbon slithered to the floor and the balloons wafted to the ceiling. "Oh, hell," he muttered.

When the phone light flashed on his desk, Max welcomed the interruption. Would it perhaps be an exciting challenge? (Something other than balloon retrieval or ribbon tying.) He felt an instant of surprise at his thought, because he was not enamored of work. In fact, Max secretly rather admired the ability of Joyce Porter's detective, Chief Inspector Wilfred Dover, to avoid undue exertions, but found Dover quite unattractive otherwise. Max also admired civility. He was more at home personally with Lord Peter Wimsey, Dorothy L. Sayers's elegant sleuth, or The Saint, Leslie Charteris's debonair righter of wrongs, who managed even the most violent encounters with studied charm and courtesy. But matters at Max's office, Confidential Commissions, had recently been slow, as in proceeding at a glacial pace, and even Max felt an uncommon sense of boredom. Confidential Commissions wasn't, of course, a private detective agency, because the sovereign state of South Carolina required either two years of work in an existing licensed agency or two years as a law enforcement officer before a private investigator's license could be obtained. Therefore Confidential Commissions was a concern devoted to problem solving—and it didn't require admission to the bar or a private detective's license to solve problems.

The only problem lately, however, had been an apparent dearth of problems among the inhabitants of Broward's Rock, the loveliest resort island to grace the Atlantic off the coast of mainland South Carolina.

So Max's voice rose hopefully. "Confidential Commissions. Max Darling."

"Dearest, dearest Max, what a delight it is to have a tiny window into your exciting world. The resonance of your voice, the very savoir faire of your agency's name—oh, it all combines to create an almost mystical sense of high drama."

Max poked a switch and his high-backed, well-padded red leather office chair eased almost horizontal, one of his favorite postures.

"Hi, Ma," he said cheerfully, an indulgent smile lighting his dark blue eyes. The balloons Annie had sent looked rather nice, clustered up there near the ceiling. "What's up?"

"Oh, the glory of it, seeking to aid those in need. Almost saintly, my dear. Do you know, I think perhaps Saint Gerasimus might be perfect!"

Max's blond brows knitted in apprehension. He was accustomed to his mother's profoundly original thought patterns, but this time he was stumped. "Saint Gerasimus?"

"To be the patron saint of detectives." A tiny gasp. "Oh, I know we aren't to call you a detective, but in our hearts we all know your calling. Seeking out wrongdoers, setting lives right again, binding up society's wounds just as Saint Gerasimus once bound up the paw of a most unfortunate lion he found limping beside the river Jordan." A pause. "Thorn in the paw," she added briskly. "In any event, dear Max, I am *here.*"

Max knew then that he was the victim of his wishes. As an old adage reminds, "Remember that you might get what you pray for." Max had hoped for excitement. And excitement, sometimes mentally unsettling excitement, always followed in Laurel's train.

But he was genuinely pleased, too. Laurel was lots of fun. He felt an immediate pang of uneasiness. Not that Annie didn't adore his mother, but—

"Dear Annie."

Had Laurel read his mind? He had an uncomfortable sense that his mother had done just that and that it wasn't the first time.

"Such a wonderful wife. A helpmeet. An inspiration. Just think of all that we have learned about mysteries from her encouragement and tutelage . . ."

True. Max hadn't perceived reality in quite the same light since he had started reading his wife's beloved genre. There was nothing like an evening with a John le Carré novel to make a reader question establishment verities.

". . . led me to ponder even greater mysteries of the spirit. And so enlightening. I feel any one of us can rise to greatness when we ponder Saint Ubald of Florence. Did you realize he went from one extreme to the other? He was quite a debauched young man, spending his time with such dissipated companions until he was thirty. And then, voilà!, the turnabout, and for the rest of his long life, a gentle and pious man!"

"Swell," Max responded heartily.

"And, of course, dear Saint Valentine, seeking to aid those in love. And we, you and I, dear Max, can count ourselves beneficiaries of his grace."

Max almost asked what she meant. It wasn't cowardice that held him back. But sometimes, the less one knew—with Laurel—the better. And, after all, it was Valentine's Day. Perhaps it was simply a generic comment.

"So you're here, Ma. That's terrific. You'll stay with us—"

"Dear Annie has already insisted. I just called to say how much I am looking forward to being with you this evening—and I'm preparing a little love feast for us three."

This evening. Max's mouth opened, then closed. What a perfect out! He'd been trying to think of a way to extricate Annie and himself from tonight's party at the Cahills. But he certainly didn't want Annie to think that he invested any significance in this morning's encounter with Sydney Cahill. To duck the invitation would make too much of it. But now he had a perfect excuse! An unexpected house guest. Of course, he and Annie *couldn't* leave his mother at home the first night of her arrival. Max nodded in satisfaction, eyes on Annie's ruby-colored gift balloons. As soon as he got off the phone with Laurel, he'd call the Cahill house and make their apologies. Be more fun to spend the evening with Annie and Laurel, anyway. And he had this terrific present for Annie. Everything would work out perfectly for a cheerful end to Valentine's Day.

"For a day that started off so lousy, it's ending up pretty spectacular," Annie said over the whistle of the wind through the open windows as Max gunned his gleaming Maserati. The gate dropped in place behind them.

"Yeah. The fog's all gone," her handsome spouse agreed.

Annie's lips twitched. Max did believe in avoiding unpleasant topics. But that was all right. His news that he'd made their apologies—house guest and all that—to the Cahills certainly added a sparkle to her afternoon. If he wanted to attribute her good humor to the subdued crimson splash of the setting February sun, that was all right, too.

She smiled as they passed the turnoff to the Cahills. Everything was coming up roses. Or maybe Valentine balloons. Max had been pleased by her gift and had even confided that she, too, had a gift in store. A surprise. Annie adored surprises.

And she loved their new home. She leaned forward in anticipation as they jolted onto the as yet unpaved lane that led to their house. It was such a marvelous house!

The dusty gray lane, in dark shadow now from the overbranching limbs of the live oak trees, curved right—and there it was.

Home. Their home.

Annie reached out, touched Max's arm.

Windows, windows, windows. The multilevel, sand-toned wood house shimmered with glass expanses, the rectangular two-story entry with its inset door of stained glass, the front wall with graceful Palladian windows recalling South Carolina's colonial heritage, the roof's three curved skylights. And in the back, French windows opened onto a gray rocked terrace overlooking their patio and pool and a dusky lagoon lorded over in season by an enormous black alligator. He hibernated from December to March and Annie was in no hurry for him to shake off his winter slumbers.

As the Maserati crunched to a stop on the crushed shells by the front steps, the varicolored door burst open and Laurel darted down the steps. She was gloriously lovely, her Nordic blond hair glistening like molten gold in the sunlight, her perfect patrician features glowing with love. She greeted them each with a kiss and a flurry of chatter, as she shepherded them with, Annie could not resist feeling, entirely too proprietary a manner into their own terrazo-floored front hall.

Annie scarcely had time to glance with still-awed pleasure at their tiled fountain, decorated with jaunty gargoyles, when Laurel's report began to register.

". . . so pleased Henny's back in town and she can come to the party, too. So *nice* to have neighbors, such an old-fashioned feeling. Though, I'm afraid, perhaps Saint Pelagia the Penitent might recognize a kindred spirit before conversion. But then I'm not sure that is truly a Christian thought on my part. Still, I am only an *admirer* of saints."

"Saint Pelagia?" Annie asked sharply, though somehow, and this was painful, too, she was only too sure of the answer.

"The notorious harlot of Antioch, of course." A woeful headshake at Annie's ignorance. "As celebrated for beauty as for the disorder of her life. And your neighbor has quite that same kind of beauty, the sort that causes a great deal of heartbreak. Though indeed I may misspeak, so we will say no more of it, and she is a generous creature to be sure, coming over herself to invite me to come to the party with you and Max and to urge us to bring anyone we should like. So I called Henny at once. And now," Laurel caroled, "we can all be so happy."

"Happy?" Annie croaked.

"My dear, we can go to the party. All of us. Oh, I do so love parties!"

FIVE

As Annie handed Laurel a glass of sherry, she was rewarded with a beguiling smile, the intensity of which immediately made her suspicious.

"I feel that I must draw upon the wisdom of Saint John de Britto," Laurel said meditatively. "Such a brave man. And so perceptive. Centuries ahead of his time."

Dark blue eyes regarded Annie encouragingly.

Annie wanted to resist, but it would have been rude not to ask. "Oh? In what way?"

"He went native. In the very best sense."

Annie had no idea how to respond. So she sipped her sherry.

"A missionary. To India. He lived a life identical to that of the natives, adopting their dress, attempting in all manners to understand their attitudes, their prejudices. I want to do the same."

Annie stared in befuddlement at her elegant mother-in-law, bewitchingly lovely in a blue satin gown. "You want to go to India?" She darted a desperate glance at the stairs. Why did it take Max so long to get ready to go out? All he had to do was take a shower and put on a tuxedo! Where was he when she needed him?

Laurel laughed gaily. "Not to India. Not tonight. I merely thought we might take a walk. I know how long Max takes to get ready. Dear boy. So immaculate. We'll have plenty of time for a lovely ramble." She finished off the sherry, avoiding even an appearance of a gulp, flowed to her feet, and headed determinedly for the door that opened onto the patio.

Annie was so relieved at this prosaic turn that she put down her glass and hurried to catch up with her mother-in-law. A walk. Surely that was innocent enough.

Enough warmth lingered from yet another summery day—it hit 72 degrees at four o'clock—that they didn't even need sweaters. A thin slice of moon silvered the imposing pines that loomed on either side of the back lawn, but only emphasized the darkness of the lagoon. Annie resisted the impulse to pinch herself. Living in the Scarlet King compound was still so much like a dream. The rustling pines, the ever mysterious lagoon. One night last week, she and Max had spotted a gray fox slipping into the woods and heard the call of a red-throated loon. She breathed deeply of the pine-scented evening with its overlay of pond vegetation, pickerelweed, lizard's tail, and marsh beardtongue, and hurried to catch up with her mother-in-law, who seemed to know exactly where she was going. How far had Laurel explored this afternoon?

Far enough, Annie realized, when she joined Laurel on their pier, to have a good sense of geography.

"So *enclosed*. So self-contained," Laurel observed, gesturing toward the homes that bordered the lagoon.

Annie looked, too, with a vague sense of surprise. Actually, she'd never thought about it in that way because she and Max had been so enchanted by the sense of privacy and isolation engendered by pine-woods that separated each property—on both sides—from the next.

But looking at the area from the pier did give a different perspective.

Six homes were sited around the lagoon, each with back lawns that stretched to the water. The intervening pinewoods were so thick with undergrowth that the only access between the homes was provided by the blacktop path that circled the lagoon, cutting through the wooded swaths. Or, of course, by rowboat across the water. Each property was equipped with a pier.

"Now, Annie dear, tell me all about our neighbors. I do so want to feel a part of this *lovely* little community. And as dear Saint John de Britto made clear, one must *immerse* oneself in the local culture."

Annie's first instinct was to retort that the natives were not all that different from Laurel's neighbors in Connecticut. She opened her mouth, closed it.

Actually, they were damn different.

Annie peered suspiciously at Laurel. Her mother-in-law was the most socially adroit person Annie had ever encountered. Why should she suddenly feel any need to prepare herself to meet anyone? But there was a ring of sincerity in Laurel's voice. She seemed truly to want to know all about Annie and Max's neighbors. Unfortunately, the light from the single yellow bulb at the end of the pier was not nearly bright enough for Annie to see Laurel clearly. She could see enough, however, to discern an oddly intent expression.

Why?

Annie riffled through their conversation, if that's what it could be termed. Saint John de Britto. Brave man. Gone native.

"That house, Annie. Who lives there?" Laurel pointed directly across the coal-dark water of the lagoon at a single light that marked a pier. Behind it, dimly visible in the moonlight, was the dark hulk of the Atwater house.

Annie had the feeling—dammit, she was sure—that she was being manipulated. To what end? But what possible harm could it do to describe their neighbors? Was she getting a trifle paranoid in her dealings with her mother-in-law?

Her answer was clipped. "Dorcas Atwater. A widow."

"A merry widow?" A silvery laugh floated in the night air.

Annie desperately tried to sort swiftly through Laurel's marital entanglements. But she'd never been good at logic problems, so she gave up trying to remember which of her mother-in-law's marriages had ended in death and which in divorce. But it was such a telling phrase. Annie began to smile, until she thought of Dorcas Atwater.

"Unmerry as all hell, Laurel."

"Such a waste," Laurel murmured. "Life is meant to be enjoyed. By everyone. As Saint Francis de Sales so aptly remarked, 'A sad saint would be a sorry saint.'"

Annie's response was so immediate and so strong that it surprised her. She hadn't realized what an impression Dorcas Atwater had made the last time she'd seen her. "Not sad. Mad. Mad as a scalded cat."

"How *interesting.* How unusual."

Once again Annie felt a quiver of surprise at her mother-in-law's uncanny ability to go to the heart of the matter. Dorcas's attitude *was* odd, and this had never before occurred to Annie.

What was Dorcas mad about? Because her husband died? Surely that was a strange reaction.

"Laurel, you're right. That's weird. And *she's* weird. Dorcas used to be pretty, in an inbred sort of way. A pale face, bony like a horse, and light blue eyes. But stylish, always wearing the latest thing. Not anymore! I saw her last week when I was jogging on the path around the lagoon, and I hardly recognized her. Stringy hair, almost all gray. No makeup and a ratty housedress. She looked like something out of a Ruth Rendell novel."

"Surely not typical of your neighbors," Laurel observed.

Annie felt called upon to defend the sartorial splendor of the residents rimming Scarlet King Lagoon, and, before she knew it, she was deep into a good old-fashioned gossip about her neighbors.

"Lord, no. Now look. To the left of the Atwater house." Annie pointed across the lagoon at a blaze of lights. Enormous baseball-park lights topped poles at six points in the backyard, throwing the entire lawn into clear, sharp relief. "That's where the Burgers live. Billye Burger goes to the kind of shops where you have to have an appointment! She wears Bill Blass originals. Billye always looks like she just got out of the beauty shop and dropped by Cartier on the way home. And her husband is the kind of Texas Rich you read about in D. R. Meredith's *Murder by Impulse* and *The Sheriff and the Branding Iron.* He's the reason it's so hard to get into the compound. I mean, I don't like to call it a compound, but that's what it is. You know how wild everything is, the undergrowth pruned just enough to keep it from killing the trees. Vines and ferns and shrubs everywhere. You'd have to have a machete to hack your way to any of these houses, except by road or along the lagoon path. The gate's to keep out strangers. Buck Burger was a criminal lawyer who made enough enemies to make Al Capone nervous. And enough money to have a home here and another in Dallas and I think one in Aspen."

Laurel gazed with interest at the starkly illuminated landscape. "That's the yard with the watchman."

"Watchman?"

"Yes. Rather a large man. And *not* charming. I encountered him when I took a walk this afternoon."

A watchman. Why did the Burgers have a watchman? Annie had lived in the Scarlet King compound for a whole week and been unaware of this interesting fact about her neighbors.

"I didn't see Mr. Burger," Laurel added.

"You didn't miss much." Annie brushed away an invisible cloud of no-see-ums and thought irritably that enough was enough with the screwy weather. They shouldn't have to put up with gnats in February! "He's loud, vulgar, overbearing, and thinks he's God's gift to women."

"Vulgar," Laurel repeated. "No, no."

"Oh yes he is," Annie insisted.

"I'm sure," Laurel said brightly, leaving Annie confused. "Such variety. That next house?" she asked. Her tone indicated disbelief.

Annie grinned. "The architect must have grown up in a modern tract house and been reacting against it ever since. Have you ever *seen* more gingerbread?"

"Only dear Hansel and Gretel," Laurel said cheerfully.

"The oddest part is that the owner isn't a Mother Earth nut or an old lady. It belongs to a dentist, George Graham, a *GQ* yuppie."

"*Not* a dentist, thank heaven."

Annie ignored this comment. Laurel really wasn't making sense tonight.

"A yuppie," she said firmly. "Fortyish, blandly handsome. The toothpaste ad type."

"So apropos," Laurel observed. "You are so descriptive, Annie."

Annie ignored that comment, too, and continued doggedly. "Drives a Mercedes, of course. Plays tennis. Jogs. And has a young, second wife, Lisa. And a teenage son, Joel. He drives a jeep." Annie didn't add that Joel paid a little too much attention when she jogged by their house. She enjoyed admiring glances; she didn't enjoy lascivious looks. "Lisa drives a Mercedes, too. And plays tennis and jogs." Annie tried not to sound tart, but she had a natural sympathy for first wives. Though certainly Agatha Christie was a prime example of how betrayal in a first marriage, though heartbreaking at the time, could lead, ultimately, to a second, much happier union. Perhaps the first Mrs. Graham was grateful for her release.

Laurel was already swinging about to look on the other side of the lagoon. Obviously, the Grahams didn't fascinate. Second marriages (and third and fourth and fifth) were nothing new to Laurel. She peered into the darkness.

"Can't see the other two houses from here. Too many pines. The farthest one," Annie pointed toward dense pinewoods across the pond, "was the original home on the property, antebellum. It belongs to a retired general and his wife. Second wife." Might as well be accurate.

"A general." There was a note of fondness in her voice. One of Laurel's husbands had been in the military.

"Nasty old coot. Glowered at me the other day when I jogged by. Guess General Houghton thinks the whole path belongs to him." It had been no ordinary glower. Annie wouldn't quickly forget those dark, burning eyes or the pulse that throbbed at the temple of that ancient bald head. "Don't see how his wife stands him." Annie paused. "Second wife." Not that Eileen Houghton was all that young. Early fifties, probably. Attractive enough in a matronly way. Annie realized that she and Billye Burger were in the minority as first wives. For all that it mattered. "Eileen used to be a nurse or something like that, so I guess she knows how to put up with impossible people."

"Annieee! Laurel!" Max's tenor boomed from the patio.

"Coming," Annie called happily. And so what if she had to go to Sydney's party. She would have fun. She always had fun with Max.

As they hurried back toward the house, Laurel asked urgently, "The last house, the other one we can't see. Is that where we are going to the party?"

"Yes. The Cahills." Annie avoided mentioning Sydney's name.

Laurel didn't know it was verboten. "Sydney Cahill?"

"Yes."

"A beautiful young woman. But so sad."

Annie didn't think Sydney was the least bit sad. To her mind that was on the order of describing a blood-lusting pit bull as playful. "Sydney's —" Annie took a deep breath. She didn't want to get into it. She walked faster. There was Max on the terrace, absolutely gorgeous in his tux.

Laurel kept pace. "Sydney's husband. I suppose he's older?"

"Another second marriage," Annie said briskly. "A disastrous one, from all I hear. Howard's first wife died and he fell for a pretty body. He's handsome as all get-out, in a rugged way. And rich. Sydney lucked out."

"Party time," yodeled that cheerful tenor.

Annie waved a greeting.

"Disastrous," Laurel said cheerily.

Annie detected a note of satisfaction, but dismissed it. After all, why should Laurel care about Howard Cahill's marriage?

Max acted as tour guide as they took the lagoon path to the Cahill property.

"The name of the compound is taken from the lagoon, Ma. Scarlet King Lagoon."

"What a romantic name!" Laurel exclaimed.

It wasn't that Laurel's romanticism irritated Annie, but she felt honor bound to be factual. "The lagoon's named for some snakes that live there." To be fair, she grudgingly added, "Nonpoisonous. And pretty, if you like snakes. A red nose and yellow bands set off by black."

The path angled away from the lagoon, passed a charming gazebo, and wound into the gardens.

Laurel beamed. "I'm sure Saint Francis would be enchanted. He loved *all* creatures. And so should we."

For the first time, Laurel's preoccupation with saints began to worry Annie. She had no desire to find all God's creatures welcomed to her new house. There was no telling how far Laurel would go when in the grip of a new enthusiasm. She opened her mouth to warn Laurel about consorting with snakes, because the island hosted four poisonous species, cottonmouths, eastern diamondback rattlers, timber rattlers, and copperheads, but Laurel spoke first, her tone tinged with awe. "What a *remarkable* house!"

Laurel rarely evinced amazement, but Annie understood. The Cahill mansion evoked a stunned response from even its most worldly visitors, which would certainly include Laurel. (Annie was convinced that "worldly" was quite an appropriate description of her mother-in-law, though perhaps Max might not appreciate some of the nuances involved.)

In the moonlight, the Moorish influence was evident. Three-story, crenellation-capped stucco walls glistened with whitewash. Sharply pointed towers loomed at either end. A golden flood of light spilled from enormous arched windows onto the luxuriant gardens below. Annie made a mental note to bring Laurel back in the daytime when she could truly appreciate the scope of the gardens. The azaleas were beginning to bloom and by April would be in full flower, dazzling masses of pink, lavender, rose, and crimson. The plantings, like those at the famed Magnolia Plantation, were planned for year-round color. Camellias, canna lilies, crape myrtle, daffodils, day lilies, dogwood, forsythia, gardenias, hibiscus, honeysuckle, hyacinth, jessamine, oleanders, pittosporum, bougainvillea, rhododendron, and wisteria bloomed in season.

"No one can say the Yankee robber barons were the only Americans to engage in unmitigated conspicuous consumption," Max observed wryly.

"Oh, but it's *lovely,*" Laurel cried and she skipped ahead of them, holding up the long skirt of her satin gown. In the pale wash of moonlight and the glow from the windows, Laurel's smooth hair gleamed like a golden cap. As she sped along with unselfconscious and enchanting grace, she was a figure from the heroic past, a Diana, a Helen of Troy.

For the first time in her life, Annie was struck by a foreboding, a distinct sense of imminent disaster. (Generations of had-I-but-known heroines would have understood.) She reached out, gripped Max's arm, and almost urged him to run after Laurel, catch her.

Then what? Her practical mind intervened. Laurel had her heart set on going to the Valentine party. What could Annie say? And now it was too late to turn back. Laurel had reached the floodlit front steps.

"What?" Max asked.

Annie hesitated. The huge bronze front door swung open. More light blazoned a welcome. Laurel turned and waved for them to hurry. Other guests, the women in bright dresses, the men in tuxedos, were arriving.

"I stumbled," Annie said. She gave her husband's arm a squeeze and quickened her pace.

The moment passed.

The Cahill mansion was no less imposing inside, with its colorful tiled floors, enormous marble columns, hanging tapestries, ornate bronze sconces with lighted candles, and enough priceless antiques from all around the world to fill a small museum. The Cahills greeted their guests at the base of the majestic marble staircase that curved to second- and third-floor balconies. A suit of knight's armor glinted beside the staircase. Someone had taped a bright red heart on his metal chest.

Sydney Cahill stood on the first step, her husband, Howard, on the second. Sydney was breathtakingly lovely tonight. Her raven black hair was a lustrous frame for magnolia-soft skin. She wore a long-sleeved dress of pleated ivory silk, two swaths falling from her shoulders to cross over her breasts, creating a plunging neckline. A glittering necklace, intertwined strands of rubies, emeralds, and diamonds, emphasized the delicate grace of her neck.

Howard Cahill was darkly handsome, a smooth, olive-skinned face, eyes so brown they looked black, black hair touched with silver. His face was memorable, a broad forehead, once-broken nose, blunt chin. Annie immediately decided she would have cast him as Philip Marlowe for a movie. He greeted his guests formally, with a quick nod and observant dark eyes, but without warmth. There was an aura of power about him, a reserve that forebade familiarity. Only an insensitive clod would ever clap Howard Cahill on the shoulder.

As the line inched forward, Annie glanced from the Cahills to the armor. Light from the glittering chandelier rippled off the visor, creating—just for an instant—an illusion of life and movement. Annie wondered sharply what it must have been like for the owner of that suit of mail. Damned hot and uncomfortable. The owner had been small to heft such a load, not more than five and a half feet. But dangerous. In one steel hand, supported from below by a stand, lay a mace, a heavy, medieval war club crowned by a spiked metal head. Annie shivered. What destruction had that weapon wrought centuries ago? How bizarre it was to view its killing weight on display during a night of gaiety in celebration of love. The faint sound of orchestra music from above mingled in her mind with the imagined grunts and clangs of mounted combat.

She and Max and Laurel reached the foot of the stairs.

Sydney murmured, "So very glad you could come. Everyone is gathering in the third-floor ballroom for dancing, but do feel free to wander about as you please. Howard has so many lovely works of art, and he does enjoy sharing them with our friends." She took Laurel's hand, but her eyes moved past Laurel and Annie to Max and fastened there with a hopeful eagerness that would have infuriated Annie, had she not been too startled by the look on her mother-in-law's face.

Laurel glowed. Although Annie had always accorded her mother-in-law full marks for extraordinary beauty, she hadn't realized just how lovely Laurel could appear, her lake-blue eyes filled with warmth, her perfect mouth curved in gentle wonder, her classic profile softened by emotion.

Oh, dear Lord. Because it was only too obvious to Annie who was the object of this adoration.

Howard Cahill's face, too, revealed a man Annie had never glimpsed —or imagined. As she watched in horrified fascination, Cahill's normal appearance of icy reserve melted, replaced with intense absorption. Annie had always appraised their new neighbor as a man to be reckoned with. A fabulously wealthy shipowner, their host had a reputation as an aggressive, combative businessman, never willing to lose once he joined a battle. But the tentative warmth in his dark eyes as he looked at Laurel revealed a man longing for intimacy.

It was only an instant of time that the tableau held, Laurel and Howard looking at each other without pretense, as if they were alone.

Laurel said softly, "I knew we should meet again. Fate has ordained it."

Over the chatter of newcomers behind them, Annie heard his gruff reply that was a dramatic beat slow in coming. "Perhaps you're right. Though I've always said a man holds his fate in his own hands."

"We shall see, shan't we?" and Laurel swept on up the stairs, in an alluring rustle of satin.

Cahill turned to watch her go.

Annie and Max followed Laurel up the stairway. Annie grabbed Max's arm and hissed, "That's the man!"

Max looked at her in surprise. "Sure. You've met Howard. Hey, listen to that music." Max had a passion for slow dancing, although she'd never been altogether sure it was the music that entranced him.

"Listen, Max," she began, but her protest was lost in Max's whistle of surprise when they stepped into the immense ballroom. Sydney had taken her and Max on a tour of the Cahill house shortly after the Darlings had moved into their new home. But the ballroom had undergone a magical transformation from an echoing, cavernous, empty room to a brilliant mélange of color, light, movement, and life.

The change was extraordinary. Crimson velvet curtains decorated with lace-edged satin hearts marked alcoves along the walls. Artfully placed lights illuminated brightly colored ceiling frescoes, vivid scenes of exotic ports: Zanzibar drowsing under a torrid summer sun, Marseilles abustle with shipping, San Francisco wreathed in fog, New York a hundred years ago, a fleet of Roman warships taking on stores at Alexandria. In each fresco stood a couple, not part of the central vigor and movement, but separate, absorbed in each other, lovers soon to be parted, who mirrored, despite differences in time and culture, the passion that seals a man to a woman. The effect of the whole was subtly erotic, implying the urgency of desire, the foolishness of delay, the relentless passage of time, a reckless haste to seize the moment.

The dimly lit ballroom added dramatic intensity to the illuminated frescoes and an air of mystery to the dancers, most of whom were masked. And such marvelous masks! They were definitely not five-and-dime cardboard but creations in papier-mâché especially for the Valentine party. She spotted Mickey and Minnie Mouse, George and Martha Washington, Cleopatra and Antony, Lauren Bacall and Humphrey Bogart, Charles and Di, even Héloïse and Abélard. Guests gathered in excited knots at long tables on either side of the ballroom. Every so often a couple would break free, triumphantly waving their trophies. What fun! Who could she and Max be? But first, she had to make Max understand about Laurel, who had plunged into the milling crowd and was lost to view.

"Howard Cahill," she hissed. "It's Howard Cahill."

"Are you all right, honey? Sure that's Howard Cahill. You've met him a dozen times."

"Didn't you see him and Laurel *look* at each other?"

Max touched her cheek. "You aren't feverish, are you?"

Annie barely restrained herself from stamping her foot. Sometimes Max, even though he was as handsome and delectable as a grown-up Joe Hardy, could be utterly maddening, more obtuse than Chet Morton at his worst.

"The man who helped Laurel get the rental car out of the ditch. It was *Howard.*"

Max smiled benignly, craning his neck. "Good old Howard." He spotted the bar. "Makes me thirsty, climbing stairs. What would you like? Spritzer?"

If she couldn't fasten her hands around his throat and throttle him, a spritzer would be second best. Apparently having about as much social antenna as Mike Hammer, Max had missed the interplay when Laurel and Howard met. Of course, that was the point. They hadn't just met. Howard was the man who had evoked such lyrical excitement in Laurel that morning. An Elaine Raco Chase heroine could scarcely evince more enthusiasm. Annie's heart sank.

Laurel had neglected to tell Max that she was in love with one of their neighbors. Obviously, Howard would have introduced himself when he gallantly rescued Laurel from the ditch. Just as obviously, there was no need for him to say exactly where he lived. But why hadn't Laurel made the connection when Sydney came by to urge them all to come to the party? Of course, it would be just like Sydney to introduce herself simply as Sydney with no surname. So Laurel didn't know the name of her host and hostess until tonight on the pier when Annie obligingly spewed forth information about the residents of the Scarlet King compound.

"Saint John de Britto, my foot! Immerse oneself in a culture, my—"

She broke off as the masked figure next to her—a much too chubby Marilyn Monroe—turned toward her inquiringly.

Annie bared her teeth in what she hoped looked like a gracious smile. "Thought I saw an old friend, John Britton," she babbled. "But no such luck." She turned determinedly away and glared at the bar. It couldn't have been any more jammed if it had been the saloon aboard the SS *Karnak* in *Death on the Nile*. She waited impatiently for Max's return. She had to make Max understand that Laurel was obviously— Oh. Wait a minute. Cool reasoning overtook impulse. How could she tell Max that his mother was flinging herself at a married man? Annie foresaw difficulties.

The band eased from a Cole Porter love song into a Viennese waltz. Elizabeth Taylor and Eddie Fisher swept by, but Annie would recognize that blue satin dress anywhere. She wondered who Laurel's partner was. Not Howard, because he and Sydney, *sans* masks, had just appeared in the ballroom. But body language shouts. Obviously, Laurel's partner was smitten. Annie raised an eyebrow. Had true love already taken the final count? But no, as the couple dipped past, Laurel blew a kiss in the general direction of Howard.

Sydney, once again, was oblivious to her husband. She scanned the dancers, her face alight with eagerness. Howard's dark eyes followed Laurel.

But not only Laurel looked toward Howard, Annie realized.

A young man with tousled curly hair and an almost overcivilized face —too long eyelashes, a sensitive mouth, a delicate mustache—watched, too, a young man who would have been handsome if he hadn't been scowling. He stood a few feet away from the clot around the bar, hands jammed in the pockets of his tuxedo, shoulders hunched.

Howard's stride slowed when his glance met that of the sour young man. Sydney moved on ahead and was lost among the throng of guests.

Once again, the look in Howard's eyes surprised Annie. He might be the richest shipowner in America; surely he was also one of the unhappiest. He stretched out his hand, but the young man pivoted on his heel and walked away.

Howard's hand slowly fell to his side. Then Laurel appeared. Rising on tiptoe, she murmured in Howard's ear, one beautifully manicured hand resting lightly on his shoulder.

Annie surveyed those nearby. Thank God, the music was loud, the voices louder, and nobody was paying any attention to their host.

Where was Sydney?

It would be pretty awful if Sydney noticed her husband's deportment with Max's mother. But what could Annie do? Besides, she wasn't Laurel's mother. Which conclusion left her more confused than ever.

Because she felt this urge to *do* something. But when she turned back, Laurel and Howard had disappeared.

Annie felt a beading of sweat on her brow. She'd better see where Sydney was. Then maybe she could find Laurel and detach her from Howard.

She had already covered a half dozen steps when she heard Max. "Annie, hey Annie, where're you going? I've got your spritzer."

He caught up with her. Annie accepted the glass, drank half of it in a gulp, then looked up into Max's surprised face.

She felt on the other side of an abyss from him. He had no idea about Laurel. Annie couldn't tell him his mother was— No, she couldn't.

"Let's go get some masks," she said brightly and headed for the nearest table.

The mask seekers were just this side of pushing and shoving in their eagerness to make a selection from the tantalizing array.

With one distinct exception—their not-so-charming neighbor, General (retired) Colville Houghton. He leaned on his ebony cane and surveyed the masks and the guests with equal distaste. His wife, Eileen, attired in a formal gown that would have found favor at a DAR banquet —a lace-covered bosom and a skirt with sweeping folds that gave no hint of the body beneath—fingered the cameo at her throat and turned a carefully schooled face toward the dance floor.

Annie didn't blame Eileen for distancing herself from the old brute, in spirit if not in fact. He looked like the skull at the feast, deeply socketed eyes, prominent cheekbones, downturned mouth, clipped gray mustache.

"Sodom and Gomorrah," he intoned in a deep, gruff voice.

A full-bodied redhead in a dress that started low and finished high drawled, "Lighten up, Pops," which sounded odd issuing from the lips of Little Bo Peep.

The general's face took on an unhealthy hue, his sallow skin flushing purplish red.

Eileen Houghton began to speak in a smooth, social tone. "I do believe I see the McKenzies across the room, Colville. Yes, he's waving to us. I'll go fetch them."

Annie didn't blame her. She'd get the hell out, too.

The general didn't move.

Annie and Max stepped past him. At the table, guests jostled one another, eagerly grabbing up masks, trying them on, discarding, trading, amid bursts of laughter and comments, some ribald: "Who's this?" . . . "Hey, I always wanted to be a general. Who matches? Mamie or Kay Summersby?" . . . "You mean Columbus actually had red hair?" . . . "Listen, everybody, I've got Romeo and I'll trade for Rhett Butler."

The papier-mâché masks were light enough to wear comfortably.

Velvet straps, with Velcro strips, extended from the temples of each mask, making it possible to adjust for size when they were fastened.

Annie rejected the Bonnie and Clyde masks. There were, she felt, definite limits to her enthusiasm for crime. Actually, she didn't care at all for true crime and Bonnie and Clyde had been distinctly unattractive. Just about as charming as Billy the Kid, despite the varied literary efforts to make that teenage killer seem appealing. Apologists might see him as the avenger of his patron's murder. Annie saw young Billy as a cold-blooded murderer, who had as much empathy for his victims as a stalking gray fox for marsh rabbits.

As the masks were snatched up and passed around, matching pairs were quickly separated. Annie ended up with Marie Antoinette and Max with Lord Byron. Not, Annie decided, the most propitious possibilities.

That's when the evening began to get complicated.

A trumpet tattoo erupted from the bandstand. Sydney Cahill hurried up the steps as a spotlight centered on her. She turned to look down at the guests, and the trumpet sounded again. Most women would look wan, their color leached out by the sharp brightness of the spotlight. Not Sydney. The diamond-white light merely enhanced her vibrant dark beauty. A faint flush of excitement stained her cheeks becomingly.

"Everyone, it's time for adventure." Her voice, deep and soft and eager, held the promise of torrid nights and languid mornings. "So often we don't know where we can find love. Just for tonight, let's search for the heartbeat of love. We are all so afraid to be open, to reveal ourselves, so let's see what chance can do and what we may discover behind the masks." She leaned forward and the necklace of rubies and diamonds and emeralds glittered against her softly rounded breasts. "Here's what we are going to do. I want all the ladies to gather in a circle." She gestured encouragingly and the matching bracelet on her arm flashed like city lights sliding beneath a midnight flight. "Gentlemen, form a circle around the ladies." The drummer tapped lightly but steadily. "And now," Sydney called out, "ladies, send your masks three to the right. Gentlemen, send your masks three to the left, then"—she paused for dramatic emphasis, her voice dropping lower—"then seek out the proper match and discover the partner fate has chosen for you tonight!" The band broke into "Some Enchanted Evening."

Amid a great deal of laughter and false starts, the newly remasked guests milled about, merrily seeking their partners.

Annie was next to the bandstand, adjusting her new mask as Queen Victoria, when Sydney started down the steps. The tousle-haired young man, a pettish look on his face, stepped forward, his hand outstretched, offering a mask to Sydney.

After an instant's hesitation, surprise evident in her arching brows,

Sydney reached eagerly for the mask with its ice blond hair piled high in a careful coiffure, then looked hopefully at the giver. "Carleton?" she asked tentatively. Annie saw uncertainty in her soulful green eyes. And a hunger for kindness.

"Madame de Pompadour," the tousle-haired young man enunciated carefully. Too carefully. He held an empty drink glass in one hand. Annie felt sure it wasn't the first.

Sydney looked from his face to the mask and back again.

"Slut," he said distinctly. "Perfect for you."

Sydney's emerald eyes filled with tears. Her lovely mouth trembled. She said pleadingly, "Carleton, please. Please don't."

"One slut deserves another, right?"

"Carleton." Her voice shook. "I'll tell Howard."

" 'Carleton, I'll tell Howard,' " he mimicked in a high, drunken voice. "You just go right ahead and do that. Tell the old man. See if I care." And he turned and stumbled away.

The anguish on Sydney's face drained away all the anger and disdain Annie had previously harbored against her beautiful hostess. Because there was pain here. Too much pain. To her own amazement, Annie suddenly felt extremely sorry for Sydney Cahill.

"Syd—" she began, when a firm hand grasped her arm and she was whirled onto the dance floor, her Queen Victoria mask slipping sideways. "Queen, my Queen, my place is forever at your side. Hey, you're cute."

Albert turned out to be a visiting tennis star, Manfred Schutz. Manfred danced like a dream, if a bit too closely, and he misinterpreted her twisting to look about the floor in search of Sydney. When an elbow in his ribs didn't persuade him to back off just a bit, Annie said crisply, "I'd like you to meet my husband. He's that big guy right over there." The distance between them increased perceptibly. With a clear understanding of Manfred's intentions, she found an unmarried friend, also a tennis player, and left them together. Manfred bent close and expertly began to maneuver his new quarry toward a curtained alcove.

Annie again began looking for Sydney. She would have, she knew, no difficulty identifying Sydney's spectacular dress and cleavage. But when she finally spotted her, ten minutes later, Annie's new-found compassion received a jolt. It was disconcerting to find the object of her good intentions in the arms of the Cowardly Lion (aka Max Darling). Of course, she knew the man was Max. She would know that body anywhere. What she could see of it. Sydney was plastered against him closer than Bertha Cool to a dollar.

Annie took off her mask, the better to see. Her eyes narrowed.

Well, she would give Max a *little* credit. He was backpedaling, and that wasn't his normal mode of dancing. It was that morning all over again, a voracious, full-bodied woman doing everything but say, "Take me, I'm yours." And for all Annie knew those very words, or a slightly more subtle equivalent, might be issuing from Sydney's delectable lips right this moment. Compassion disappeared faster than a mint Christie at a classic mystery sale.

Madame Bovary thrust a drink into Annie's hands. "Want me to see if Miss Melville is available?" The protagonist of *Miss Melville Regrets* is one of the world's most unusual assassins.

"Not funny, Henny." She took a deep gulp and realized Henny had given her a gin and tonic, which she loathed.

"Actually, I'd say Sydney is getting nowhere fast," Henny judged.

Annie was too cool to be outwardly proud of her husband, but inside she felt a warm glow. Max was, literally, unhanding himself, removing Sydney's beringed fingers from his shoulders and stepping pointedly away from an inviting alcove.

Henry VIII tapped on Sydney's shoulder. She turned eagerly. Annie wondered if beneath the mask of Marlene Dietrich, Sydney's lips were curved again into a hopeful, vulnerable smile. Sydney stepped coquettishly into the man's arms and tilted her head to one side inquiringly. Obviously, she didn't recognize her partner. They danced a few feet, then Sydney reached up to lift her partner's mask.

Annie saw the face, too, and was perhaps more surprised than the hostess, who must have known that all of the Graham family was invited. Joel Graham, the dentist's son, winked sensuously at Sydney. It might have looked absurd, a horny kid mimicking a Hollywood come-on. But the lusty twist to his full lips and the hot light in his heavy-lidded eyes exuded confidence and experience. Joel might be just a senior in high school, but he was eighteen going on twenty-eight. He bent closer to Sydney, who had gone rigid in his arms, and whispered something. She pulled away, stumbling in her high heels as she did so. Annie would have bet that Joel said something no nice young man said to a nice woman.

She hoped it got him in some hot water at home. Lisa Graham stood near the bandstand, a Bess Truman mask in her hand. Her expression, as she watched Sydney hurry away from Joel, was enigmatic. Annie wondered what she was thinking.

It was from that point in the evening that Sydney's almost frantic progress from man to man became painfully apparent to anyone who watched.

That decided Annie. Sydney, no matter how her lower lip might tremble at times, was clearly up to no good. Annie no longer felt any urge to run up to Sydney and commiserate because somebody, obviously with very good reason, had called her a slut. As for Laurel's pursuit of Howard, Sydney was too immersed in her own pursuits to notice even if

Laurel slung Howard over her shoulder and disappeared into the swamp. Annie decided to cool it. She put her mask on and stood invitingly by the dance floor. When the Scarlet Pimpernel bowed and asked her to dance, Annie happily acquiesced and spent a good five minutes trying to guess her companion's identity. He knew her at once, which added a little pressure. His resonant tenor voice was familiar. He was taller than average and a graceful dancer. But she couldn't give her whole mind to the exercise. Despite her good intentions, she was only too aware of Sydney Cahill and her prowling progress from man to man and the almost equally blatant attraction between her mother-in-law and their host.

Then she realized her partner was waiting for an answer, and she hadn't heard the question. "I'm sorry," she said. "I was looking at Sydney. Her dress is so lovely."

Their hostess stood across the ballroom near an alcove, deep in conversation with a stocky Rudolph Valentino. She leaned languorously close. The man's right hand, huge and thick-fingered, slowly slipped from Sydney's shoulder to her breast and lingered for a long moment before sliding to her waist. A fiery red ruby ring glittered on his third finger. Sydney pressed against him.

"Sydney. Ah, Sydney." The voice behind the Scarlet Pimpernel mask was amused. In a snide fashion.

She knew him then. Their dentist neighbor, George Graham. His voice had held that same sardonic tone—a patronizing little-woman inflection—the last time she and Max played mixed doubles with the Grahams at the country club and Lisa double-faulted.

Annie wondered if George, too, had seen that lingering, public caress.

"Our hostess gives her all, doesn't she?" Graham asked lightly. A pause, then the smooth addition. "To be sure her guests have fun."

Graham hadn't missed it.

"Apparently so," Annie agreed dryly. She immediately felt like a mean cat. But, dammit, Sydney asked for it, didn't she?

Yes, but Annie didn't enjoy the feeling that she was sharing an unkind critique of her hostess with George Graham. Enough was enough. "Are you and Lisa playing much tennis now, George?"

They were, of course. Annie heard more than she wanted to know about their reaching the quarterfinals of the New Year's Day mixed doubles tournament.

She went then from partner to partner. The party had a fervid atmosphere, a combination of sensuous Latin music, loud, excited talk, and the telltale billowing of the red velvet curtains as couples slipped in and out of alcoves. Annie wondered if the dimness and the masks had weakened accustomed reserve, setting free an eroticism foreign to the staidness of Broward's Rock. (She had to make it very clear to one unknown

partner, Samson, that she wasn't up for grabs, of any kind.) Masks were
traded several times more. She ended up once with Max (he was too tall
to be George Burns!) and that was the most fun of the evening.

"I'd rather dance with you forever," he murmured, his breath tickling
her ear.

Sweet.

"Damn good thing," she said briskly.

He chuckled. "Where's your sense of romance?"

"Don't believe in it."

"Are you the Grinch of Valentine's Day?" he demanded.

"Nope. I don't believe in romance. But," and her arms tightened
around his neck, "I do believe in love."

"Have to cut in here. No fun when the married folks stick together."
A robust laugh. "They can do that in private. Come on, little lady, let's
have at it."

Not even a Lancelot mask could add polish to Buck Burger. His voice
rumbled from a massive chest. His huge hands fastened on her clumsily, one engulfing her right hand, the other a bit too low on her hip for
her liking. As she clapped her hand firmly over his, she saw the winking
red ruby ring on his middle finger. A well-traveled hand, she realized.
She briskly resettled it, and he laughed good-humoredly.

Buck's idea of dancing was a jerky stop-and-start progress a half beat
behind the rhythm and a running commentary on the party scene.

"Have to hand it to old Sydney. Woman's a fool but she can come up
with the goods sometimes." A lustful laugh. "In addition to the original
package. But this blowout's the first time I've enjoyed a party since I left
Texas. People finally letting their hair down. About—"

Annie had no desire to pursue their common ties to the Lone Star
state.

"—time. Course old Sydney was born with her hair down. Look at
her now, cuddlin' up to some guy like it was twenty below and a bliz-
zard outside. One hot lady." There was no rancor in Burger's voice.
Apparently he didn't mind sharing.

Annie twisted her neck to see. One man in a tuxedo, when masked,
looked like almost any other man. But it wasn't Max. Then she spotted
Laurel dancing with Howard. Neither wore a mask and Annie wished
fervently they hadn't put them aside. They danced superbly together
and that was enough to attract attention, their bodies in perfect tan-
dem. But their faces, absorbed and intent, trumpeted an attraction far
out of the ordinary. Annie's heart sank.

"Hey, get a load of Howard. Shit, who's—"

Annie broke in before it was too late. "That's Max's mother."

It gave Buck pause, as she had hoped it would.

"She's visiting us," Annie added noncommittally.

"Yeah, well, we'll have to have you folks over. I'll have Billye give you a holler."

Thankfully, the number ended and Buck lurched to a stop.

"Such fun," Annie said insincerely. Masks did have some advantages. She didn't have to create an insincere smile, too. "Believe I'll slip away for a moment now."

"You women," he said with heavy jocularity. "Go to the john on the way to heaven."

Annie didn't even try to answer that one. As the music started again, she headed for the perimeter of the dance floor, looking eagerly about for Max.

It took only another moment's survey to realize that not only was Max absent, so was Sydney.

Okay, José, there were limits. Annie had reached hers. She plunged through the ballroom's huge archway and headed for the stairs. By the time she reached the bottom floor, she was in control. Honestly, there was no telling what she might have said or done had she discovered her husband—that delectable blond aka old white meat—in a tête-à-tête with Sydney in a quiet corridor on another floor.

By the time she reached the gardens, she decided she was overreacting, but she was in no mood to hurry back upstairs. The gardens were delightful—cool and quiet. Annie breathed deeply, enjoying the scent of moist greenery. Her steps crunched on the oyster-shell path as she passed the shadowy gazebo. The air was much cooler now, but far from cold. She strolled out onto the pier and leaned against the railing. The water was still as dark as pitch, the low-watt yellow bulb at the end of the pier futile against the dark night.

The hoarse, venomous whisper came without warning.

"Bitch."

Annie stiffened.

It came again, harsher now, clearer.

"Bitch!"

An oar slapped against water.

Annie looked down.

The woman hunched over the oars steered the boat past the pier. The boat gently rocked to a stop, the paddles splashing deep in the water. The rower, a shadowy figure with stringy hair and a bony face, looked up.

Slowly the hatred seeped from Dorcas Atwater's face to be replaced by indifference.

"You aren't Sydney."

"No," Annie said gently. "I'm Annie Darling."

"I know." Her tone said it didn't matter, nothing mattered.

"Dorcas, shouldn't you go home? It's late."

"Home?"

Annie's hands tightened on the railing at the sudden gurgling sound. It was a terrible moment before she realized it was laughter, a horrible kind of laughter.

"Home. Oh, that's funny, that is. Shouldn't I go home?"

The oars splashed violently, the boat jerked around, and the hideous laughter echoed across the water.

Annie turned and ran for shore.

On the ground-floor marbled foyer, she paused to catch her breath, then started rapidly up the steps.

She heard the click of high heels as she neared the second floor and Max, his voice admiring, say, "I'd love to see your collection."

She sped to the landing, every nerve alert. What did Sydney collect? Men's Jockey underwear?

Her relief when she recognized Max's companion made her effusive in her welcome. "Billye! How wonderful to see you! You're looking lovely. As always. Younger every year."

Buck Burger's wife welcomed Annie with the stylized embrace common to her circle, a glancing hug and one cheek pressed for an instant against Annie's. The unmistakable scent of Diva wafted over Annie.

Billye's lips curved in a perfect smile, which suited her porcelain-smooth face. Her white-gold hair was perfectly waved and looked about as real as the papier-mâché mask she held in one heavily ringed hand.

"Annie, honey, you're the sweetest little thing this side of the Red River." She took Annie's arm in a feather-light grasp, and they started up the stairs to the ballroom.

Max followed, grinning at the exchange of feminine nonsense. "Hey, Annie, Billye and I've been looking at Howard's collection of pointillist paintings. She's invited us over next week to see her collection."

"Why, I'd just love to show you all my paintin's," Billye said happily. "Buck doesn't pay them any mind, and it would be so lovely to show them to people who really care."

Annie smiled warmly at Billye.

"And I just know it's goin' to be so wonderful to have you young people as neighbors. You'll add so much to the Scarlet King compound."

They paused in the great archway. Billye gave them a friendly farewell smile. "I'd better round up Poppa and get us started home."

Annie was all for that. "Max, let's see if we can find Laurel. It's almost midnight and—"

She broke off, eyes widening. Had the general lost his mind?

General Houghton stalked toward a curtained alcove not far from the bar, his harsh face intent, eyes steely, lips grimly compressed. One gnarled hand held his ebony cane high in the air. He didn't hesitate when he reached the alcove. The cane sliced viciously through the air, and the curtain and its heavy bronze rod clattered to the hardwood floor.

Every guest close by turned to look.

The couple embracing in the darkness of the alcove jerked apart.

No masks.

Even in the dim light, Annie could see the smear of lipstick on George Graham's face.

Sydney Cahill, her eyes enormous with shock, fumbled to pull up the portion of her dress that had slipped to reveal one breast.

Howard Cahill stood only a few feet away.

Conversations stopped.

The orchestra came to the end of a medley from "Phantom of the Opera," and an awkward, tense silence ensued.

Howard, his face devoid of expression, turned away.

The general thumped his silver-tipped cane on the floor. "What kind of man are you?" he called after Howard contemptuously.

Howard kept on walking.

Every eye followed him.

"Maestro," a husky voice called, "it's time for a finale. 'When the Saints Go Marching In,' if you please!" Laurel ran lightly to Howard, stood on tiptoe and whispered in his ear, then lifted a sweeping hand to encourage the orchestra. "Everyone now, all together, form one long line." She placed Howard's hands on her hips and began to lead a high-stepping march to the infectious, irresistible blast of music.

Annie was caught up in the growing line. The old, familiar chant sounded as the line of dancers snaked about the floor.

It was a hell of an end to a hell of a party.

SIX

As Max unlocked the front door and stood aside for Annie and Laurel to enter, Laurel paused and beamed at them. "I might just run back. For a moment. Dear Howard. If he ponders Saint Bernard, I know it will be a comfort."

Max's hand shot out with incredible speed. "Tomorrow, sweetheart. It's late now. Past midnight."

Annie had a vision of an enormous dog, which she knew revealed a depth of ignorance, but she couldn't resist. "Saint Bernard?"

"Not, of course, any resemblance in personality at all. Between Bernard and Howard. Bernard, of course, was such a *driven* man. Given over to scourging and really so hard on his monks. *Very* little food. But he faced discouragements with such bravery. You see, the Second Crusade was a *disaster*. And it was Bernard who had rallied the West to besiege Damascus. I do feel Howard must accept defeat and rise above it. Though not withdrawing from society, as Bernard did. Bernard was quite opposed to light-mindedness. But then," and she laughed lightly, "we don't want Howard to be a saint, merely to be inspired."

"Not tonight," Max repeated firmly, still gripping his mother's elbow.

Laurel shot him a flashing sapphire glance, but Max had his stubborn look. Annie agreed entirely.

It wasn't all that easy, of course. They made several trips to the kitchen *("A little fruit before bedtime. So good for mental lightness"),* shared a final glass of wine, agreed that it had indeed been a delightful party (so many thoroughly nice people), and promised not to give Laurel a thought in the morning *("Just do your regular thing, my dears. Whatever it is.")* before Laurel was finally settled in the pink and gold suite.

In their own room, Max closed the door, looked at Annie and said simply—"God."

She nodded, not sure whether it was a prayer, a plea, or a benediction.

She was opening her mouth, ready to rehash the night (and how could she tactfully suggest to Max that his mother should be caged?), when she saw the package in the middle of their king-size bed.

"Oh, Max. Max!"

He grinned happily.

Annie could demolish a wrapped package faster than Spenser could pump iron.

"Oh, Max!" She stared down at the lovely pin, a two-inch ivory dagger with a jeweled hilt and a ruby at its tip. "Max, it's lovely!"

"Just a little memento for Valentine's. Can't say love isn't celebrated in mysteries. How about Patricia Wentworth's *The Ivory Dagger*? Love always wins out."

Her eyes misted. Dear Max. How much trouble he must have gone to. And obviously he had consulted Ingrid. No way would he have known about Patricia Wentworth and her prim sleuth, Miss Silver, who was so adept at righting an upside-down world for lovelorn couples. His taste ran more to Jeremiah F. Healy's John Francis Cuddy or Nicholas Freeling's Henri Castang.

What a jewel of a present.

What a thoughtful lover.

She stepped into his arms and their true Valentine celebration began.

• • •

Annie smiled sleepily and touched once again the ivory pin, firmly attached to the yoke of her soft cotton nightshirt. (That, too, had been a gift from Max. He visited rather often at the shop next door to Death on Demand and seemed intrigued by the assorted stock at Lingerie for Loving Ladies, often bringing her a gaily wrapped package. She did so enjoy packages, though some of his choices seemed impractical to an extreme. Flimsy.)

A lovely end to a day that had begun— Her eyes snapped open. Oh yes, what a beginning. But all's well that ends— Annie lifted her head and looked toward the open French windows and the balcony that overlooked their patio. She and Max enjoyed the cool night air and the sounds that drifted from the lagoon and the thick stand of yellow pines that separated the properties. Sometimes the noise could be piercing. Winter is the hootiest season for owls. Since female owls have a higher tone than the males, it was possible to tell when romance—or acrimony —was in swing. Their pines were home to a courting pair of Florida barred owls whose avian conversation was a mixture of hoos, cackles, barks, chortles, and aws. They were, in fact, hooting away, but there was nothing in their repertoire which sounded like the slap of tennis shoes against stone.

The luminous dial of the bedside radio clock read 12:50 A.M.

Slipping out of bed, Annie hurried to the open windows and stepped out onto the balcony. In the faint moonlight, the pool was a dark octagon. Water burbled softly in the spa. Nothing moved the length of the stone patio, but shrubbery quivered where a path entered the woods, though there was not a breath of wind. As Annie watched, the foliage ceased to move.

Oh, damn.

Laurel, of course.

As to where she was headed and why, Annie preferred not to speculate. But Annie knew she had to go after her mother-in-law. It wasn't safe to roam about in the woods at night. Not, of course, for the same reason that one avoided solitary wanderings on night-shrouded city streets. Laurel would understand those dangers. But was she prepared to meet a hungry, perhaps irritable and love-starved raccoon? Or, worse yet, a gray fox out courting? Or a predatory wild boar? Male boars could weigh as much as four hundred pounds and their razor-sharp tusks could be lethal.

Stepping back into the bedroom, Annie glanced at her sleeping mate. She didn't want to wake Max and tell him that Laurel was on the loose. In more ways, she thought primly, than one. It would be better by far if she could retrieve her mother-in-law and perhaps suggest that it was a little unseemly to seek out a married man in the middle of the night, no matter how noble her intent.

It did take time before she could set out in pursuit, even though she hurried. She slipped off her nightgown, pulled on a sweatshirt and pants and a pair of Reeboks. Downstairs, she stopped in momentary confusion. Where had they put the flashlight? In her treehouse, its customary spot was atop stacked, seldom-used blankets in the closet next to the bathroom. The new house had three bathrooms on the second floor and two on the ground floor and— Oh, of course. The kitchen pantry. Retrieving it, she carefully skirted her way across the room, still not quite sure where everything was. As expected, she found an open French window by the patio. Outside, she shivered in the cool, damp air, then headed for the pines.

It was very dark. An occasional shaft of moonlight pierced the canopies of the trees. Every few feet, a dim light burned on a tree trunk, courtesy of the Scarlet King Homeowners Association since the path around the lagoon was considered property in common. That made it possible to follow the path but also made the woods beyond seem even darker and more threatening. Annie almost turned on the flash, then decided to wait. It would be better if she could spot Laurel before she advertised her own presence. When the path forked, Annie turned right without hesitation, heading toward the Cahill property.

A sudden hoo-ooo at her shoulder made her jump convulsively. Another owl. That brought to mind other denizens of the forest who were about at night. Like cougars, who could measure nine feet from nose to tip of tail. Annie broke into a careful trot, hoping she didn't stumble over a vagrant tree limb. She tried hard not to think about cougars. Or bobcats. Or skunks.

"Oh, Jesus." It was a man's voice, hoarse and shaken.

Annie froze. She strained to see through the darkness, but there was nothing but shifting shadows. Motionless, she listened hard.

Ragged breathing.

Oh Lord, where was Laurel and what in the hell was going on?

Annie was afraid to go ahead and determined not to go back alone. Was Laurel all right? She cautiously edged ahead. Through the trees, she saw a gleam of light and heard running footsteps.

In a city when frightened, the best course was to make noise. Scream. Blow a horn. Shrill a whistle. Scare off an attacker.

Annie flicked on the flashlight and yelled as loud as she could.

Her first effort came out as a strangled whisper. Heart thudding, she began to wave the light and jump up and down and, finally, she got it out. "Help! Help! HELP!"

As the beam of the light swung back and forth, she saw she'd come much farther in the darkness than she realized. She had reached the end of the forest path where it gave way to the Cahill gardens and their lovely Victorian gazebo. A small shaft of light pointed from the gazebo.

Annie's light swept over the gazebo steps.

Her shout died in her throat.

Waveringly, Annie brought the beam back to the steps and focused it on the blood-drenched figure crumpled there.

SEVEN

The quiet was ominous, freighted with horror.

Blood glistened obscenely against magnolia-white skin and creamy silk, clung viscously to the diamond-brilliant necklace.

Shakily, Annie took one step forward, then another. She had to see if . . . But when the light focused fully on that crushed head and what remained of a no longer lovely face, she knew there was no need to hurry. Help would be forever too late for Sydney Cahill.

Shrubbery rustled to her left, toward the lagoon.

Whirling, Annie swung the light in that direction. Was there a darker shadow past that clump of azaleas?

"Who's there?" Her voice rose in panic.

No answer.

Annie had had enough. Not for her the perilous sleuthing of an Anne Maybury heroine. She bolted toward the path to home, running as fast as she could go.

From the lagoon, she heard a splash.

"Max, wake up! Wake up! Sydney's dead, and I can't find Laurel." She shook him like a terrier with a rat.

He came flailing up from a deep sleep and grabbed her in his arms. "It's all right," he said groggily. "Bad dream. Everything's all right, Annie. I'm here. Just—"

"Max, listen! Something awful's happened and Laurel isn't—"

"Did I hear my name?" Laurel stood in the open doorway to their bedroom.

"Oh my God, I was afraid—" Annie sank to the bed in relief, then looked sharply at her mother-in-law. "Where have you been? What have you been doing?"

Laurel looked fetching in soft pink warm-ups and matching pink sneakers. A few pine needles clung to the jacket. She waggled one hand in a delicate, airy gesture and said vaguely, "So helpful sometimes to walk about. Just to breathe in the night air. And so much warmer here in February than in Connecticut. Though the crunch of icy snow has its own charm. Still, a foray at night there can be too frosty. Here, the night air ̣othes and refreshes. It doesn't have noxious fumes, of course. That's merely an old wives' tale."

"Laurel," Annie cried. "You've got to tell us where you've been. Someone's killed Sydney." She turned anxiously toward Max. "At the gazebo. Someone . . . We have to call Chief Saulter. Oh God, we've got to tell Howard!"

Laurel gasped. "Sydney dead? But she was fine when—" A sorrowful shake of her golden head. "What a tragedy. Poor dear girl. Oh, I must go to Howard."

"Mother, wait a minute." Beneath its blond stubble of beard, Max's face tightened with worry. "Where have you been?"

"Round and about. Hither and yon. But that is of no moment." She took a deep breath and refused to meet his eyes. "My dear, if what Annie says is true, you are wasting time. You must contact the authorities. And I shall go inform Howard."

"Oh no," Max said. "That's the last thing in the world you should do. After the way you and Howard ogled each other at the party tonight, to have the police find the two of you together now would be a disaster."

Laurel drew herself up to her full five feet two inches. "I find that statement to be beneath contempt. Of course I shall go to Howard. It is my duty. As Saint Scholastica made abundantly clear—that lovely moment in her last meeting with her brother, Saint Benedict, when she called upon God to prevent Benedict from leaving. Benedict felt he could not spend a night absent from his monastery, but almost immediately the most enormous tempest erupted!"

At their noticeable lack of response, Laurel deigned to draw the moral. "Human relationships are so much more important than petty rules of behavior." She turned on her pink heel and sped toward the stairs.

"Annie, Annie, catch her!" Max yelled as he flung himself toward the closet and clawed for warm-up pants and a top.

Annie obediently started toward the doorway, then stopped. "What do I *do* when I catch her?"

The wail of a siren drowned out Max's vigorous response.

The police chief of Broward's Rock flicked a switch, and three battery-powered lights hummed to life, casting a sickly glow over the gazebo steps and the small group gathered close by. Frank Saulter gave a satisfied grunt and scrambled up from his knees. He directed one more troubled glance at Sydney's body, her blood-spattered, creamy skin a muddy sulfur in the yellowish light, then cleared his throat and looked into the frowning face of her husband.

"Sorry to ask you to remain here, Mr. Cahill. For right now, I'm the only man here. I've got a call in to my assistant, and he should arrive soon. Until then I'll have to ask you and"—Saulter's eyes skipped over the gathering—"and everybody else at the scene to stay here."

"Certainly." Cahill stood as if at parade rest, feet apart, hands clasped behind his back. He still wore his tuxedo, but his shirt was tieless and open at the throat. He didn't look toward the gazebo, but stared somberly at his dusty shoes, ignoring them all. Laurel was just close enough to the unmoving—and unmoved?—widower to be grouped with him. Annie longed to shake those pink-clad shoulders until Laurel's perfect teeth rattled like castanets. Did she deliberately want to attract Saulter's attention? But it would only underscore Laurel's proximity to Howard if Annie and Max tried to separate Laurel from him now.

As Saulter rapidly sketched the crime scene, Annie's eyes were drawn again and again to the sundial and the young man who leaned against it. He stood with his back to the gazebo. Annie recognized him at once—the almost handsome man with a face as lovely and vacuous as Albert Campion's, the man who had said viciously, "One slut deserves another," and made Sydney cry. He rubbed his head as if it hurt. No doubt it did, considering how much he had apparently drunk earlier. Occasionally he shot a furtive look toward Howard, then nervously brushed at his thin mustache. Who was he? Why was he here? She shot a glance at her watch. The party had broken up after the raucous march. That was almost two hours ago. He, too, still wore his tuxedo.

As for the other occupant of the clearing, what was he doing here? How did he have the nerve to come onto Howard Cahill's property after his behavior at the ball? General Houghton's burning dark eyes devoured the crime scene, returning time and again to Sydney's body. His cadaverous face, clipped iron-gray mustache, and balding head with a thick blue vein pulsing in his right temple belonged in a Count Dracula horror flick. A pistol butt stuck out of the right pocket of his tattersall robe. One wrinkled hand rested on the pistol butt, the other on his ebony cane. General Houghton cleared his throat peremptorily.

"Be glad to pitch in, Chief. Came because I heard cry for help. Can set the time exactly. One oh eight—"

Cry for help. With a shock, Annie realized Houghton was talking about her. She opened her mouth, then closed it. There would be time enough when Saulter took their statements.

"—any event, came prepared." The general patted the pistol. "Be glad to convoy this party to my residence. Can keep them sequestered until further notice. Rouse my wife. Hospital trained. She can escort ladies to rest facilities, if need be. Won't permit communication."

Saulter quickly accepted the offer. "Appreciate it, sir. No need to subject"—he looked at Howard—"everyone to this." He glanced at each person in turn. "Cooperate with General Houghton. I'll be along to talk to each of you as soon as possible."

The general efficiently placed Annie, with her flashlight, at the head of the column, then marched them single file to the lagoon where, at his direction, they turned right. Once again, the path plunged into a thick tangle of greenery, loblolly pines, live oaks, stiff waxey-leaved yaupon holly, water oaks, and clumps of saw palmettos. Annie's flashlight made a frail assault against the deep darkness. As the pines began to thin, she could see the Houghton house, its ground floor blazing with light. As they neared the steps to the rear piazza, the back door burst open.

"Colville, where—" Eileen Houghton stopped on the top step and began to button her quilted red cotton robe, hiding her buxom figure beneath its shapelessness. Graying blond hair hung straight down to midback. Her pincushion-plump face was bare of makeup. Pale blue eyes widened in amazement.

"Bad business, Eileen." But wasn't there a note of satisfaction beneath the somber report? "Sydney's been murdered. Gazebo. Authorities there, but need site for witnesses to await interrogation. Offered our library. You can see to coffee, whiskey."

Apparently Eileen Houghton was accustomed to taking orders from her elderly husband. She nodded obediently and turned on her heel. Silently, they followed her down a broad central hallway, typical of an antebellum house, to the library.

The general gestured with his cane at the assortment of easy chairs and sofas. "Hope everyone can be comfortable. Damn awkward situation." He cleared his throat. "Damn sorry, Howard." Again the words were correct, but Houghton's eyes waited avidly for Cahill's response. Howard made none. A flush edged up the general's sallow cheeks. He turned his piercing gaze toward the young man with the tousled brown hair. "Don't believe we've met, sir."

But it was Howard who spoke. "My son, Carleton, General Houghton."

Annie recalled the drunken taunt. *"Tell the old man. See if I care."* My God, she thought. Howard's son. Sydney's stepson.

Carleton stuck out a trembling hand.

The general pumped it briefly.

"Carleton teaches in Minnesota. He's visiting us—" Howard stopped.

Us. Not now. Not any longer. "He's here for a few days over spring break."

The general looked toward Laurel. It was one of the few times in Annie's memory that a male, of whatever age, evinced no pleasure in that act. In fact, his eyes narrowed, though he spoke civilly. "Didn't make your aquaintance earlier this evening, madam." So he had at least noticed her at the party.

"My mother, Laurel Roethke," Max said clearly. "She's visiting Annie and me." He cleared his throat and added forcefully, "She arrived only today. Well, yesterday morning now."

Laurel gazed thoughtfully at the general. "Such a shame when love is thwarted. I'm sure you agree, General?"

Annie doubted that it happened often, but Houghton had no response. His dark brows drew together in an irritated frown.

"It does seem to me—and I do bring some *years* of experience to my judgment—that this tragic occurrence must be a result of one of the darker faces of love," Laurel mused regretfully.

"What the hell are you talking about?" Carleton's voice lacked the deep timbre and authoritative note of his father's voice. He sounded querulous, where Howard would have been combative. His face was very pale.

Laurel smiled benignly. "So difficult sometimes for the young to differentiate between love and passion, commitment and jealousy, desire and lust. And it *does* make a difference."

"Enough nonsense," the general barked. The blue vein at his temple throbbed. "People stay in their own beds, follow the rules, world'd work damn sight better."

Howard Cahill, sitting in a red leather wingback chair, ignored the comment, his face grim.

That was the extent of the conversation for an incredibly slow-moving hour. Max sat on the chintz-covered sofa beside Annie, his arm supportingly around her shoulders, but his dark blue eyes moved again and again toward his mother. If anyone started to speak, the general shook his head briskly. "No communication. Difficult, but necessary. Operational procedure, you know."

Eileen Houghton, dressed now in gray slacks and an orchid high-necked blouse, her blond hair up in a tight coronet braid, offered whiskey or coffee. Everyone but Laurel accepted coffee.

"Perhaps chamomile tea?" she asked brightly.

Eileen Houghton brought that, too.

Laurel settled with her tea on an ottoman close to Howard. Occasionally, she reached out and patted his arm in gentle commiseration. When he looked at her, his haggard face softened. Annie wondered how in God's name Max could have a mother with such a total lack of native cunning. Didn't she understand how serious this was? Didn't she grasp the fact that a particularly brutal murder—Annie tried not to remember the shattered cranial bones of a once beautiful woman—had taken place? And the victim had been the wife of the man Laurel was now so publicly supporting.

What was Laurel going to tell the police? Annie felt a wave of panic. Surely Laurel wouldn't guilelessly reveal her sudden infatuation with Howard? Or admit she'd gone on a midnight foray to seek out a married man?

Would she?

Their gazes crossed. Laurel's exuded confidence, good cheer, and reassurance with an overlay of distress for the dreadful circumstances.

Annie stared hard at Laurel, who responded immediately, of course, with an inquiring glance. There were no flies on Laurel when it came to picking up vibes. Just like Dorothy Gilman's Mrs. Pollifax.

Effective communication without words was tricky. Annie inclined her head in a quick, tiny nod toward Laurel—meaning *you*—pointed with a circumspect index finger at her own midriff—meaning *me*—placed one hand conspicuously in the other and clasped them—meaning *together*—and began to hum that old familiar hymn, a standby to generations of campers, "In the Garden."

Laurel beamed delightedly. "How sweet you are, my dear. And so *clever*. But I came to the garden alone. We must all tell the truth, mustn't we?"

Max stifled a groan. Carleton's head jerked toward Laurel and his eyes had the look of a startled wild animal. Howard frowned.

"Here now," the general said sharply. "Quiet."

Annie would have enjoyed delivering Laurel into the evil hands of some rogue on the order of Casper Gutman, Auric Goldfinger, or Dr. Fu Manchu. So let Laurel paddle her canoe right over the dam. See if Annie cared.

Annie's face felt hot, and she knew it probably matched the rich rosy-reddish hue of the library's cypress paneling and bookshelves. She tried to concentrate on surveying the general's remarkable collection of books, primarily histories of warfare from the Gallic Wars to the present, but Max kept looking at Laurel, his concern undisguised. So, despite Annie's irritation and the grainy feel of fatigue, she forced herself to consider the possibilities.

Laurel, who was going to say God only knew what, was likely to be in a hell of a spot. The police, both real and literary, from criminal-turned-Sûreté-chief Arsène Lupin to cigar-chewing, Nero Wolfe–pawn Inspector Cramer to Wilkie Collins's dull-witted Superintendent Seegrave, have a definite bias for the obvious. Of course, Frank Saulter knew them and knew Laurel. Still, he couldn't help but look very closely at everyone who had been in the vicinity of the crime.

Okay, Annie thought, Max was out of it. She could swear he had been asleep when she left the house and still asleep when she returned, after finding Sydney's body.

That left Annie, Laurel, Howard, Carleton, and the general, all of whom had been on or near the scene very early on.

Annie knew she hadn't done it. And she knew that Laurel was innocent. Laurel might be spacey, Laurel might be unpredictable, but Laurel could never hurt a living creature. Annie knew that without any doubt.

Would Chief Saulter know it?

Of course.

It was so obvious.

But people would talk and Chief Saulter would hear about Laurel and Howard at the party and their unmistakable infatuation.

Surely that would direct suspicion at Howard, not Laurel.

Still, Annie didn't feel good about any of it.

Where *was* Laurel when the murder occurred? What, if anything, did she know? When it became apparent that Laurel—and Annie, too, of course—had been wandering about at the time Sydney was struck down, would that make the killer nervous?

Annie swallowed.

She knew she was tired and she'd been scared to the core, then horrified by her gruesome discovery. So maybe she wasn't thinking too straight.

But she had a god-awful feeling that maybe she and Max had better think about this one and think hard. And fast.

Who could have killed Sydney?

Three men had been near the gazebo when death stalked.

The widower, Howard Cahill.

His son, Carleton, whose nasty comment had made Sydney cry.

The general.

And, of course, the dark grounds could easily have harbored someone unseen, someone as yet unknown. The skin on the back of her neck prickled. What about Dorcas Atwater? Of course, it was much earlier in the evening when Dorcas rowed near the Cahill pier. She could have returned. But without doubt three men had clear opportunity and must be considered as possibilities.

Helen Reilly's Inspector Christopher McKee believed that observation of suspects could provide the key to a crime. Well, here she was with at least three suspects to observe. Annie looked at Howard Cahill. Even tonight, obviously under stress, he appeared competent and in control of himself. He sat deep in thought, distinct lines furrowing his

broad forehead and making deep indentations to either side of his firm
mouth. He looked tough, determined, wary—and worried.

There was not even a trace of grief in his demeanor.

If he had murdered his wife, surely he would parade grief as publicly
as possible, like a Freeman Wills Crofts villain with an unbreakable alibi.
But he was making no show of emotion, of any kind.

He wasn't a stupid man. Far from it. Annie knew little about him, but
that little—he was a self-made multimillionaire who had fearlessly and
shrewdly faced down governments, unions, competitors, and terrorists
in building his great shipping fleet—argued superior intelligence.

An intelligent man who decided to murder his wife would know that
the police always look at the husband first, and plan accordingly.

Of course, superior intelligence often is accompanied by overweening
arrogance.

Perhaps feeling her gaze, Cahill suddenly looked directly at Annie,
and she knew abruptly that despite his unaffected appearance, he was
riven with emotion. For just an instant, their glances locked and in his
dark eyes she saw despair and fear, a soul harrowed by unspeakable
visions.

"Dear Howard," Laurel soothed, "don't lose heart. We must ever
carry with us the memory of Saint Colette. Such *hostility* when she
began her great work of returning the Poor Clare nuns to their original
strict rule of life. So hard to persuade them to forgo the pleasures of the
world, but she refused to be discouraged, no matter how daunting her
trials."

"The saints," Howard said bitterly, "were never hostage to love."

"Oh, but they were, they were," Laurel contradicted gently. "Love
made them saints. They take the Gospels quite literally. That is what
mankind finds so fascinating, yet so frightening about them. 'Love your
neighbor as yourself.' So simple. So very, very difficult to do—and it
requires such sacrifice. But that is their credo, and love made life so
difficult for them. As it does for everyone, but then what would life be
without—"

"Madam." The prominent blue vein pulsed in the general's temple.
"Quiet, if you please."

Annie didn't think she liked the general very much. But men who
become generals, for the most part, probably care little whether they
are liked. They prefer to be feared. The general's truculent eyes, prominent beak of a nose, and downturned mouth exuded no charm. He
looked ill. There was a grayish blue cast to his skin and he was too thin,
his hands bony, the skin of his cheeks flaccid. But his every act underscored his will to dominate, to control, to survive.

Why would he kill Sydney? Did he see her as a Jezebel, as a shameless woman? Was he a zealot who felt the world was well rid of women

like Sydney? Or had his exposure of her at the party, locked in George Graham's embrace, been the act of a frustrated lover? Had he been attracted to her, then rebuffed? That wouldn't jibe with his graceless comment about people staying in their own beds . . . . In context, surely it referred to Sydney and that was an ugly slur to make with her husband listening. But the general had said it. A hateful man. The general, she decided, was well worth considering.

She looked next at Carleton Cahill, who had to be high on any list. Obviously, his relationship with Sydney didn't fit the accepted pattern between stepmother and stepchild. Carleton, after a little too much to drink, hadn't bothered to hide his contempt for Sydney. Had, indeed, made a point of it. It is not unusual for children to resent a remarriage, a second wife. But he was no child. Just how much had he disliked Sydney? Was it dislike verging on hatred? At the party he had seemed equally hostile to his father. Carleton was no longer glaring at Howard, but he was clearly uncomfortable, darting nervous, uneasy glances around the room. There was no vestige of grief.

Annie sighed wearily. What a mess. Max gave her shoulders a quick squeeze. "Tired?" he asked softly.

"I'm okay."

The general glared at them.

Max glared back. "Look, it's almost two in the morning. I think—"

Footsteps sounded in the hall. The general nodded toward his wife, who scurried to open the door. Two men entered. Annie gripped Max's hand. Oh no. No. But it was.

Circuit Solicitor Bryce Willard Posey strode forward, his bulging blue eyes glistening with eagerness. Posey was without doubt and without question the most odious man she'd ever known. Despite the late hour, he was freshly shaven and exuded the sweet smell of cinnamon after-shave. Did he think a photographer might show up? But, of course, the murder of the wife of one of the island's wealthiest residents would bring the news services, and Posey was already prepared. He'd crammed his six feet three inches, two hundred and fifty pounds into a blue suit that would have looked better on a leaner man. With a light blue shirt for television. Annie looked past him at lanky, khaki-clad Chief Saulter, whose corrugated face was a mass of unhappy wrinkles. He looked as lugubrious as Phoebe Atwood Taylor's Syl Mayo when his cousin Asey, the famous Codfish Sherlock, was pestered by State Trooper Hanson.

Posey knew every eye was upon him. He puffed his cheeks, as full of himself as Erle Stanley Gardner's Hamilton Burger when addressing a jury, and surveyed his audience. It was, Annie thought sourly, like watching a pouter pigeon preen.

Howard Cahill wasn't intimidated. He sat calmly in the wingback chair, his face inscrutable.

Carleton Cahill hunched forward in his chair, his hands balled in tight fists. One blue eye jerked in a nervous tic.

The general nodded in satisfaction, his duty discharged, and fastened his cold, venomous glance on Carleton.

Annie wondered how Eileen could stand being married to such a hateful old man, a man at least twenty years her senior. Annie looked toward Eileen, and her sympathy shriveled. Eileen's eyes glistened with a kind of eager slyness as she watched Howard. Her plump face radiated an avid interest. She leaned forward in anticipation and her blouse pulled taut, outlining the fullness of her breasts. It was obvious that she was looking forward to the coming unpleasantness, to this slice of raw drama that had erupted in her no doubt incredibly boring and repressive life.

What a charming couple, Annie decided.

Laurel was smiling kindly at Posey. No doubt, Annie concluded, Laurel's study of the saints had infused her with a determination to be kind to life's unfortunates. There should, Annie thought dourly, be a legal limit to charity.

Max, of course, was his handsome, endearing, wonderful self, though she hoped he would refrain from his tendency to bait Posey. Her husband's dark blue eyes shone with a familiar sardonic gleam, which made her heart sink.

"Ladies and gentlemen, I am Circuit Solicitor Bryce Willard Posey, and I have come from the mainland to take charge of this investigation." His voice boomed sonorously in the library. "I shall not rest until I have incarcerated the perpetrator of this hideous crime of passion."

Slowly, Howard stood. "Who killed my wife?"

The somber question hung between the two men. The contrast in their demeanor, Posey's arrogant posturing and Cahill's restrained intensity, made Posey look foolish. He realized it immediately. His heavy jowls reddened. "We shall find her killer, Mr. Cahill, you can count on that. We have already determined one important fact." He waited until every eye was on him. "We are," he said ponderously, "looking for a man."

Carleton Cahill began to laugh raggedly.

His father called out sharply, "Carleton!"

Carleton lifted trembling hands to his face, pressed them there for a long moment, then let them drop.

Moving his bulk quickly for so large a man, Posey crossed to stand directly in front of the younger Cahill. "What's so funny?"

Carleton didn't answer. He shook his head miserably back and forth.

Howard was there in an instant. "Back off."

Posey swung to face him.

Chief Saulter stepped close enough to intervene, if necessary. Max came swiftly to his feet.

Posey and Cahill were both big men, but the prosecutor ran to fat and the shipowner had the stocky, well-muscled build of a man who had worked hard and kept fit.

"My son is upset," Howard said quietly.

"Interesting," Posey replied. "He's upset—and you aren't? It was *your* wife."

For just an instant, Howard's shoulders slumped and a look of pain touched his eyes. In that moment, he looked much older. Then it was past. Once again he stared at Posey with self-possession and control. "Yes, Sydney was my wife."

"My stepmother," Carleton said contemptuously.

"Carleton." His father's chiding voice wasn't angry, was, in fact, gentle.

"Oh, Jesus," Carleton said. "How did something like this ever happen to us?" He struggled to his feet, reached out to his father. "Dad, how did this ever happen?"

Howard gripped his son's arm for a long moment, then shook his head wearily. "I don't know."

"Well, we're going to find out just what did happen," Posey trumpeted. He pulled a small notebook from his pocket and flipped it open. "Now, let's see. The call came in at twenty-two minutes past one o'clock."

Saulter broke in. "I arrived at the entrance to the Scarlet King properties at approximately one thirty-three and was met by Mr. Howard Cahill at the gate. He—"

Annie didn't even think before she spoke. "The gate!" she demanded. "Was the gate open?" She hadn't even thought about the gate!

Posey turned a meaty red face toward her, but Saulter said hastily, "Good question, Annie. The gate was closed. Moreover—"

Howard interrupted. "The gate was open all evening for the party." Sudden hope flickered in his eyes.

"Who had a party?" Posey demanded suspiciously.

"We did," Howard responded. "My wife and I. We had almost a hundred guests. I hired several young men from the country club to help park cars. One of them was at the gate all evening, to be sure no one but residents or guests entered."

"Pretty exclusive, huh?" Posey sneered.

Howard looked at him in disgust.

The general cleared his throat. "Easily misunderstood. Private property, of course, from the turnoff through the Scarlet King compound.

Gate matter of security. Compound developed by Buck Burger. Used to be criminal lawyer. Lots of enemies. Security," he concluded.

"Do you suppose," Eileen interrupted, "that someone from the party was an old enemy of Mr. Burger's—or even of Mr. Cahill's? You made a lot of enemies, didn't you, when you broke that strike in Long Beach?" She had a soft, unctuous voice that sounded as though she'd spent years saying reassuring things she didn't mean. "I read about it in *Hoity Toity.* Anyway, do you suppose someone killed Sydney to get back at Howard? Or maybe they thought Sydney was Billye Burger. Maybe it was an attempted kidnapping and Sydney—"

Saulter broke in briskly. "The gate was in place at ten minutes to one when the last Paradise Caterers truck departed. It was driven by Hutch Kennedy. He and his partner, Ben Dunstan, drove toward the main road and just before they reached it, they had a flat tire. They were just finishing changing it when I came in. They said not a single car or a single person had passed them from the time they left the Cahills."

"I see," Howard said wearily.

"The road is narrow, with bar ditches on either side," Max observed. So there was no place for a car to park where it wouldn't have been seen by the caterers. No place at all.

"If no car came in," Eileen began, her eyes narrowing in thought, "that means—" She drew her breath in sharply. "That means it's someone inside the compound, someone who lives here! Oh, my God!"

"Grim," the general said gruffly. "But," he patted his sagging robe pocket, "don't be alarmed, my dear. No danger for you while I'm here."

It might, given his age, have sounded rather pathetic. But it didn't. Annie thought she detected a gleam of eagerness in those dark eyes. He'd damn well enjoy blowing somebody away.

Posey turned gallantly toward Eileen. "Don't be frightened, Mrs. Houghton. We will protect you. Besides, the ferocity of the attack upon Mrs. Cahill is characteristic of a crime of passion. Generally, crimes of passion are committed by those with a close personal relationship with the victim." His heavy head swiveled back to Howard. "Mr. Cahill, did you give your wife a valentine?"

Howard's iron composure cracked. "What the hell kind of question is that?"

Posey's thick lips curled in a pleased smile. "A very important question, Mr. Cahill."

Howard jammed his hands in his pockets. "All right, Mr. Posey, if it's so goddamned important. No, I did not give Sydney a valentine."

"Oh." Satisfaction oozed from Posey. "You did not give Mrs. Cahill a valentine." He leaned forward, relishing the moment. "What were your relations with your wife?"

Carleton scrambled to his feet. "Dad, you don't have to answer questions like that." Carleton glared at Posey. "Why are you wasting time? Why don't you get a search started? It's probably too late already. Why don't you start looking for Sydney's murderer?"

Posey didn't bother to answer. He ignored Carleton, who flushed a deep red.

Howard took a deep breath. "For the most part," he said carefully, "my wife and I maintained a very cordial relationship."

"You didn't mind if she was screwing around with another man?"

Howard stood very still, his face a frozen mask. When he answered, there was a steeliness in his voice that hadn't appeared before. "Carleton is right. I don't have to answer these kinds of questions. Chief, isn't anything going to be done to find out what happened?"

Posey was not to be ignored. "You can answer questions here, or you can answer them at the jail. Take your pick, Mr. Cahill. And I'll tell you one thing"—he shook a bulbous finger in Howard's face—"money can't buy your way out of a murder charge, not as long as I'm circuit solicitor and I—"

"Such a *mistake* to lose sight of the ultimate goal," Laurel said kindly, insinuating herself between the two men. "Dear Saint Michael—I know you are familiar with him," she trilled to Posey, "the patron saint of policemen—he would remind us, I'm sure, that we should attend to first things first. Who *could* have killed poor dear Sydney? Howard can't be included among those with such an opportunity because he was seeing me to the front door of my son's house at almost the very moment the murder must have occurred. Therefore, it is a clear waste of your time and energy to bombard him with questions. In fact, I might suggest that a study of the time element is essential because—"

Posey erupted. "What do you know about any of it?" he demanded angrily. "You talk as though you were there and—"

"But I was."

The circuit solicitor's watery blue eyes fastened on Laurel like a diamondback rattler sighting a particularly tasty rabbit.

Max moved swiftly to Laurel's side. "Mother. Laurel. Wait a minute. Don't—"

"Max, dear, it is clearly my duty to share what I saw. Such a lovely evening—at least the weather was quite clement. A delightful change from Connecticut, so I decided to view the gardens in the moonlight. Howard had told me I was quite welcome to wander through them. At any time." She smiled at him.

"I'm sorry you're involved in this at all," he said somberly.

"Perhaps we should be grateful. If I had not come, you might face a difficult period. One is so often truly led, I do believe." She flashed a disarming smile at Posey, who regarded her with deep suspicion.

But Howard didn't look relieved. If anything, his face was more somber than before.

"You came over to his house in the middle of the night?" Posey demanded. "What time? When?"

"I left my room at Max and Annie's house at precisely twelve forty-five," she said crisply. Her tone was assured and businesslike, very different from her usual airy patter. "I had a pocket flashlight with me. I walked quickly and I reached the property next door at twelve fifty-three. Precisely."

Everyone looked at her curiously.

She raised a golden eyebrow. "I looked at my watch."

"Why?" Saulter inquired, his gaze intent.

"Because I heard voices."

She certainly had everyone's attention.

Especially that of Howard and Carleton. The widower raised a hand, as if to stop her. Carleton's eyes widened and he looked as if the shades of hell had materialized before him.

"My dears," she said sweetly, "I know it is difficult to relive those last moments, especially since Sydney was so upset. And you were both so angry."

Posey licked his porcine lips in anticipation. "Why was she upset?"

"Sydney was childlike in so many ways—"

Annie recalled that voluptuous body and Sydney's behavior and thought, Oh, sure.

"—and so her confrontation with Howard in the library upset her very much. She was close to tears."

Saulter unobtrusively began to write swiftly in a dog-eared notebook.

"Of course, I well understand Howard's feelings. He was very forbearing, but Sydney simply went too far when she trifled with another man at their very own party." She beamed at Posey. "A dentist, I understand. George Graham. A very active man. In any event, Howard's patience was at an end and he told her that he intended to file for a divorce."

"You bitch! Shut your mouth before—"

"Carleton!" Howard said sternly.

"Howard, it's quite all right." Laurel directed a benevolent look at Carleton, whose face was livid with anger. "Carleton doesn't understand that the truth always outs. And it does, you know. Lots of people will be happy to tell the police about Sydney's interlude in the curtained alcove with Graham. Sydney was distraught with Howard's pronouncement. She sobbed that it was all Carleton's fault, that he had been so ugly to her. Then she ran toward the open library windows and said she would find someone who loved her. And she burst out into the garden and headed for the gazebo." A wisp of a sigh. "Poor dear child. She ran to love. And found death."

Saulter wrote furiously, and Posey looked like he'd won the Florida lottery.

"But, the important point," and once again she was crisp and direct, "I arrived outside the library window at twelve fifty-four, in time to see Sydney storm from the room, out into the garden and onto the path leading to the gazebo. At the same time, Carleton burst out of the library and began to walk rapidly to the right."

Annie sorted it out in her mind: Sydney on the path to the gazebo, Carleton heading for the tennis court and pool.

"I turned away, feeling that I had arrived at an inopportune moment. I started up a path leading in the general direction of my son's house. I didn't want to return by the lagoon path as that was the way Sydney had gone. I walked on for no longer than a minute or two; then I heard Howard's voice behind me. He joined me and said he hoped my pleasure in the gardens hadn't been affected by the episode I'd witnessed. He was quite in command of himself. Grave and weary, but not angry. I knew that he would not wish to discuss those moments, so we spoke about the loveliness of the night. We walked on together and in a moment or so we were at Max and Annie's front door and he said good night. It was just five minutes after one when I entered the foyer. General Houghton heard a cry for help at eight minutes after one. So you see, Howard could not possibly have killed Sydney. There simply was no time."

"But that was me," Annie cried. "I mean, I yelled for help when I found Sydney; then the bushes rustled and it scared me, so I ran home."

"Then it's even clearer," Laurel concluded happily. "Sydney was already dead at eight minutes after one. Howard is completely in the clear."

Posey looked like Nero Wolfe when an orchid died.

Saulter was nodding slowly.

But Howard Cahill had no aura of a man saved from the gallows. Instead, his eyes dark with pain, he slowly shook his head. "Laurel, my dear, you are such a lovely person. Please don't misunderstand me when I say I appreciate your efforts. I wish we could have met another day, another way."

Posey's head swiveled from one to the other.

"What the hell? Is this phony? What's going on?" He glared at Howard. "What happened when you came out of that library? Where *did* you go?"

Howard looked like a man en route to the gallows. "I decline to answer any questions until I can talk to my lawyer."

Laurel's eyes widened in surprise. She bit her lip, sighed, and said, "Oh, my dear!"

EIGHT

The unseasonable February weather—highs in the 70s rather than the 60s—had persuaded a huge pileated woodpecker that it was March and mating time. He drummed on a hollow limb of a towering pine that stood right next to Max and Annie's patio and their outdoor breakfast table. Little pieces of bark crackled free and fell, pelting them. He sounded more like a jackhammer than a bird. Annie brushed tree debris from her hair, already ruffled by a gentle early morning breeze, and glared up at the boisterous suitor. His red crest flamed in the early morning sun, and his black wing feathers glistened like polished ebony.

"He's driving me crazy. How can he stand to make so much noise? Why doesn't that incessant banging addle his thimbleful of bird brains?" she groused as she reached for another peanut butter cookie. (If Max and Laurel wanted to eat oat bran for breakfast, so be it. What was wrong with peanut butter cookies?)

"Another of nature's miracles," Laurel said sweetly but loudly enough to be heard over the rat-a-tat-tats. "Thick muscles around his brain provide cushioning. Just like a crash helmet. Isn't that dear?"

Max lowered his newspaper and grinned. "Face it, Annie, he'd rather die than stop. He knows there's a lady woodpecker out there somewhere who will think those are the niftiest sounds she ever heard."

"Such a *strong* urge," Laurel murmured.

Annie felt a moment of panic as two handsome faces beamed at her. Mother and son. How in God's name could they both look so calm, so happy, so certain that goodwill surrounded them? Laurel, who apparently never suffered from fatigue, was as fresh as ever this morning, her dark blue eyes shining with eagerness, her patrician face unlined. She looked about sixteen in a soft cream cotton blouse and green poplin pants with a batik design. Her golden hair shimmered like an August beach. Max might have his mother's blond hair and dark blue eyes, but, thankfully, he wasn't the least bit ethereal. To the contrary, he was solidly there, every well-built muscle of him in a blue-and-white-striped polo that emphasized the breadth of his chest and khaki shorts that revealed stalwart legs any woman would notice. He was damned attractive. If Laurel weren't here— But she was. And so was the reality of murder next door. How could Max look as unruffled as Lord Peter Wimsey (aka Death Bredon) in *Murder Must Advertise*?

"Look, we've got to get busy," Annie said briskly, pouring another round of French-roast coffee into their cups.

Two sets of dark blue eyes looked at her inquiringly.

"You do recall," she said with heavy irony, "that we've had a homicide next door."

"That ass Posey," her husband replied; then he rattled the newspaper. "It says here that this is the warmest and earliest spring we've—"

"Max, who cares? What's wrong with you two? Last night Laurel couldn't wait to jump into it and defend Howard. And, Max," she said irritably, looking at her handsome husband, "what's with you? Last night you were worried sick about Laurel and don't pretend you weren't because I know better."

Max folded the paper and put it on the wicker tabletop. "Of course I was worried. I didn't know where she'd been or what she might have seen, but once Laurel told us, that made everything all right."

Laurel was nodding in agreement.

"I hate to be dense—"

Laurel murmured, "Like dear Captain Hastings."

Max popped the last morsel of his oat bran muffin into his mouth. "Or Sergeant Heath. Or Tony Abbott."

Annie restrained herself from assault. Ever since Laurel took a class on the mystery, she'd prided herself as an expert. "—But would you please explain why it makes everything all right."

"Laurel's out of it," Max said cheerfully. "She wasn't anywhere near the gazebo after Sydney headed for it, so the murderer won't get nervous. And Howard saw Laurel leave for our house, then caught up with her, so I don't see how Posey can get any crazy ideas about Laurel being involved. No problem."

"But Posey hauled Howard off to the mainland last night for further questioning after Howard all but admitted Laurel made it all up," Annie objected.

"I beg your pardon," Laurel said politely.

"The alibi. Your alibi and Howard's. You made it up."

"No." Laurel was firm.

Max stared at Annie in total surprise. "Of course she didn't make it up. Laurel doesn't lie."

"Of course not." Laurel took a dainty sip of coffee.

Annie studied her mother-in-law. Did Laurel always tell the truth? God knew that was difficult to determine. It all depended upon how one defined truth. Laurel's mind moved like quicksilver and was as impossible to grasp and hold. And could anyone ever have confidence in her recollection of times? Despite how often she claimed to have checked her watch.

Laurel reached across the table and patted Annie's hand. "You must have faith, my dear. Look at the wonderful examples given to us by the dear saints." A tiny frown marred her beautiful brow. "Although, to be sure, so many of them met with great obstacles despite their noble intentions. I know Saint Augustine must have felt sorely tried when it appeared that the Church to which he had given his all would come to naught." She looked at them inquiringly, sighed at their evident lack of comprehension, and amplified, "You will recall that Rome had already fallen to the barbarians and there seemed to be no hope for what remained of the Christian world. The invading Vandals were at the gates of Hippo when Augustine died."

Max's eyes glinted with mischief. "Actually, all I remember of Saint Augustine was his rather understandable plea, something on the order of 'Lord, make me chaste—but not yet.' "

For once Laurel was speechless. Annie decided not to speculate on the reasons. She avoided looking at Max. Sometimes he was eerily like Laurel in his ability to divine her thoughts.

Besides, it was time to get back to the point. "So neither one of you is worried." Annie still didn't understand it. Oh, she understood Max's relief. He had been concerned on Laurel's account. Now that he felt sure she had been nowhere near the scene of the crime, he was quite relaxed. But how could Laurel be so untroubled?

Annie tried to put it tactfully. "Uh, Laurel, I'm afraid that when Howard refused to corroborate your statement, Posey assumed you were—uh—mistaken."

Laurel was undisturbed. "Right shall prevail."

"Doesn't matter what Posey thinks," Max added, wistfully eyeing a peanut butter cookie.

"Push the edge of the envelope," Annie murmured, placing one on his plate.

He munched happily. "An alibi's an alibi. Let's see Posey prove it isn't true."

Laurel patted her lips with her napkin. "What a delightful repast, my dear. Now, I believe I will—"

Footsteps crunched on the crushed oyster-shell walk to the side of the house, and Chief Saulter came up to the patio.

"Morning, Max, Annie. Mrs. Roethke. Glad I found you all here. Like to get your statements about last night, if you don't mind."

Annie bent to one side to look past Saulter, but glory be, Posey wasn't there.

Max stood and walked forward, offering his hand. "Sure, Frank. Come have some coffee."

"That'd be mighty fine."

Annie brought not only a cup and saucer but a plate and a basket filled with croissants.

"How'd you know I hadn't had any breakfast?" Frank asked. Then he looked reluctantly at Laurel. "Guess I'd better tell you folks about Mr. Cahill first. You might not want to invite me. Posey arrested Cahill this morning as a material witness."

"Posey's an ass," Max said calmly. "Howard has an alibi."

"He certainly does," Laurel agreed. "Oh dear, I suppose I'd better run over to the mainland, make it clear—"

"Uh, I wouldn't do that," Saulter said quickly. His weathered face crinkled in embarrassment. "Not a good idea. In fact, Mrs. Roethke"—he cleared his throat uncomfortably—"Posey said if you repeated that, uh, that claptrap—that's what he called it—he said he'd throw you in jail too on a charge of conspiracy."

Laurel frowned. "I am puzzled. Hasn't Howard given a statement yet, agreeing with mine?"

Saulter shook his head. "His lawyer came, flew in on a private jet from Atlanta. Don't know what they talked about, of course, but the upshot is—Cahill won't say a damned word. Not a word about what happened after he and Mrs. Cahill had that spat in the library. Won't even admit to that. Posey says he's guilty as hell, must be, otherwise why would he clam up? So Posey thinks you made the alibi up."

Max frowned. Laurel looked thoughtful, rather than outraged, which increased the niggling worm of suspicion wriggling in the back of Annie's mind. Not, of course, that Laurel would ever deliberately tell a falsehood. But Laurel had an incredible capacity for seeing the world precisely as she wished it to be. However, if the alibi was fake or—to be charitable—mistaken and Howard was guilty, why didn't he leap on it? It was a little difficult to picture a ruthless businessman as overburdened with rectitude. George Washington, maybe yes; Howard Cahill, probably no.

Annie's mind gnawed on the problem.

1. Was Howard keeping quiet because he expected to be arrested and tried and would not testify—the defendant is not required to do so—counting on Laurel's testimony to convince a jury of his innocence?

2. Wasn't that hypothesis incredibly convoluted?

Not, she decided, for a man who had the wit and Byzantine abilities to run a worldwide shipping business.

Unfortunately, Annie had too lively an imagination and could foresee dire consequences if that scenario unfolded and was successful (Laurel marrying a man who was really a murderer). She recalled with a shudder Leslie Ford's *Trial by Ambush*.

Annie grabbed another peanut butter cookie. For mental invigoration.

Laurel thoughtfully tapped beautifully manicured fingers on the tabletop and gave a vexed sigh. "Dear Mr. Posey, so *sure* of himself. And we all know what goes before a fall!"

Saulter eyed her warily.

"In fact"—she leaned closer to Saulter—"it sounds very much as though the circuit solicitor has no suspect other than Howard. Am I correct?"

"Uh. The investigation is continuing," he replied carefully.

"Of course it is. And that's why *you're* here." She clapped her hands gaily. "You are in need of aid."

The chief moved uncomfortably in his chair. "Actually, I want to take your statements."

Laurel placed a hand over her heart. "I shall do my utmost to serve justice." She looked dreamily toward the lagoon. "Chief, it is up to us— all of us—to preserve our dear circuit solicitor from embarrassment, humiliation, and obloquy. I cheerfully accept that charge." She hitched her chair closer to his. "Here are your suspects: George Graham, his wife, General Houghton—" She looked at Saulter inquiringly. "Is your pen broken?"

Saulter licked his lips and began to write.

"Carleton Cahill, Buck Burger, and Billye Burger."

There was total silence when she finished. Max looked at his mother admiringly. Annie stared at her in astonishment. Saulter gaped.

But Annie knew an opening when she saw it. "Chief, that's not all. Add Dorcas Atwater. And Joel Graham, George's son."

Saulter obediently wrote the names, then tried to regain control. "I sure appreciate all this help, but, thing is, I got to get your statements and get back to the mainland."

"Certainly, certainly," Laurel agreed. "We are cooperating to our utmost."

Annie had to hand it to the old girl. Laurel cooperated with the élan of the Saint scaling a chateau wall. Despite Saulter's occasional efforts to redirect her, Laurel succeeded in her objective.

Annie could see Saulter's scrawled notes:

GEN. HOUGHTON—*Obsessed with sex. Nasty temperament. Accustomed to killing (war record). Did he want Sydney or want to rid the world of Sydney? Act in bringing down alcove curtain almost unbalanced. Very handy on the crime scene.*

JOEL GRAHAM—*When Sydney recognized him, she pulled away. Why?*

GEORGE GRAHAM—*Obviously involved with Sydney. Lovers' quarrel?*

LISA GRAHAM—*She saw Joel and Sydney together. Did she see Sydney in her husband's arms?* ("She's the jealous type," Annie offered. "She keeps a close rein on George on the tennis courts.")

CARLETON CAHILL—*Hated his stepmother. Why? Ugly scene at band-*

stand. (Saulter didn't write down Laurel's summation of Carleton: "Actually, a dear boy, I'm sure. Just so emotionally vulnerable.")

BUCK BURGER—*Involved with Sydney?* (Laurel had no doubt. "You see, Chief, I know a great deal about love. And men. And the way Mr. Burger"—she cleared her throat delicately—"touched Sydney was quite revealing. Not for the first time, I'm quite sure." Annie didn't look toward Max at all during this portion of Laurel's statement.)

BILLYE BURGER—*Jealous as hell?* (Laurel put it more delicately: "Some women's entire existence is defined by the man whom they marry. His loss through divorce could be shattering!") *Tenuous.*

As Laurel concluded her statement, she heaved a delighted sigh and looked quite angelic. "So you see, dear Chief Saulter, there are ample suspects in addition to Howard. And I cannot reiterate too often my utter conviction that the timing was such that Howard had no possible opportunity—"

"Fine, fine, Mrs. Roethke. That's enough—I mean, thank you for your cooperation." He turned in relief to Annie.

Annie affirmed Laurel's observations. "She's right, Chief. Lots of people might have wanted Sydney dead. And listen, I want to tell you about Dorcas Atwater. She hated Sydney. And Dorcas is—odd. Maybe more than odd."

He was interested in Annie's description of Dorcas, lurking near the Cahill shore in a rowboat, though he pointed out the time difference.

"She could have come back, Chief," Annie insisted.

"Or maybe she never left," Max suggested.

"Such an unhappy soul," Laurel murmured.

Saulter was glad, finally, to get to the crime scene itself.

"Now, Annie, if you could tell me what you saw."

It didn't take long, but she was startled by Saulter's excitement when she described the splash she'd heard as she ran toward home.

"A splash? Hey Annie, wait a minute. What kind of splash? Different from a frog startled by your running?"

Annie struggled to remember. At the time, she was frantic to be gone, to get away from that ominous rustling of the shrubs— "The bushes—the bushes made a noise!"

"You think somebody was there? Could have been a raccoon."

"No. Someone was there, I'm sure of it." She hadn't realized until she said it with such conviction, but she was positive somebody *had* been there. The murderer?

"Oh, hell," Max said grimly.

"But what would anyone throw—" Annie looked sharply at Saulter. "The weapon! What killed Sydney?"

"You didn't see a weapon when you found her?" Saulter asked.

"No." She shrugged. "But I didn't really look. It was dark in the gazebo, and I wasn't thinking about it. I just came close enough"—she paused, swallowed—"to see that Sydney was beyond help."

She remembered the scene too vividly. But there was no weapon where she had looked.

"Didn't you find anything, Chief?" Annie tried to envision what implement had been used. What could have caused such enormous damage to Sydney's face? A bat? No, the skin had been gouged and bones shattered. An ax? A blade would have cut, not gouged. An ax head? Perhaps. The gruesome possibility made her shudder.

"Nothing," Saulter admitted. "Not a trace. Deputies from the sheriff's office are searching the house now. We got a warrant."

"There wasn't time to hide . . . Oh, that's the point. The murderer could have thrown it in the lagoon."

Saulter nodded. "Can I use your phone?"

Max took him inside to make his call, and Annie looked at the milky green lagoon, basking in the unseasonable warmth. Cattails and sawgrass rimmed the bank. She wouldn't want to scuba dive among the tangle of water lilies. Two American egrets, spectacularly lovely with their flowing plumes and snow-white color, poked bright yellow bills into the murky water, searching for minnows, frogs, or even young cottonmouths. It was a scene of quiet island beauty, the kind captured on a thousand canvases.

She looked to her right, even though she knew the Cahill house, gardens, and gazebo weren't visible from their patio because of the pinewoods. The trees ran all the way to the lagoon. The path that circled the lagoon and linked all the properties cut through the woods. The recreation areas behind each house had been cleared, of course, affording an excellent view of the lagoon.

A chair scraped.

Startled, Annie looked around, then jumped to her feet. "Laurel, where are you going?"

Laurel paused, "My path is not yet clear to me. But direction will come." She patted Annie's cheek. "As our dear American saint, Elizabeth Seton, once wrote, 'Troubles always create a great exertion of my mind and give it a force to which at other times it is incapable.' "

On this utterly disturbing note and with a final benign nod, she headed toward the house.

Annie was uncertain of her proper course. She hated like fury to leave Laurel unsupervised. But, after all, Howard was in jail. Therefore, if he was the killer, Laurel was safe. If he wasn't, surely Laurel wouldn't do anything to alarm the murderer, who would be as somnolent as a sunning alligator with Howard taking honors as the prime suspect. Besides,

Annie couldn't attach herself to Laurel like Harold Merefield to Dr. Lancelot Priestley's telephone. So, despite her concern, she and Max adhered to their regular schedules, parting on the boardwalk, not foggy this morning, with Max en route to Confidential Commissions and Annie hurrying to Death on Demand.

As she unlocked the front door and flipped on the lights, an eager bundle of white fluff launched itself from the cash desk and landed on Annie's shoulder.

"Dorothy L.!" she exclaimed. The kitten wobbled unsteadily on her perch, tiny claws fastening to her cotton sweater. A huge purr rumbled in Annie's ear. Laughing, she reached up and unhooked the kitten. "You are a sweetheart," and she nuzzled a white ruff.

A gut-wrenching growl erupted, louder than the roar of exhaust from Black Beauty, the Green Hornet's miracle automobile.

Guilt-stricken, Annie immediately thrust the kitten behind the cash desk and turned to reach for Agatha, who stood on the special display table in the middle of the central aisle.

The black cat hissed, sounding like an enraged hognose. However, unlike that fairly charming nonpoisonous reptile, which will roll over on its back, poke out its tongue, thrash about, then play dead if its hiss doesn't succeed in scaring off an approaching human, Agatha met Annie's hand with unsheathed claws, scored her palm, then, with another hiss, turned and careened through the February book exhibit. Books tumbled in every direction. Which was deliberate as hell, Annie knew. Agatha was totally sure-pawed.

Dorothy L. rubbed up against Annie's ankle.

As Annie hurried to the coffee bar to wash her hand and hunt for some Band-Aids, she called out, "Bite the hand that feeds you. That makes a lot of sense."

It was dark in the American Cozy area, between the south wall with its shelves full of mystery classics and the angled bookshelves holding the Christies, Espionage/Thriller, and Romantic Suspense, but Annie could see two eyes glowing like the fires of hell.

"Agatha, love," she said gently, and slowly, very slowly, she walked forward, unwounded hand outstretched. When, finally, she held the slender black body in her arms, she massaged behind the delicate furry ears until a tiny, grudging purr began.

Laurel was right. Love wasn't easy for anyone, not even cats.

Of course, the tentative rapprochement didn't last long, because Dorothy L. rollicked into view. Agatha stiffened, hissed, launched herself with a massive kick from her back paws into Annie's stomach, and chased the kitten up the corridor.

"Friends, girls," Annie called. "We're all going to be friends."

Annie tried to ignore the clatter the cats made. Surely Agatha wouldn't really harm a kitten. She slapped the Band-Aid onto her palm and put the coffee on. When it was done, she returned to the front of the store and began to set the February exhibit to rights. Five famous mystery writers were born in February: Janwillem van de Wetering, February 12, 1931, in Rotterdam; Elliot Paul, February 13, 1891, in Malden, Massachusetts; Georges Simenon, February 13, 1903 in Liège, Belgium; Gregory Mcdonald, February 15, 1937, in Shrewsbury, Massachusetts, and Ralph McInerny, February 24, 1929, in Minneapolis, Minnesota. She picked the books up, two by each author: Van de Wetering's *The Corpse on the Dike* and *The Mind Murders,* Paul's *The Mysterious Mickey Finn* and *Mayhem in B-Flat,* Simenon's *The Methods of Maigret* and *Maigret's Boyhood Friend,* Mcdonald's *Fletch* and *Confess, Fletch,* and McInerny's *Her Death of Cold* and (writing as Monica Quill) *And There Was Nun.*

She stepped back, admired her arrangement, then found a fresh notepad (from a competitor, Scotland Yard, Inc., but Annie loved the pads with the quote from Philip Guedalia at the top in green script: "The detective story is the normal recreation of noble minds"), filled a coffee mug (inscribed with the title *Before the Fact*), and settled at the table nearest the bar.

There was much to be done. First, the timetable. She wrote *Timetable* with a flourish, glad to address facts for a moment. Reggie Fortune would have approved. As he so often stated, he had a simple faith in facts and utter disdain for imagination. Annie wouldn't quite go that far, but it was nice, for the moment, to deal in times and logistics.

Not that it was easy. In fact, she crumpled three pages and was at work on the fourth when the phone rang.

She would have ignored it—Death on Demand wasn't open yet—but she lacked the self-control of Leonidas Witherall, who found it quite easy to ignore a growing pile of Western Union telegrams in *Dead Ernest.*

"Death on Demand."

"Annie, why didn't you call me? I can't believe I had to find out from the radio." Henny's voice throbbed with outrage.

The radio. Oh, of course. There would have been nothing in the morning papers, but this afternoon's *Gazette* would have the story. "Henny, it was two o'clock in the morning before we got home and—"

"Did you find her? What happened? Who bumped her off? Is Howard really in custody? What the *hell* was she doing in the gazebo at that hour? What was the weapon? It said she was bludgeoned to death. Did you know they're calling it 'the Valentine Murder'? And what's the cryptic bit about 'material at the crime scene indicated the lovely Mrs. Cahill was anticipating a romantic rendezvous'? Annie, what's going on?"

Annie felt a pang of sympathy for her best customer. Henny was always on top of the news. To be forced to admit she knew nothing was a terrible loss of face. Moreover, Henny was as determined as Christie's Inspector Slack ever thought about being. So, taking a deep breath, Annie began, "I heard footsteps on our patio about a quarter to one . . ."

The heart-shaped balloons from Annie bobbed cheerfully in a corner of Max's office, stirred by his passage as he paced up and down on the elegant rose and cream Persian rug. So yesterday he'd hoped for a problem. He should have known Laurel's arrival would result in more problems than anyone would care to face. Not, of course, that Sydney Cahill's murder was Laurel's fault. But Laurel was totally involved emotionally. She was trying to alibi Howard Cahill. If the police refused to believe her, she would go to any lengths to prove his innocence. And that, Max said to himself, was where he came in.

Dropping into his well-padded, high-backed swivel chair, he ignored the controls (the chair could be tilted almost horizontal and contained a vibrator and heating element) and reached for a legal pad and a pen. His hand flew as he printed in block letters:

COMPOUND GATE CLOSED 12:50
ROAD UNDER OBSERVATION UNTIL SAULTER'S
    ARRIVAL AT 1:33
Ergo:
MURDERER DID NOT ARRIVE BY CAR
Inference:
MURDERER A RESIDENT OF SCARLET KING
    COMPOUND
Any other ingress possible?
BY FOOT OR BICYCLE FROM GOLF CART PATH?

It took almost half an hour, because Max took pains with it, but his map—to his eyes—was a thing of beauty upon completion. He studied it, then made a couple of phone calls. And narrowed down the list of suspects to a frightening few. Wow, did he have news for Annie!

"And that's *all* you know?" Henny demanded.

Annie's throat felt as dry as St. Mary Mead when it was after hours for the Blue Boar. "That's it."

"There's a lot to find out," Henny said happily. Annie could imagine her fox-sharp nose wriggling in anticipation. "You know, this may be

one of those murders with many hidden motives. Well, painstaking
detective work will succeed. Just like Police Lieutenant Joe Gunther."

Annie didn't say anything. Gunther?

Henny's voice was silky. "Brattleboro police."

It didn't ring any bells.

"Why, Annie, don't you know Gunther?"

It wouldn't do any good to fudge. Henny would back her to the wall,
demanding title and publishing house.

"No." Short, crisp, irritated.

"Oh my dear, I thought you kept up. Really so important to know the
field."

"All right. What book? Who wrote it?"

"Open Season by Archer Mayor. A first novel. Marvelously well done.
I'll have to send you a reading list, my dear."

Annie hung up on Henny's chuckle. Then wished she'd snapped
something about not having taken a trip around the world with a stock
of new books. But the telephone talk had been useful, helping her
organize the night's events in her mind. She was just finishing her
listing of times when the bell sounded as the front door opened.

"Hey, Annie."

"Back here." She felt the old familiar surge of delight upon hearing
Max's voice. Which was ridiculous, wasn't it? After all, they'd been
married almost five months now. But she hopped up to hurry and meet
him.

Max waved a sheet of yellow paper. "I've made a map."

Annie pointed to the table and her notebook. "Come look at my
timetable."

Armed with freshly filled coffee mugs, they settled at the table.

Max studied the timetable:

TIMETABLE

12:45—Laurel leaves house.

12:47—Annie hears footsteps on the patio.

12:53—Laurel reaches the Cahill gardens.

12:54—Laurel is outside Cahill library and overhears angry exchange.

12:54—Sydney hurries onto the terrace and takes path toward
gazebo.

12:54—Carleton storms outside and turns right, heading toward
tennis court and pool.

12:55—Laurel takes a path in the direction of the Darling house.

12:56—Howard catches up with her and walks with her.

12:56—Estimated time of Sydney's arrival at the gazebo.

12:57—Annie leaves Darling house.

1:05—Annie is halfway down the path.

1:05—Laurel enters the front door of the Darling house. Howard turns toward home.

1:08—Annie hears a noise, yells for help.

1:08—Annie's cry arouses Gen. Houghton.

1:09—Annie finds Sydney's body.

1:10—Bushes rustle, frighten Annie. She runs for home.

1:12—Annie hears splash. (The weapon?)

Annie looked over the map. She traced the golf cart path.

"It isn't lighted after dark, is it?"

Max shook his head.

"So if anybody came that way, they would have to have carried a flashlight."

"And worn a raincoat," Max added.

She looked at him in surprise. It hadn't rained in almost a week.

He tried not to look too proud of himself. "Checked with the club pro. Sprinklers turned on at midnight to take advantage of nonpeak usage period. Ran until two A.M. No way anybody could have made it to the fourteenth hole"—Annie nodded; they could see that green from their patio—"without getting wet. Or leaving some kind of tracks. The pro was out early this morning. No indication anybody had walked over the course after the water started. No bike treads anywhere either."

Annie thought back to the gazebo, seen in the light of her flashlight. No puddles. No spots of water. Nothing to indicate the murderer had been splashed. She looked once again at the map, at the entrance to Scarlet King, at the road which dead-ended, at each house in order: the Houghtons', the Cahills', the Darlings', the Grahams', the Burgers', and Dorcas Atwater's.

Then Max handed her a second sheet in his distinctive printing:

SUSPECTS IN THE MURDER OF SYDNEY CAHILL
(within compound at time of murder)

Gen. Colville Houghton

Eileen Houghton, general's wife

Howard Cahill

Carleton Cahill, his son

George Graham

Lisa Graham, his wife

Joel Graham, his son

Leroy Williston (Buck) Burger

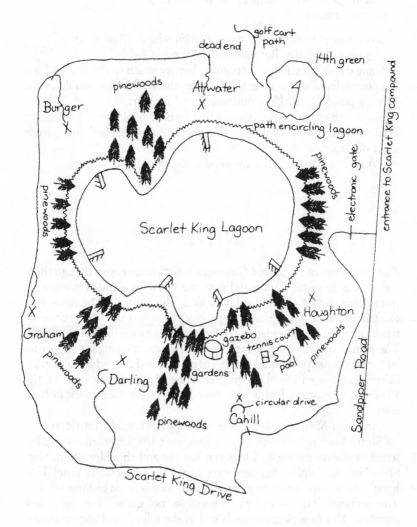

Max's Map

Billye Burger, his wife
Jim Tom Marshall (Live-in butler at the Burgers. Laurel's watch-
    man? Only live-in help in the compound.)
Dorcas Atwater

"Max, this is terrific!" She paused, then added, "And scary."

"A pretty short list. But one of those people did it."

Annie didn't question his certainty. Any approach to the Scarlet King
compound from other than the road or the golf course would entail
crossing pathless, trackless pinewoods and swamps.

"Right," she said crisply, echoing that favorite rejoinder of Lieutenant
William Weigand of New York Homicide. Annie reached for a fresh
sheet of paper.

"Okay, Max, here's what we need to do."

NINE

The newsroom of the *Island Gazette* radiated tension even though there
was very little sound. Annie did note the muttered expletives erupting
from the occupant of the third desk along the left wall. The nine-year-
old *Gazette* was quite proud of its modern newsroom, the clatter of
typewriters long ago replaced by the noiseless video display terminals.
The printer did clack at the far end of the room, spewing forth copy on
long continuous perforated paper sheets. Vince Ellis, editor and pub-
lisher, discouraged use of the printer, since all editing was done on the
VDTs, but reporters had a tenacious desire to see their work in hard
copy.

Annie and Max hesitated in the doorway, feeling like intruders.

"Shit!" Marian Kenyon's fingers flew over the keyboard as she listened to the phone wedged between her ear and shoulder. "Shit. Shit.
Sh— No, no, Ralphie, not you, sweetheart. It's the goddam time! That
horse's ass knows we go to press at noon. So who's he playing to? The
wire services? The *New York Times*? No, no, go on. I've got a few
minutes." Her fingers never slackened as she talked, and she continued
to swear in a steady monotone as she listened and wrote.

Vince clawed at his curly red hair (clearly from its untidy state it was
not the first time), then gingerly tapped Marian's shoulder and pointed
at the wall clock.

Marian ignored him. "Okay, okay. Got it." Banging down the receiver, she shot a single withering glance at Vince. "If I go any faster, I'll
self-destruct."

Vince nodded and backed away. He almost spoke again, then shrugged, and turned toward Annie and Max.

"On deadline," he explained unnecessarily, crossing to meet them. He shook Max's hand, but his eyes were on Annie.

"What were you doing in your neighbor's garden at one o'clock in the morning?"

Not knowing what information had been released by the police, Annie felt at a distinct disadvantage. She murmured vaguely, "Oh, a noise. Then when I went down the path, it came out at the gazebo and I found Sydney." She doubted that even Laurel could have managed it better.

But Vince looked like he'd been gashed by a stingray. *"You* found the body! Oh God, the stuff we got says Howard found her." He swung around. "Wait a minute, Marian!"

Annie grabbed his arm. "Hold on. It's okay. He must have come on the scene right after I'd left, because he called the police. I had run home and was going to call for help."

"Jesus Christ almighty," Marian bellowed, her voice rasping like a nail file. "I can't write if—"

"Okay, okay," Vince soothed. "Go with it. We'll stick to the official version." He looked at the wall clock. Three minutes to noon. "Come on," he said to Annie and Max. "Let's go to the coffee room. I need something to eat."

They settled at a Formica-topped table, Vince with a Coke and a Baby Ruth from the candy machine, Annie with a root beer and a Hershey bar, and Max with a Perrier and a sack of peanuts.

Max glanced at her selection. "Temporary surge of energy," he commented.

"I'll take it," she replied.

Vince drank the Coke halfway down and bit off a good third of the candy bar. "What a morning," he mumbled, "but we've got a hell of a story. Marian even managed a sidebar with 'intimate' details of Sydney's life. Poor bitch. Now"—he took another bite and continued indistinctly—"what can I do for you?"

"Let us in on whatever you got from the cops," Max said quickly.

"You mean, like extra background that's not for pub right now?"

"Everything," Annie urged. "And we'll give you the inside scoop on what the crime scene looked like."

"They'd taken Sydney to Charleston for an autopsy before we even heard about the murder," Vince groused. "We don't have a shot of the gazebo. We used a file photo of the house. Saulter could have called me." Vince thought for a moment, then stuck out his hand. Annie grabbed it, then Max. "It's a deal."

A heavy throbbing shook the building.

Vince grinned triumphantly. "The press run. Hold on a minute, and I'll get us a paper."

He returned waving it triumphantly and with a dark smudge of ink across his freckled nose.

"God, look at this. Terrific, huh?"

The entire top half of the front page was absorbed by the crime. A three-column photo of the Cahill home ran in columns 1, 2, and 3. Inset at lower left and right were mug shots of Howard and Sydney. A three-column headline topped the lead story.

ISLAND SOCIALITE BRUTALLY SLAIN
IN OWN GAZEBO: POLICE HOLD HUSBAND AS
MATERIAL WITNESS IN VALENTINE DEATH
By Marian Kenyon

Sydney Cahill, 34, was found beaten to death Wednesday in the early morning hours by her husband, Howard Cahill, 59, millionaire owner of the Med-Pacifico Shipping Lines and a resident of Broward's Rock since 1973. Mrs. Cahill's bludgeoned body was found about one A.M., crumpled on the steps of the gazebo in the famous Cahill gardens.

Circuit Solicitor Bryce Willard Posey announced Wednesday that Cahill was being held as a material witness. The prosecutor declined to state whether the detention was an effort to protect Cahill or whether Cahill was considered a suspect in the brutal murder of his second wife. His first wife, Chelsea, well known on the island for her charitable works, died of cancer in 1983.

Although no motive has been established for the brutal slaying, police have ruled out theft as the victim's jewelry, a necklace and matching bracelet of intertwined strands of diamonds, emeralds, and rubies, was still in place when the body was discovered.

The Cahill mansion had been the scene Tuesday evening of a spectacular Valentine Ball, with more than 100 guests in attendance.

A grisly footnote to the holiday celebration was the homemade valentine found clutched in the dead woman's hand. Police attribute her presence in the gazebo at the late hour to the valentine message:

ROSES ARE RED,
VIOLETS ARE BLUE.
WAIT IN THE GAZEBO,
I'LL HURRY TO YOU.

IN THE STILL OF THE NIGHT,
OUR HEARTS CAN TAKE FLIGHT.
WHEN THE CLOCK STRIKES ONE,
OUR TIME WILL HAVE COME.

YOUR SECRET ADMIRER

When and how Mrs. Cahill received the valentine, if known, has not been revealed by the authorities. Neither has its author been identified. The *Gazette* has been unable to reach the widower for a statement.

The Cahill mansion, built by the shipping magnate in 1974, is a part of the exclusive Scarlet King compound, which may be entered only with permission and is not open to the public. The only road into the compound is barred by an electronically operated gate. Only residents possess the number code which operates the gate. The police report states the gate was in place Tuesday night before Mrs. Cahill was killed.

Annie scanned the rest of the story. Nothing they didn't know—the body to Charleston for an autopsy, the lack of a weapon at the crime scene, the short list of residents of the compound, and the to-be-expected pompous declaration by Posey:

An intensive investigation is underway. As soon as it is completed, I shall file charges. Island residents may be assured that no stone will be left unturned in the search for the perpetrator of this heinous crime. Anyone with information that might pertain to this brutal slaying or who can aid police in their search for motives is encouraged to contact the circuit solicitor's office. Neither high estate nor low shall affect the course of my investigation.

But the zinger was the valentine clutched in the dead woman's hand.

Annie pointed at the paragraph. "Was the valentine printed, typed, or written?"

"They were being cagey about that," the newsman explained. "Actually, I was surprised they gave out the info at all, but Marian said she figures they want to stir up people who know anything about Sydney's extracurricular activities."

"The obvious implication," Max observed, "is that Sydney went to meet a lover in the gazebo."

"And either Howard followed and killed her in a jealous rage or the lover, for reasons unknown, did away with her," Annie added. "I don't suppose her secret admirer's going to sally forth and bare his breast."

Vince raised a bristly red eyebrow. "You've got to be kidding. Has to be a married man."

"Oh now, how can you say that?" Annie objected. "With her winsome ways, it could be damn near any male on the island."

"The gate. Oh, the famous gate," Max said softly.

Which brought them back to the short list, the very short list, of residents in the Scarlet King compound.

"Except," Annie pointed out, "for Howard's son, Carleton, and the Graham teenager. What's his name?"

"Joel," Max supplied absently. He tapped the paper. "Looks to me like Posey's already decided on Cahill. I wonder why he hasn't charged him yet."

Vince gulped down the rest of his Coke and crushed the can. "Let's huddle with Marian. She can read Posey like a palm."

Marian sank into a plastic chair like it was a hammock, shook her curly gray hair away from her face, took a cup of coffee black, and, between drags on an unfiltered Camel, assessed the prosecutor's case.

"Dead cert Posey's going to charge Cahill. But Posey's got the willies. I mean, Cahill's the Onassis of the U.S.A. Posey knows he'd better play it right. What if the guy's innocent, for God's sake." She jerked her head to blow smoke away from her listeners. Marian had a dried-up face like a prune and brown eyes that glittered with intelligence and more than a little malice. "But Jesus, what's with this stonewall routine? Baby, you don't play that game when you're riding with the angels. Anyway, I think that's why Posey went public with the valentine. See, that will get the calls started, the whispers about who Sydney played house with, and, once the public gets the idea this was a roundheeled broad, they'll figure Cahill's guilty as hell and the pressure will build up for his arrest. That's the way I see it." She puffed at her cigarette; smoke wreathed her face. "And if they can find the weapon and pin it to Cahill, he'd better hire himself a street brawler of a lawyer." Taking a final deep drag, she stubbed out her cigarette, pulled a small notebook from her pocket, and fastened hungry eyes on Annie. "Listen, the cops won't ante much on the crime scene itself. They said the body was on the steps. Well, where? Was she going up, coming down, standing at the top. Where was the blood?"

Haltingly, Annie described what she had seen, and Marian sketched, prodding her with more questions. "Face up, face down? On her side, back, front? Where were her hands?"

When Annie'd finished her description, she checked Marian's sketch. "That's right. Except her right hand was hidden beneath her right leg. It was bunched up a little bit."

"Valentine in that hand."

The reporter's brusque comment made Annie wince. Valentines. She had a heart full of memories of valentines, silly, cute, sweet, simple, gaudy, or elaborate, but one and all brimming with vitality.

Annie knew she never wanted to see the valentine that Sydney had held so hopefully.

"Oh, yeah, yeah, yeah," the reporter muttered. Eyes narrowing, she erased, redrew, then jerked her head at Annie. "Get down on the floor. Pretend this is the top step and this chair"—Marian jumped up, pushed her chair to Annie's left—"this is the first pillar as you walk up."

Macabre as it was, Annie understood Marian's objective as soon as she took the pose. Dr. Thorndyke would have been proud of them.

Scrambling to her feet, Annie pointed at the drawing. "Oh my God," Annie exclaimed, "I can see it now. Sydney walked up the steps into the gazebo and wham, the murderer bashed her. See, look at the blood on that pillar to her left. She sagged into the pillar and the murderer hit again and she toppled backward down the steps. She was lying with her feet on the top step, her legs and torso on a diagonal and slightly turned to the right. That accounts for her right hand being hidden from view."

"She never had a bloody chance," Marian rasped. "The bastard was waiting for her. Premeditated all the way."

Max said grimly, "If Cahill killed her, it wasn't a jealous rage. He planned it."

"But how could Howard have reached the gazebo first?" Annie protested. She hesitated, then told Marian and Vince about Laurel's arrival outside the library. "After Sydney started down the path to the gazebo, Laurel headed for our place. Howard caught up with her pretty quick." Annie hauled out her timetable. "Look, Sydney probably reached the gazebo about twelve fifty-six. If the murderer attacked her immediately, she was dead by twelve fifty-nine. Laurel said good night to Howard about five past one. So it can't be Howard."

"No way," Max agreed.

Marian fished out another cigarette, lit it. "Depends," she said, mildly for her, "if this Laurel was telling the truth."

"Oh now," Max began.

Marian shrugged. "Or maybe Sydney took a long walk. Wasn't she supposed to be upset? Maybe she didn't go straight to the gazebo. Maybe she wanted to cool down, be in a romantic mood to meet her secret admirer. Poor bitch. All it would take was a few minutes. If Howard hurried like hell, he could have got there first. Thing is, people can be mistaken about times, even though they're sure as hell themselves. And one thing you have to remember, people lie a lot in murder cases." Her cool green eyes studied the sketch. "Another thing. The murderer must have been inside the gazebo and facing the entrance, right?"

They nodded.

"So the first blow slams Sydney into the pillar to the killer's right. What does that tell you?"

Vince got it immediately. "Left-handed. The killer's left-handed."

"Maybe," Marian responded. "But look at the next blow. Sydney collapses backward *to her right.*"

"Hey, that doesn't make any sense!" Annie objected.

"Switched hands. Weapon in the left hand for the first blow, switched to the right hand for the second blow."

Vince frowned. "Come on, Marian, that's too damn fancy in the middle of a murder."

"Had to be," the reporter said stubbornly. She blew a dribble of smoke, reflectively. "Kind of interesting. Saw Cahill play in a doubles tournament last fall. He's ambidextrous. Doesn't have a backhand. Switches his racket from his left to his right. Hits everything forehand. Including a hell of an overhead smash."

If *they* had figured it out, the police lab would see the same scenario. Everything pointed to Howard Cahill. Annie didn't look at Max. She didn't want to see the beginnings of doubt in his eyes.

But Max could be stubborn, too. "I don't see it. For either Cahill or his son. Look, we've got some times figured out—"

But he never got to finish. The door to the coffee room burst open. An excited young man with a voice that quavered cried, "Vince, Marian, they just arrested some dame in the Cahill homicide! Somebody named Roethke!"

Max paced the prosecutor's office madder than Travis McGee when The Busted Flush was threatened. "By God, Posey's gone too far this time. He can't keep her in jail. Who the hell does he think he is?" He shot a hostile glance at Posey's university, law school, and bar certificates on the paneled wood wall behind an immaculate desktop.

"The chief investigating officer of this county, Mr. Darling," Posey announced unctuously, as he entered from a side door. "Discharging my duties to the citizens of the great state of South Carolina."

Posey did move just a bit quickly to put his desk between him and Max, and he glanced back to be sure Saulter was close behind.

Max turned on Saulter. "What the hell's going on here, Frank? Have you ever heard about false arrest? By God, before I'm finished, you'll wish you'd never heard my name."

Annie gazed at her husband in admiration. She knew many facets of Max, but this was the first time she'd ever seen him sound like Philip Marlowe, with overtones of Perry Mason.

Saulter's face furrowed unhappily. "Max, one of our deputies found her trying to conceal evidence."

Posey sat down behind his desk. He was attempting to look judicious, but he couldn't conceal his glee.

"Bloodstained evidence, Mr. Darling. A jacket that clearly belongs to Mr. Cahill—has his initials monogrammed inside, on the right front lining—and guess what? The jacket's all crumpled and splashed with blood. We're waiting on the lab report, but I don't think it's going to come as any surprise when the blood type matches Mrs. Cahill's."

Max looked at Saulter.

Saulter nodded reluctantly. "Doesn't look good." The police chief pulled a notebook from his pocket and began to read. "Trooper Lensgraf saw subject"—he glanced apologetically at Max—"Mrs. Roethke—depart from Cahill mansion by side door at eleven oh three A.M. today behaving in suspicious manner. Looked in every direction, hesitated, then hurried toward front of house. Trooper Lensgraf followed circumspectly. Suspect, carrying a bundle wrapped in newspaper, proceeded in surreptitious manner to exit Cahill grounds, crossing to adjacent property of Mr. Maxwell Darling. When called upon to halt, suspect plunged into thick stand of pines. Trooper Lensgraf immediately blew his whistle, summoning fellow officers. A search was instituted and suspect, affecting surprise at her accostment, was discovered sitting on the branch of a live oak tree, reading a newspaper. That is, to be precise, she was holding six crumpled pages of day before yesterday's *Gazette.*"

Saulter paused, cleared his throat.

"No law against that," Max snarled.

Annie had a vivid picture of that confrontation. There was a particular expression of Laurel's—a combination of amazement, incredulous delight, and otherworldliness—with which Annie was quite familiar. Her mother-in-law often employed it when she had no intention of saying what was really on her mind.

"However," Saulter continued with a studious lack of emphasis, "Trooper Lensgraf distinctly recalled the newspaper being in the shape of a bundle, so after taking the subject into custody—"

"On what possible grounds?" Max demanded furiously.

"Trespass on a crime scene, failing to heed an officer's command to stop," Posey trumpeted.

"—Trooper Lensgraf deployed six searchers in the area of the detention. Trooper Edward Benz found a man's suede jacket partially stuffed into a hole halfway up a nearby live oak. Trooper Benz called for crime technicians to photograph the evidence and remove it to the police laboratory."

"No proof whatsoever that she ever possessed that jacket," Max said triumphantly.

Saulter reached toward his shirt pocket, then plunged his hand into his pants pocket and pulled out a hard candy. Annie remembered that he had recently quit smoking. Again. Saulter deftly unwrapped the cellophane and popped the candy in his mouth and spoke around it. "Traces of newsprint on the jacket, Max."

Annie knew Max's legal training was getting the better of him. He could wrangle back and forth for hours on minute points, but what mattered was the jacket itself.

"Frank," she asked, "you're sure it's Cahill's jacket?"

"Yep."

"It has blood on it?"

"Splatters across the front and on both sleeves."

Both sleeves. Another indicator that their switched-hands analysis was correct.

"Well, where did she find it?" Annie demanded.

"Find it?" Posey interposed. "We have no evidence that Mrs. Roethke 'found' the jacket. She was caught trying to dispose of it. The simplest interpretation is that she received the jacket from Mr. Cahill."

"Oh, hell, Posey," Max objected immediately, "that doesn't make any sense. You've had him in custody since right after the murder last night."

Posey's snoutish face suddenly looked like the Pig Woman in the Hall-Mills case, bellicose, threatening, and intensely hostile. "That's correct, Mr. Darling. Which would indicate that Mrs. Roethke must have received the jacket shortly after it was worn during a murder of unparalleled ferocity, that she willingly, actively, and knowingly abetted, aided, and conspired in the commission of a brutal crime against a defenseless young woman—a woman who stood between Mrs. Roethke and the man with whom she had become hopelessly enamored."

"Nonsense," Max barked. "If she had it right after the murder, why would she be leaving the Cahill house with it the next morning? You can't have it both ways, Posey."

"What does Laurel *say?*" Annie demanded.

"Gibberish," Posey retorted, his watery blue eyes glinting with anger. "But it is calculated!" he stormed, waggling a pudgy finger at them. "The woman is trying to set up an insanity defense, you mark my words. But I and the sovereign state of South Carolina are not deceived."

Max ignored Posey and demanded crisply of Saulter, "Has she been afforded counsel?"

"She has a call in to Jed McClanahan," the island police chief said quickly.

Posey glowered.

Max sighed.

Annie understood his response, but didn't quite share it. McClanahan claimed to be the best trial lawyer in the state of South Carolina. That might be a little exaggerated, but the feisty lawyer would hone in on Posey just like John J. Malone, though McClanahan was partial to bourbon, not rye, unlike Craig Rice's hard-drinking lawyer hero.

Still, Laurel was in a dreadful mess. She probably needed counsel more on the order of Fredrick D. Huebner's Matthew Riordan or Ed McBain's Matthew Hope. Or possibly they could convince Haughton Murphy's Reuben Frost to end his retirement.

"But certainly in my endeavor to represent all the citizens of our fair state, I am justly acclaimed as a temperate man. Therefore, Mr. Darling, I will be happy to grant Mrs. Roethke another opportunity to explain her suspicious actions this morning at a crime scene." Posey punched the intercom on his desk. "Hortense, have an officer bring Mrs. Roethke to my office."

A strained silence ensued until Laurel's arrival.

Annie had to hand it to her mother-in-law. No other woman could wear a bright orange cotton jail shift *sans* jewelry and *sans* makeup with such élan. Laurel beamed impartially at them all.

"Max, my sweet, you shouldn't have interrupted your day. So many fine goals to pursue. And Annie, I know this is the off season, but I heard you say how *badly* you needed to unpackage and shelve all those wonderful new reference works: *A Readers Guide to Classic British Mysteries* by Susan Oleksiw, *Myself and Michael Innes* by J. I. M. Stewart, *Silk Stalkings* by Victoria Nichols and Susan Thompson, *Crime and Mystery: The 100 Best Books* by H. R. F. Keating, *The Spirit of Australia* by Ray B. Browne, *In—*"

"Mrs. Roethke, I would like for you to focus your mind upon this morning," Posey interrupted. His tone was appropriate for dealing with someone like the easily unhinged killer in Joan Banks's *Death Claim.*

"Oh, come off it, Posey," Max said impatiently. He looked at his mother, who appeared especially diminutive and charming next to the bulky policewoman at her side.

Laurel smiled kindly.

"And you come off it, too." Max gazed at her sternly.

"My dear, you are too, too exercised. This is all a minor problem of misunderstanding."

Posey leaned forward. "You can easily clear it up, Mrs. Roethke. Just tell us how you obtained that jacket and why you were trying to hide it."

Laurel gazed at the prosecutor with limpid blue eyes. "I do so wish I could be helpful. You see, there are so *many* difficulties. But"—she paused until every eye was focused on her, building on the silence with a fine sense of drama and an implicit promise of great tidings to come— "I am confused on so many points. I have known Mr. Cahill for such a short time. I do not *know* that the jacket is his. I have no idea how the

jacket became stained with blood. In fact, I do not have in my posses-
sion *any* proof that Mr. Cahill wore the jacket or even touched it last
night. Nor do I know of my *own* cognizance how the jacket was transported from the gazebo. If it was. You see, I am adrift upon a sea of
speculation. But if I could speak to Mr. Cahill alone for a few moments,
I—"

"Maybe you'd like to talk to the Queen of England, too?" Posey asked
with heavy irony.

"Oh, certainly," Laurel said agreeably. "That would be delightful. You
know the royal family has always been so fond of mysteries. And indi-
rectly responsible for the longest-running play in the world. You see, the
BBC asked Mrs. Christie if she would do a short radio sketch for a
program arranged for Queen Mary. Mrs. Christie agreed, of course.
The result—my dear Mr. Posey—the result was "Three Blind Mice"
and that radio sketch was the basis for *The Mousetrap,* which has been
on stage in London since November 25, 1952. Now, isn't that wonderful?"

"Oh Jesus Christ, what a lot of crap!" Posey exploded.

Laurel fixed him with a piercing gaze. "That good saint, Louis of
France, quite detested profane and blasphemous language. He *never*
used it himself and would not tolerate it in others."

There was a small silence, then a red-faced Posey turned on Max.
"You see? Well, you may all think she's pretty damned funny, but she's
going to be funny behind bars until she comes clean." He jerked his
head at the officer who had accompanied Laurel.

"Mother . . ." Max began.

She blew a kiss to him and another to Annie as she walked toward
the door. "Be of good cheer, my dears. But you must understand that
when one has given one's word, well, one must keep it. But Saint Vin-
cent de Paul was so correct when he reminded us that bitterness has
never served any other purpose than to embitter. However, as Saint
Teresa of Avila once remarked, oh so wisely, "All things pass.""

" 'One's word,' " Posey mimicked, jumping to his feet. "That sounds
mighty like conspiracy to me, madam. You may be an old hag by the
time you get out of jail."

Laurel paused in the doorway, arching one perfect blond brow. "I do
quite understand Saint Jerome's point." A tiny smile crossed her face.
"It was he who said, 'A fat paunch never breeds fine thoughts.' "

TEN

"Did you see his face?" Max erupted in laughter again.

Annie tensed, ready to grab the wheel, until he veered back into his lane. Max usually was an excellent driver, but he was in such high spirits over Laurel's quashing of Posey—as Max saw it—that he was totally absorbed in reconstructing the scene they'd just witnessed in the prosecutor's office. As a sympathetic (and intelligent) wife, she forbore to remind him that she too had been present. Max was having too good a time. She made appropriate comments— "That's right," "She sure did," "Certainly made a fool out of him!"—but with only a portion of her attention.

Should she tell Max? That was the question. She was tempted. But she also felt sure that she could better handle the delicate task that lay ahead by herself. Although she was a little surprised Max hadn't picked up on it, because it seemed to Annie that Laurel's clue, craftily inserted in her farewell chatter, was almost as obvious as *The Footprints Under the Window,* which had hooked generations of Frank and Joe Hardy readers.

But perhaps not.

Just for an instant the horrid idea occurred to Annie that she was developing thought patterns similar to those of her mother-in-law.

"Hey, Annie, don't you agree?" Max was looking at her in surprise. Obviously, she had missed his latest pronouncement.

"Absolutely," she replied, with a warm, admiring smile.

Satisfied, he looked back at the road in time to avoid a possum that had rolled over and played dead at the car's approach.

Max chortled as he swerved the car and pointed at the furry body. "The only mammal known to mankind to be dumber than Posey."

Dumb Posey might be, Annie thought, but right now he had the upper hand. She and Max were going to have to be as perceptive as Kate Fansler and Homer Kelly combined to free Laurel and, perhaps, Howard. Distracted for a moment, she envisioned the pairing of those detectives, the brilliant creations of Amanda Cross and Jane Langton. Now that would be a creative collaboration.

". . . going to check out the neighbors. Right?"

Annie nodded, glad she'd picked up on his comment. "And you'll get busy digging up background on everybody?"

"You bet."

Annie gave him a thumbs-up signal as the Maserati rolled onto the ferry to cross to the island.

Yes, indeed, she intended to canvass their neighbors.

Especially one.

Funny how lonely and quiet the house seemed. And it wasn't just because Max was at Confidential Commissions. Annie hated to admit it, even to herself, but, dammit, she missed Laurel, missed that engaging smile, missed that endless stream of observation, query, comment, hope, and kindliness which constituted Laurel's conversation, missed the flash of those spacey but appealing dark blue eyes.

Annie felt lonely even though she was in her favorite spot in their new house, their garden room which opened onto the patio. Banyan trees glistened as greenly as in a Central American jungle. (Mary Jo Adamson, who vividly evokes the lushness of Puerto Rico in her Baltha-zar Marten mysteries, would feel right at home.) Chintz-covered sofas and chairs, lime with twining roses, were scattered across the brick flooring. Annie sat in a cane chair beside a jade green bamboo table, jotting down or re-creating everything she felt to be pertinent, the time-table, Max's map of the Scarlet King compound, Marian Kenyon's sketch of the crime scene, observations about the suspects Annie had seen:

Howard—tough and capable. Upset, though he tried to mask it. But was his distress caused by the murder?

Carleton—obviously distraught, easily angered. He'd glared at his father at the party, then eyed him uneasily at the gazebo. What was he thinking?

General Houghton—mean-looking old bastard. A man who saw everyone but himself as immoral. A religious zealot? Or a spurned suitor? His wife, Eileen, wasn't at the crime scene, but she'd eagerly awaited Posey's attack on Howard. A bit of spice in an otherwise dull life?

And brief summaries about the remaining residents of Scarlet King (and Valentine party attendees) whom she intended to talk to as soon as possible:

George Graham—the bland-faced dentist. Would she ever forget the stark silence after the general unveiled moral depravity in progress and everyone near that alcove in the Cahill ballroom saw Graham smudged with Sydney's lipstick? Obviously, Graham knew Sydney well. Was he grieving for Sydney? Or had *he* worn the lover's false face and greeted her in the gazebo with blows instead of caresses? Annie inked thick black question marks after his name.

Lisa Graham—a rich man's second wife. What had been her thoughts when her stepson apparently said something vulgar to Sydney?

Where was she when the general's cane revealed her husband embracing Sydney? And just how angry might she have been? Lisa was a superb tennis player. She, too, had an excellent overhead smash.

Joel Graham—George's son by his first wife. From Annie's occasional glimpses of him during their first week as residents of the Scarlet King compound, Joel had seemed on the surface to be a typical high school senior, with stylishly baggy khaki trousers, a leather belt left dangling, blond hair spiky in front, long in back. But there had been nothing boyish about the way he spoke to Sydney at the Valentine party or, for that matter, about the look he'd given Annie one day when she'd jogged past him. That odd little encounter with Sydney—it seemed all wrong. Oh, not his sexual awareness of her. What man, young or old, was not sexually aware of Sydney? It was Sydney who had surprised her, Annie realized. Sydney had seemed jolted by that moment. But surely Sydney had been around the block too many times to be shocked by youthful lewdness. Unlikely as it seemed, had Sydney backed away because Joel was young? Could Joel have misinterpreted some earlier exchange? Could he have killed Sydney in a fury because she rejected his advances? Annie marked another series of question marks.

Buck Burger—he'd pawed Sydney at the party. So what else was new? Buck would paw any woman who let him. It might not have meant anything more than that. But Annie would have bet her first edition ($100 approx.) of Jim Thompson's *Cropper's Cabin,* Paperback Original Lion Book 108, that Buck knew Sydney damn well. She tapped the sheet with her pen. Buck was going to be a real challenge. Sure, his reddish face radiated geniality, but the warmth never reached his swamp-green eyes. As a flamboyant former criminal lawyer he had the edge, but she relished the prospect of going head to head.

Billye Burger—a very rich woman, who flaunted wealth as Sydney had paraded sexuality. From Billye's white-gold hair to her red lizard-skin high heels, from starburst diamonds to Hal Ferman originals, she was the epitome of the finest money can buy. Annie had no idea what kind of woman existed beneath the facade. Or whether she knew her husband was a womanizer.

Dorcas Atwater—Annie drew an oblong, dotted in wildly flared eyes and a droopy mouth, added straggly hair. And a rowboat. And tried to quell the creepy feeling that wreathed in her mind like London fog on a Jack-the-Ripper night. Dorcas hated Sydney. Why?

The phone rang.

"Hello."

"The bottom line is—" Henny paused.

Annie wasn't sure what was expected. Henny's voice had a smart-ass tone, and only an actress of her abilities could have invested four words with such a California nuance.

"Yeah?"

"I'm on the case, and I can't be bought off. You can't trust anybody."

Of course, Henny, as was her custom, was exhibiting various investigative personae. This one was for sure a resident of the Golden Gate state. Problem was, Annie didn't have any idea who was on stage at the moment. California teemed with fictional sleuths from Ross Macdonald's aloof L.A. observer, Lew Archer, to Marcia Muller's first-of-her-kind woman private eye, San Franciscan Sharon McCone.

"Uh—Jacob Asch?" Annie guessed.

"Not even close. Paul Marston, of course."

Annie's hand tightened on the receiver. She wished it were Henny's neck.

But she might as well get it over with. "First novel?" she said sourly.

"Sure. *The Bottom Line Is Murder* by Robert Eversz." A sly chuckle. "So sorry you are missing so *many* good books."

Sure, she was sorry.

"All right, Henny. Spit it out."

"Sure. The bottom line is that Sydney bed-hopped. I hit pay dirt at the club. I talked to Nicky Quentin, the tennis pro. It took some work, actually he's rather gallant, doesn't like to talk about his ladies, but he did finally admit, when I promised to be the soul of discretion, that he had a fling with her shortly before she married Howard. Nicky said, 'You know, she really was beautiful and basically kind of plain-vanilla nice, but she stuck to you like glue. And she was so sappy, always wanting everything to be so romantic. That's okay for a little while, but it gets old fast. Thank God, with Sydney, there was always some other guy out there, hot for her body. Which was—' Then he turned bright red." Henny added, a trifle put out, "Funny how young men always assume older women don't know anything about sex. Why, I could tell him—but no point in destroying his illusions. I wonder if it could be the same kind of situation as the victim in so many of Leslie Ford's books."

Annie processed that suggestion. "Hmm, I don't think so. Ford's seductive victims were stronger characters than Sydney."

"Annie, that's brilliant!"

Although it was always agreeable to be admired, Annie was a little uncertain as to her worthiness, at least in regard to this particular judgment. As a matter of fact, she'd thrown the remark out without a lot of thought. It was more of an automatic response.

But Henny was excited. "That cuts to the core of the matter. Just like Allison Moffit."

Annie didn't say a word.

"Such a *strong* personality."

"Don't know her." Annie dropped the words as if she were casting out spoiled food from the refrigerator. (That seemed to happen to her too often. Could she help it if she forgot mundane things like the survival time for tomatoes?)

"Oh, my dear! Such an outstanding new writer. Mary Lou Bennett. Author of *Murder Once Done.*" A telling pause. When she continued, her accent was suddenly quite Mayfair. "Do read it when you have a moment. And think about what you said. I'll get back to you soon, of course. There's so much to be discussed. Really, quite an interesting crime. Ta ta."

Annie slammed home the receiver, though she did recognize the final reference. Tessa Crichton, Anne Morice's sleuth. Henny was going to push her too far one of these days. And what was brilliant about Annie's analysis of Sydney?

Abruptly, she grabbed up her papers. She knew what needed to be done. And there was no putting it off any longer. No matter how difficult she envisioned the encounter.

As the extension number buzzed, Max weighed the options. Should he be a reporter, an insurance agent, an accountant, or a lawyer? This was even more fun than community theater, although, of course, telephone work didn't afford full scope for his talents. He recalled with pleasure his wonderful rendition of Mortimer Brewster in *Arsenic and Old Lace.* Now, there was a part. And he got to kiss the pretty girl, too. In fact, he—

"Personnel Records, Adeline Perkins speaking," a nasal voice announced irritably.

Max warbled the first line of the old barbershop quartet song in his clear tenor, then boomed avuncularly, "My horoscope assured me I should be in contact with a musical soul today and I feel certain that prediction has come true."

"You some kind of nut?" The nasal whine quivered with apprehension.

"My dear Adeline Perkins, of course not. This is Reginald Van Mackey"—he felt the Van added class—"a member of the Bluffton Men's Dinner Club and I am calling to obtain information about our esteemed member, General Colville Houghton. I have been directed to you, Miss Perkins, as the sole individual in the Pentagon with the necessary expertise and intelligence to assist me. It is the happy task of my committee to be charged with the responsibility of writing a skit depicting the highlights of General Houghton's life for presentation at our annual Founders' Day Dinner."

Adeline Perkins turned out to be an Aquarius and "the funny thing is my horoscope said I'd receive an unusual communication today!"

Information spewed forth on General Houghton and his career. Max damn near got writer's cramp.

Carleton Cahill's blue eyes had all the warmth of twin ice holes in a frozen Minnesota lake. He shoved back a thin lock of darkly blond hair with a shaking hand.

"All women are alike. They lie their goddam heads off. Goddammit, she promised not to tell." His thin voice shook with anger.

"She didn't," Annie replied quietly. Laurel's reference in her parting words to bitterness and to a promise she'd made was not telling. Not exactly. It took someone of Annie's subtlety (she refused *absolutely* to consider the possibility she had a similar thought pattern to Laurel's) to divine the message: Laurel got the jacket from that bitter young man, Carleton Cahill, but promised not to tell anyone. Actually, it was sweet of the old thing to ask for help. Annie felt flattered.

"Oh, sure." His mouth twisted sarcastically beneath the scanty mustache. "I suppose a little bird told you."

"Nobody told me. But she had to get that jacket somewhere. She was caught going away from this house. Who else is there?" And who else was bitter?

"Are you going to the cops?" Fists clenching, he lurched toward her.

Annie realized abruptly that they were very isolated in the enormous Cahill mansion. Would anyone even hear a scream? She looked past Howard Cahill's angry son. The French windows of the library were closed and the thick green velvet curtains drawn, unlike the night of the murder. Behind her, the heavy oak door rested solidly in its frame.

She stood her ground and stared determinedly up into his flushed face.

"I could have told the police. I didn't. I wanted to talk to you. Look" —Annie spread her hands in a gesture of appeal—"Laurel wants to help your father. We want to help Laurel. Let's work together."

He glared down at her, but he looked sullen rather than threatening. Annie met his gaze calmly.

Slowly his fists relaxed. He turned and paced away from her. "Hell, that's what *she* said. I don't know what to do." He swung around, a nervous hand plucking at his mustache. "It's her fault Dad's still in jail."

Annie felt a rush of anger. What an ungrateful creep! Laurel was doing her best for his father, who was about as stiff-necked and unappreciative as a man could be. And now Carleton was blaming Laurel, for God's sake!

"Now wait a minute—"

"That circuit solicitor convinced the judge he should keep Dad and

Mrs. Roethke in jail because they would have an unparalleled opportunity to collude if they were released."

It had a ring of authenticity. Who but Posey would talk in terms of an unparalleled opportunity to collude?

Annie didn't care. She sprang to Laurel's defense. "Look, Laurel wouldn't be in jail at all if she hadn't tried to get rid of that jacket. And I know damn well she got it from you. And you're going to tell me what happened. Where did you get it?"

He dropped into a chair, his long arms and legs askew, his narrow face drooping almost to his chest. "Oh Jesus—"

Annie gasped. "Oh my God, it was you. I heard *you!*"

He looked up with tortured eyes. "I found Sydney. God, it was awful. So much blood. So much *blood.* And the jacket was lying there beside her on the steps. And the mace—" He shook his head, as if to drive away a hideous memory. "Anybody could have taken it." The plea in his voice couldn't override the dull despair. "During the party. The armor's been in the front hall ever since the house was built. The mace could be picked right up. It wasn't attached to anything."

The mace.

Annie remembered it only too clearly, remembered the heavy metal club studded with spikes atop the solid wood handle.

The metal had darkened with age.

And blood? Old blood turns black.

Now fresh blood stained it.

No wonder Sydney's cranial bones shattered and broke.

"The mace." Annie's voice was so dry her throat hurt as she forced out the words. "It wasn't there when I found her."

Carleton didn't respond. His eyes reflected remembered horror. But he didn't have to answer. She understood now. His cry at the sight of the dead woman and his father's bloodied jacket and the mace. He must have decided instantly on his course, grabbing up the jacket, gripping the handle of the weapon, and fleeing into the shadows as Annie approached.

"You made the noise in the bushes," she figured out loud. "When I ran, you threw the mace in the lagoon."

No answer.

"Have they found it yet?"

This time he looked at her and shook his head. "If you tell them"—life and anger surged again in his voice—"I'll say you lied."

"What did you do when I ran away?"

"I lit out for the house. All I could think about was getting rid of the jacket. I was afraid if I tossed it with the mace that it would come loose in the water. Maybe even float. I didn't think I had much time. I knew the police would come soon."

"You ran into the house?"

"I had to find a place for the jacket. Dad didn't stand a chance if they found it."

"Where did you hide it?"

For an instant, triumph glittered in his eyes. "Think they're so goddam smart. The Buddha in the east wing is hollow. I stuffed it inside."

Actually, Annie didn't think the inability of the police to find the jacket indicated stupidity on the part of the searchers. The house was crammed with artwork and antiques. But she didn't say so to Carleton.

He looked at Annie imploringly. "That Mrs. Roethke—she doesn't think Dad did it."

"But you're afraid he did," Annie surmised.

"No." It was explosive, angry, and painfully uncertain. "God, no. But he—" Carleton licked his lips and looked up at the oil paintings over the mantel. Annie followed his gaze.

Two paintings: Howard astride a horse, a polo mallet held high, every sinew and muscle focused on the play, and a gentle-faced woman with soft brown hair and kind blue eyes playing a piano.

The first Mrs. Cahill?

Carleton's eyes, shiny with sudden tears, clung to the woman's portrait. "That's my mother." His face hardened. "How could Dad have married *her* after Mom? Mom and Dad were crazy about each other. They were so happy. Dad cried when she died. The only time I ever saw him cry."

Poor Sydney, Annie thought abruptly. How difficult it must have been to follow in the quiet footsteps of a genuinely mourned first wife and to be met with such unrelenting hostility from Howard's son.

And Howard had shed no tears for Sydney. Yet, that night at the general's house, Annie had seen such turmoil and agony in Howard's eyes.

"Oh, for pity's sake," Annie exploded. "How could we all be so dumb!" But Laurel wasn't dumb. She'd understood from the very first.

Carleton stared at her blankly.

She suppressed an urge to shake his slumped shoulders. "Don't you see?" she demanded. "That's why your father didn't admit to Laurel's alibi. He must have seen you running up the path from the gazebo, something clutched in your arms. And your face was probably a mess. You were upset, in a panic. He knows Sydney headed down that way. So he goes down to the gazebo and finds her. For God's sake, Carleton, your dad thinks *you* killed Sydney!"

The young man's eyebrows rose and his mouth half opened. A cartoonist couldn't have broad-brushed a more classic expression of amazement. Then Carleton's face brightened. "Sure, that must be what happened! God, I've got to talk to him. That damn lawyer's got to get him out of jail." He hurried to the desk. "I'll call him right now."

"Wait a minute," Annie urged. "You'd better be careful what you say."

He flipped through the phone book, picked up the receiver. "How's that?" He was impatient to make his call. "It can't get worse than it is right now."

"Sure it can. Posey's not going to believe a word you have to say." Annie watched Carleton with clear, cold eyes. She wasn't sure *she* would believe a word he—or his father—had to say. Carleton's spirited defense of Howard could be a murderer's crafty smoke screen. After all, he had been under no compulsion to tell Laurel about the jacket. But, once he had and once he foisted it off on her, it was quite likely that events would unfold as they had, with Laurel under arrest and even more evidence piled up against Howard.

Bitterness.

Laurel had stressed that, in her parting words.

She was right.

Carleton was bitter as hell. Just how angry was he with the father who had, in the son's mind, betrayed his beloved mother's memory?

Carleton slowly replaced the receiver, brushed back a lock of fine hair with a nervous hand. "You don't think the prosecutor will understand?"

"Think about it," she said crisply.

Any fool could figure Posey's reasoning. Howard Cahill's second wife was a tramp. So much of one, in fact, that she even dallied in an alcove during a party in their own home. Howard told her after the party that he intended to file for divorce. Posey would claim that Howard's stated intention to arrange a divorce was fake, that he was a man consumed with jealousy, a man who had already decided that his wife must die, sending the fake valentine and secreting the mace within the gazebo. As for Laurel's alibi, Posey would dismiss it out of hand. Obviously, Laurel and Howard were attracted to one another, providing yet another motive for Sydney's murder. Posey might even think the flirtation with Laurel was contrived to hide Howard's murderous passion over his wife's betrayal.

Therefore, if Carleton admitted to finding Sydney dead with the jacket and mace beside her, he would only reinforce Posey's conviction that Howard was the murderer he sought.

Eagerness and hope seeped out of Carleton's face. He clawed again at his mustache. "Well, what in God's name am I going to do?"

"The only hope is for us to find Sydney's killer."

"That's crazy. That's silly."

"No. It's necessary. And you can help."

"Me?" He stared at her incredulously. "What am I supposed to do? Look for fingerprints? Hunt for clues?"

"No, your job is very simple. Tell me everything you know about Sydney."

Max sensed he was close to a mother lode of succulent details on the dark side of General Colville Houghton's life. But how to pry it loose? Melba Crawford's snippy rejoinders to his inquiries about the man whom her husband had served as adjutant indicated there was no love lost between Mrs. Crawford and the general. But her answers, so far, had been circumspect, even though suggestive.

Speaking very low, almost in a whisper, Max said, "Now I can tell, Mrs. Crawford, that you are a woman of the world. Sophisticated. Savvy. Deserving of respect. You know and I know that sometimes a reporter has to use background information. No attribution." He emphasized the last. "I know you'd like to see the truth revealed about the general. Especially since he and your husband were in the same class at West Point and your husband never got his star. Which I am sure, from what everyone has told me, that he richly deserved."

"It broke Bradley's heart. And I *know* it was Colville's fault. He was such a hateful man, so jealous of anyone with true ability. Yes, I would like for the world to know what Colville Houghton is really like. And I can tell you." Hatred rough-edged her voice. "I certainly can."

"The bitch. I knew she was a bitch." Carleton glared at Annie defiantly. "I screwed her when I was a senior in high school. How do you think I felt when Dad said he was going to marry her?"

Annie felt a sudden sympathy for this angry, immature man. Lousy, that's how he must have felt. At the same time, she felt ever more sorry for Sydney, who so desperately sought reassurance from increasingly evanescent encounters.

Carleton paced beneath the portraits. "Shit, I should have told him then. But I didn't. And he probably wouldn't have listened any better than he did—" He broke off abruptly.

Some logic problems Annie could solve. Carleton hadn't told his father about his sexual experience with Sydney before Howard married her. But he had tried to tell him at some time. When?

"You tried to tell him Tuesday night." Her tone wasn't accusatory, merely thoughtful.

He stood stiffly beneath the portraits of his parents. Where his mother was gentle and lovely, he was weak and too delicately handsome. Where his father was forceful and determined, he was obstinate. "Hell, no. I never told him."

He and Annie both knew he was lying.

That made Howard's decision to divorce Sydney even more understandable.

But it also added to Howard's reasons for anger with Sydney.

"Your dad must have been really upset Tuesday night."

"He finally saw her for what she was. A slut. And it got him, all right. But, dammit, he didn't deserve any better. How could he have put a woman like that in my mother's house? In my mother's bed?" Rage shook his voice.

"Your mother is dead," Annie said coolly.

"Yeah." The anger was gone, replaced by weariness.

"And so is Sydney," she added deliberately.

They stared at each other for a long moment, her eyes questioning, his wary.

"I didn't do it," he said sullenly. "I hated her, but I didn't do it."

Annie studied him, then nodded. "All right. You say you didn't do it. And, if I'm right and your father is trying to protect you, that means he's innocent. So who does that leave?"

"How the hell should I know?" he snapped.

Annie was tempted to say, "Hey, jerk, if you can't put your mind together to help your father, who the hell do you expect to do it?"

With an effort of will, comparable, at least in her own mind, to Miss Marple's restraint in dealing with Inspector Slack, she said in a reasonable tone, "Carleton, if you didn't do it and your dad didn't, it means someone else within this compound committed the murder. Now, I want you to tell me exactly what happened after the party was over."

Mrs. Crawford knew enough to put Max on the right track. It took another half-dozen calls before he had the whole story. And an ugly one it was.

A cloud of yellow pine pollen swirled on the afternoon breeze. Annie sneezed. It would take a nonallergic foursome to play tennis at this time of year on the Cahills' secluded court, screened by pines on all four sides. She had retraced Carleton's path from the library the night of the murder. Another path angled from the tennis court to the gazebo and yet a third ran straight to the lagoon.

She quickly followed the track from the court to the gazebo. It snaked through dense woodland and she understood better Carleton's impatience with her demand to know what he had seen that night.

Damn little, she realized, just as he had claimed.

She stopped by the gazebo, off limits behind yellow police tape marking it as a crime scene, and turned toward the lagoon. Shading her eyes, she saw a uniformed deputy in a boat peering into the murky water.

The water swirled, and a masked scuba diver surfaced. "I've got it. I've got it!" A gloved hand broke through the surface of the water, and the sunlight glinted on wickedly sharp metal spikes.

Another nail in Howard Cahill's coffin.

But she wasn't giving up yet.

Although, as she slipped along the shaded path, passing her own house, heading for the next, she wasn't altogether sure the coffin didn't fit.

But she couldn't let Laurel down.

ELEVEN

The Graham house always made Annie think of Emporia, Kansas gone mad. The two-story white frame sported so much Victorian trim that one local carpenter had retired from his earnings and moved to Key West. Annie wasn't sure how to describe the two-story protrusion which bulged in front; it was emphatically more than a bay window. In addition, a massive cupola topped the third-floor sun deck. Overall, the house had a decidedly pregnant look. However, despite its pretensions, the porched structure, complete with cane-bottom rockers, had a certain dandyish charm. She climbed up the steps, passed the Victorian bulge, and reached the front door, which was tucked in the back of the porch.

Lisa Graham, dressed for tennis, answered Annie's knock. The dentist's wife was about Annie's height, a little older, with—and Annie was proud of her own honesty—a tad better figure, more and riper curves. Her tennis dress, beige with red trim, clung to her like Bertha Cool to a retainer. She had a pleasant face, round and unlined, with widely spaced brown eyes and a firm chin. But her welcoming smile, as she recognized her visitor, slipped sideways like Sergeant Buck encountering Leslie Ford's Grace Latham.

"Hi, Annie." Lisa was too well bred to evince overt surprise, but this was not a kaffeeklatsch neighborhood at any time, much less at close to three o'clock on a Wednesday afternoon. Moreover, though she and Annie knew each other—they'd worked on the community fund drive last fall—they were by no means friends on a drop-in basis.

"Are you on your way to the club?" Annie asked. "I don't want to delay you."

"No. Just got back. Played doubles. What can I do for you?" Her tone was pleasant, but just impersonal enough to indicate that a quick good-bye was in order, given the chance.

Annie had her story ready.

"It's the crime," she said with apparent frankness. "Sydney's murder. Max and I are worried about neighborhood security. I'm canvassing everyone, and Max is talking to Chief Saulter about further safety measures. So, if I could just have a minute of your time—"

At Annie's mention of the murder, Lisa's tanned face suddenly became as smooth and unreadable as the artfully schooled visage Carmen Sternwood turned to the world in *The Big Sleep*. But Lisa's left hand, which could grip a tennis racket so expertly, tightened on the door frame until the knuckles ridged the skin.

"Security," she repeated blankly.

Annie stepped into the hall, as if confident of her welcome, chattering vacuously, "Time for us to stick together. Such a *surprise*. Of course, I didn't know Sydney very well, but it seems to me the implication is clear that she was meeting someone there. Can't imagine who."

Lisa stiffened, and she looked sharply at Annie.

Lord Peter himself could not have nattered on more innocuously. "Max thinks there must be some other way of getting into the compound. We wondered if you and George had ever seen any strangers around. We both agree"—should she cross her fingers?—"that it's absurd to suspect Howard. So, it's up to the neighborhood to come up with anything that can be helpful."

Moving as she spoke, Annie brushed past Lisa and headed for the living room.

Lisa, after hesitating at the door, finally closed it and followed.

Annie paused in the archway that opened into the living room. "Oh, Lisa, what a perfectly lovely room."

It was a vision of light and space. Overstuffed pastel furniture, in two distinct groupings, offered a pastoral view of the pinewoods through enormous floor-to-ceiling windows. Ferns spouted from hanging baskets and from earthenware pots. Contemporary paintings, vivid with splashes of topaz, burnt orange, and cherry, hung on three walls. There wasn't a single piece of Victoriana in sight, despite the ornate scotia moldings on the ceiling. Maybe it was George's first wife who had been rapturous over the 1890s. Lisa could redecorate as much as she wished, but nothing could be done about the Victorian exterior of this house.

Annie dropped into a voluptuously comfortable two-seat couch. "Whew, does this feel good. It's hot this afternoon. I'm parched."

The response, as Annie had calculated, was automatic. Lisa was a thoughtful hostess. "Would you care for a drink? Gin and tonic? Coke? Iced tea?"

"Tea would be wonderful."

"Of course. I'll be right back."

Alone, Annie popped to her feet and prowled, seeking a better insight into her neighbors' lives. But even Sherlock Holmes would have been stymied by this impersonal room, luxurious but uncluttered. No family photos. No obvious mementos. She knew no more when she finished her circuit of the room than when she began. It bespoke money and quiet good taste, no more.

Footsteps sounded in the hall. Annie sped back to her seat. Lisa entered with a tray, tall crystal glasses filled with ice and tea and generous sprigs of mint.

"Sugar?"

"No, thanks."

Now, safely ensconced as a guest, Annie set to work.

Sitting opposite her, perched stiffly on the very edge of a huge ottoman, Lisa fielded questions cautiously. According to her, the Grahams had known the Cahills for several years, but only casually. (Annie forbore to point out that George and Sydney's embrace in the alcove at the Valentine party had not been casual.)

Lisa forced a social smile. "We happened to get married the same year. But we didn't have much else in common."

"Did George have this house when you married?" Annie asked innocently. Lisa's nod confirmed her hunch. She wondered idly what had happened to all the Victorian furniture.

"Didn't George and Sydney play tennis sometimes?"

Lisa's eyes narrowed, like a cat's pupils subjected to harsh light. "Who told you that?"

Annie gazed at her blandly. "I thought I saw them together a couple of times when Max and I were playing."

Lisa yanked off her red towel sweatband with a little more force than was necessary. Her curly brown hair popped forward, and she brushed it back. "Oh," she said carelessly, "I suppose so. You know how casual everything is at the club. A lot of pick-up games on Saturdays."

That's probably exactly the kind of games that ensued. Annie wasn't thinking tennis. "Didn't he ever mention playing with her?"

Lisa's smile was controlled and distant. "Probably. In one ear and out the other when it isn't important."

Annie sipped her tea, and the aromatic mint tickled her nose. "Did you ever hear any gossip linking Sydney with anyone?"

Again Lisa gave Annie a probing glance, but Annie maintained her bland, friendly expression.

It was obvious to Annie that Lisa could unload on Sydney like Paul Drake reporting to Perry Mason.

Annie read it in the angry glint of Lisa's eyes, the tightening of her coral lips.

But she didn't.

That's when Annie decided Lisa had indeed seen her husband's embrace of Sydney at the party.

Lisa tossed her head, her dark curls quivering. "I really scarcely knew her."

"Oh." Annie sighed gustily. "Then you can't help us out in that direction. But you and George and Joel were at the Valentine party?"

"They invited all the neighbors," Lisa said quickly.

"Oh, of course. Did you happen to notice Sydney that night, who she talked to, that kind of thing?"

"She was like a cat in heat, rubbing up to every man in the place," Lisa snapped.

In Annie's experience, it was the toms who came after the tabbies, but she decided it might be damping to disagree, so she listened, with a mental apology to Agatha and Dorothy L.

Her eyes flashing, Lisa spewed the names of Sydney's dance partners, who at one point or another included an island lawyer, the druggist, a pediatrician, the visiting tennis player, and—much more to the point if Lisa realized it—compound resident Buck Burger. Lisa, of course, didn't mention her own husband or Annie's, though quite obviously she hadn't missed Sydney's sultry attentions to them Tuesday night. And she didn't mention Joel. An oversight? Did she consider it too unimportant—or too important?

"She might as well have waved a flag that said 'Take me,'" Lisa said bitterly. "She was absolutely—"

It was then that Annie saw the shoe in the window. Although, of course, it wasn't actually a shoe in the window. It was a reflection. Annie faced the windows. Lisa could see neither that particular window nor the portion of the hall it reflected. As delicately as Georges Simenon's Inspector Maigret absorbs atmosphere, Annie shifted millimeter by millimeter until her peripheral vision encompassed the archway opening into the hall.

The tip of a scuffed sneaker was just visible in the archway. Someone was listening to their conversation, to Lisa's denunciation of Sydney's actions on the last night of her life.

"—out of control!" Lisa paused, her cheeks crimson.

"I felt that, too." Annie leaned forward confidentially. "You know, she must have had some real problems." The shoe didn't move.

"That woman's only problem was a bad case of nymphomania."

Annie was careful not to remind Lisa that she had begun their little chat by pretending absolute ignorance of Sydney's activities. It was amazing what a little discretion could net by way of revelations. Annie was sure that if she had started off by asking about George and Sydney's clinch in the alcove, she wouldn't have learned a thing. She made a mental note to remind Max how much one could learn about human nature from reading mysteries.

Lisa abruptly recalled herself. She picked up her half-full glass of iced tea and drank. She added another spoonful of sugar and sipped again before saying, her voice once more perfectly controlled, "Of course, that's what it looked like, that night. I don't know anything firsthand."

"Perhaps it was one of those men who met her in the gazebo," Annie said brightly. "Now, this is so critical. Did you and George hear anything—any kind of disturbance that night? Do you think anyone could have trespassed on your property?"

Lisa paused, the glass midway to her lips. Then, slowly and deliberately, she drank the rest of her iced tea.

Annie tried hard not to come to attention, like a bird dog on point. Lisa was stalling. Why? Had they heard something? Why did that question alarm her?

Lisa placed the glass precisely on its coaster. "That night?" Her effort to be casual rang as false as Mike Hammer sipping a sherry. "Oh, I don't think we would have heard anything—if there was anything to hear. And she wasn't shot, was she? We watched a movie. You know how it is sometimes when you get in from a party. It's hard to unwind."

Hard to unwind? Annie plummeted into sleep like John Putnam Thatcher welcoming a balance sheet. With alacrity.

"Of course," Annie replied insincerely. "Max and I love movies, too." She didn't add that her favorites were made before 1940. She was nutty about *Woman in the Dark,* based on the Dashiell Hammett short story and *Jamaica Inn,* drawn from the 1936 Daphne du Maurier novel. "What did you watch?"

It was painful to see Lisa try to come up with a name. "Oh, one of the police academy ones," she said finally.

Sure, Annie thought, and I'm a little green man from Mars, too.

"They're so noisy," Lisa said with more assurance.

"Have you heard anything strange on other nights?"

"Oh no, no. It's awfully quiet out here." She was completely at ease now, her hands loose in her lap.

So her tension was directly connected with Tuesday night. What had happened in this house on Tuesday night? Annie was willing to bet a first edition (very fine) of James M. Cain's *The Postman Always Rings Twice,* worth a cool fifteen hundred dollars, that it wasn't a private viewing of *Police Academy* number whatever.

"You can't think of anything that would be helpful in the investigation?"

Lisa's apologetic shrug was perfect. "But you know"—and her voice reflected increasing confidence—"we're so far away from the Cahills.

I'd certainly help if I could. Such a dreadful thing to happen. And Howard's so nice."

The shoe in the hall lifted, rubbed against an ankle encased in a thick white sock.

Annie had a good idea who lurked out there.

She lifted her voice just a little. "I don't suppose it's true, but I did happen to hear someone say they saw Sydney with Joel at the club recently."

"Joel." His stepmother's tone was thoughtful.

Annie waited patiently, giving her every opportunity to mention the interlude both she and Lisa had observed at the Valentine dance.

"Oh, it would have been a tennis game, something like that," Lisa said finally. "Joel scarcely knew her." She glanced at her watch. "I'm sorry, Annie, but I have some things to do . . ."

Annie rose. "Of course, it's getting late. Thanks for talking to me. If you think of anything that might help—or if any noise that night comes to you—just give me a call."

The shoes in the hall were gone.

When they reached the door, Annie paused. "Do you suppose Joel's home from school yet? Perhaps he heard something that night . . ." She let it hang.

"Oh," Lisa's reply was careless. "I doubt it. Joel's always listening to that hideous loud music. But you can ask him. He has the quarters out on top of the garage. Because of the music. It drives George crazy. If Joel's jeep is at the end of the drive, he's home."

But Annie's luck was out. As she started down the Grahams' front steps, the jeep sped past in a cloud of dust.

Annie dialed as fast as she could.

"Confidential Commissions." Max's secretary always sounded cheerful and as if her mouth was full. Which it probably was. Barbie spent a lot of time cooking in the tiny little kitchen at the back of the office suite. Max never alluded to it, but Confidential Commissions didn't exactly teem with clients on a regular basis. It was amazing what Barbie could create in what Annie considered to be less than scintillating culinary surroundings, everything from blueberry fritters to stuffed flounder rolls with citrus sauce. Of course, as far as Annie was concerned, even a kitchen designed by Martha Stewart wouldn't tempt *her* to cook. Everyone had their interests. Annie's was eating, not cooking.

"Hi, Barbie. Can I talk to Max?"

A definite smacking of lips. "He's on the phone right now, Annie. Long distance. Want him to call you?"

"I'd better talk to him now. Could you interrupt?"

"Sure."

A buzz and a crackle. "Mr. Darling, there is an emergency call for you from Tokyo. It's about the stolen emerald necklace."

Annie grinned. Barbie must really be bored.

In a moment, Max was on the line. "Annie? What's up?"

"You've got a toothache."

Max and Hercule Poirot had this in common, they both loathed going to the dentist. Max, of course, bore up to it better than Poirot, but not by much.

"No, no, teeth never felt better," Max proclaimed emphatically. "If anybody needs to go to the dentist, it's you. Probably rotting out from too much chocolate. I found those raspberry-filled Godiva starfish hidden behind the oat bran muffins. Now, I've got to get back to—"

Max had a thing about chocolate and its ill effects. So, of course, she'd put the starfish in an inconspicuous place. It certainly wasn't fair to infer she'd *hidden* them. "Chocolate," she assured him crisply, "is the elixir of the gods. Just think, those poor Romans never had a chocolate soda. And my teeth are fine, but I don't have time to go into town." The Broward's Rock business district clustered near the ferry landing. Of course, Max's office and Death on Demand were on the other end of the island around the yacht harbor, but it wouldn't take Max five minutes to drive to Graham's office. "Too much is happening out here. Listen, Max." She told him about the movie, *Police Academy* number whatever. "Get over to George's office and pump him before she sees him and they get their story straight. Okay?"

"But, Annie, my teeth are—"

"*Lie.*" She hung up.

She dialed again immediately to prevent Max from calling back. They didn't have Call Waiting at home because Annie considered it an odious invention, almost as infuriating as the American film versions of Christie novels. The British could be counted upon to do Christie right. Joan Hickson was a Miss Marple whom Dame Agatha would have enjoyed. But most American productions of Christie novels sucked. Americans seemed unable to film mysteries without being campy. She shuddered as she recalled the made-for-TV bastardization of *Murder in Three Acts,* transplanted from the English coast to Acapulco and starring Tony Curtis. There were, of course, exceptions to this blanket indictment, notably *And Then There Were None* in 1945, starring Barry Fitzgerald, Walter Huston, and Roland Young, and *Witness for the Prosecution* in 1957, starring Tyrone Power, Marlene Dietrich, Charles Laughton, and Elsa Lanchester.

Ingrid's businesslike voice yanked her back to the present. "Death on Demand."

"Hi, Ingrid. Everything okay?"

"Oh, nothing's wrong that a cat psychiatrist might not be able to solve."

Annie's heart sank. "Problems?"

"I don't suppose it's a major problem. Unless it upsets you to have a cat stalking around like General Zaroff on a tear."

General Zaroff? The bored hunter, created by Richard Connell, sought the ultimate prey—man himself—in "The Most Dangerous Game," the classic suspense short story.

"Has she hurt Dorothy L.?" Annie demanded.

"Not yet. That isn't to say I haven't intervened a half dozen times. Now Agatha snarls every time she sees me. Annie, I tried to pet her and she almost took my hand off."

Annie sighed. "What are we going to do?"

"Give it time, I guess. That's what Henny advises. Hey, you know she's off on a new kick."

If Annie's ears could have flattened, they would have. "Yep. Who is it this time?"

"You want the whole ambience, the jingle of gold chains, the Hollywoodese, the tired tinsel?"

"No. Give it to me straight."

"Jake Weissman, a Hollywood agent in *Death Takes the Stage.*"

"First novel?"

"You got it. By Donald Ward. Henny's really laying it on that we don't know him. She says Ward's superfunny, a great new—"

"Ingrid." It was a warning growl, probably reminding Ingrid of Agatha.

"All right, all right, but Henny's so good at playing parts. And the book does sound terrific. I've ordered a half dozen. Besides, Henny's really been busy."

And Annie hadn't? But huffiness didn't become her. Henny was a damn good sleuth, so Annie tried hard not to sound pettish. "What's she come up with?"

"It's that valentine." Ingrid didn't have to explain which one. Forever after in Annie's mind, 'that valentine' could only refer to the crumpled homemade heart found clutched in the dead woman's hand. "Henny's trying to find out when Sydney got it. For starters, Henny figures it had to be on Tuesday. Because the message doesn't give a day. See, if it had come in the mail Monday, the message would have had to specify Tuesday night."

Annie recalled the verses: *Roses are red, violets are blue. Wait in the gazebo, I'll hurry to you. In the still of the night, our hearts can take flight. When the clock strikes one, our time will have come.*

Oh, sure. Of course. Annie began to feel a flicker of excitement. That narrowed it down without a doubt. Sydney *must* have received that message sometime during the day on Tuesday.

"It *didn't* come through the mail," Ingrid emphasized. "Henny talked to Sue Lee Hankins, who has that route. Sue Lee doesn't keep track of everybody's mail, of course, but there was a lot of volume Tuesday because it was Valentine's Day. She remembers the Cahill house particularly because Howard got this huge round cylinder and she was glad there wasn't any other mail, except a bunch of circulars."

"She's certain?"

"Henny says so."

If Henny said so, that's the way it was. She could ferret out facts with the tenacity of C. W. Grafton's lawyer sleuth, Gil Henry.

"Henny's hot on the trail now. She said she'll get back to you."

"Okay, Ingrid. Thanks. And listen, about Agatha. Why don't you sauté her some chicken livers. Maybe that will put her in a better humor."

"Maybe." Ingrid didn't sound convinced. "I think she'd prefer Dorothy L.'s head on a platter. But I'll give it a try."

"Thath thum." Max's neck ached, he was sure he was going to strangle, and he had the helpless feeling he always experienced when tilted back in a dentist's chair. Annie sure had swell ideas. And how the hell did she expect Max to ask questions with George's hand crammed in his mouth!

George Graham poked with a sharp tip. He was close enough for Max to count the freckles on his nose. "Looks good, Max. Can't find anything wrong. Could be a hairline crack. We'll see what the X-rays show. Does it hurt when you take a hot shower?"

Max wondered if this was the dental equivalent of a Rorschach test. "No."

"Good. So we aren't talking a root canal." And stuck his fist back in Max's mouth. Graham's tone was cheery. He exuded reassurance, dependability, a faint scent of peppermint mouthwash, and the heavier aroma of a snappy men's cologne.

Max wriggled like a stuck pig. Root canal! They sure as hell weren't. "Mumph clomph woof." The saccharine strains of "Harbor Lights" as mutilated by Muzak added to his misery.

Out came the fist. Graham began to peel off the latex gloves. "Could be a temporary sensitivity."

"I'm sure it's temporary," Max said eagerly. "But I thought I should get it checked. Just in case. Thanks a lot for working me in this afternoon."

Graham laughed, revealing even white teeth. "Wednesday afternoons

are slow. Everybody plays golf. Except me, and I'll take tennis anytime."
He looked like a tennis regular with his freckled golden skin and sun-touched brown hair.

"Slow days are one of the perks of living on Broward's Rock," Max said genially. "And Scarlet King has to be the best place to live on the whole island. Annie and I are crazy about our house." He frowned gravely. "Of course, it's hellish to think a murder happened right next door."

"Terrible," Graham agreed. He frowned, too, and for the first time looked middle-aged. Perhaps it was his perennially cheerful smile that made him look so young. For a moment, as his smile fled, he looked every one of his forty-six years. "God, what an awful thing to happen. I can't believe Howard did it. But they say nobody but the residents could have been inside the compound. So who else could it have been?"

Max stayed away from that question. "At the party, it seemed pretty clear you and Sydney were old friends."

Graham gave Max a level stare. "What the hell are you getting at, Darling?"

"I just wondered if you were the man Sydney was going to meet at the gazebo."

There was nothing equable about Graham now. The man beneath the dentist's pleasant public persona was suddenly apparent, and he was no pushover. "No way. I sure as hell wasn't."

"You mean she was making out with you in the alcove but she was also going to meet the great love of her life a couple of hours later in the gazebo?"

Graham crumpled the used latex gloves in one hand. "Don't be naive, Darling. Hell, what man on the island didn't screw her, at one time or another. You have to admit she was damn pretty. Problem was, she couldn't keep her mouth shut. I got the drift pretty quick. She couldn't wait to describe every bed she'd been in for the past year and how men were so fickle, and how wonderful it was that I was so different. Jesus. About that time, I figured out the next thing she'd do was tell Howard, so I broke it off."

"Broke it off," Max repeated neutrally. "Then Tuesday night—"

Graham stepped on a trash can lever and dropped the gloves inside. As it clanged shut, he asked coldly, "What business is it of yours?"

"None," Max agreed cheerfully. "But when the cops stop looking at Howard, they may be more than a little interested in you."

"So I got a little bit Tuesday night. Hell, why not? She was up for grabs. It didn't mean a thing."

"What did Lisa think?"

Graham stiffened. "Wait a minute. You leave Lisa alone."

"Maybe Lisa got ticked off Tuesday night when she saw you and Sydney in a big clinch. Maybe Lisa found Sydney in the gazebo."

"And bashed Sydney's brains out? Get real, Darling. Lisa was frosted all right. Mad as hell, as a matter of fact." Graham heaved a put-upon sigh. "Jesus, I don't know what women expect. They've got the goddamnedest ideas about sex. Lisa knew I wasn't any plaster saint when we met. Fact is, I was still married to Kathleen then. But suddenly when we're married, it's supposed to be a different ball game. Most of the time it is. But Sydney—hell, you know how it is."

Max knew. He also knew the dentist would be surprised to know Max's views on monogamy. Max believed in it. Not that he didn't appreciate the attraction of other women, but a deal was a deal.

"I mean, for God's sake," Graham complained, "I *married* Lisa. I didn't marry any of the others. Even signed a prenuptial agreement guaranteeing Lisa an income of at least fifty thou a year. What the hell more does she want?"

Graham, obviously, thought wedding vows had to do primarily with real-property rights.

The dentist reached in his pocket and pulled out a packet of Trident. He waved it in Max's direction. At his headshake, Graham popped a piece of gum in his mouth. "So you're right. Lisa was ticked off, but she didn't leave the house that night." He slapped his thigh in disgust. "I left the goddamned house. She locked the goddamned door to the bedroom and wouldn't let me in. So I got mad and slammed outside. I ended up out by the pool on one of those puffy overstuffed things. I got a couple of big towels out of the cabana and wrapped up. I could see the light in our bedroom, and it didn't go off till after one-thirty. From what I hear, Sydney was dead long before then. So you can cross Lisa off your list."

And Graham, too, of course. If anybody took his story as fact.

TWELVE

Max twisted like a pretzel until the hand vibrator reached the tight muscles behind his left shoulder. He was ready to quit for the day. But it was only half past four. He quirked a blond eyebrow at the picture of Annie that graced his desk. Dear Annie. Her eyes gazed at him soberly from the silver frame. Such serious gray eyes. He winked in return. Because she wasn't always serious. Her kissable mouth could widen in an infectious grin, and her eyes could sparkle with delight.

But if he went home at four-thirty with his task incomplete, those same eyes would look as mournful as Lieutenant Nathan Shapiro surveying the New York City of Frances and Richard Lockridge.

A prisoner to duty, Max clicked off the vibrator, stretched, and reached for the telephone. He glanced at his notes. Susie Dunlap, reputed to have been Sydney Cahill's best friend. He stared at the name, then smiled. Sure. It was close indeed to that of a famous West Coast mystery writer, Susan Dunlap. Annie had held a signing for her not too long ago, featuring Dunlap's latest book, *Pious Deception,* and her new sleuth, Kiernan O'Shaughnessy, a former forensic pathologist turned private eye. Dunlap was also the creator of the Berkeley policewoman, Lieutenant Jill Smith, and the remarkable gas company meter reader, Veronica "Vejay" Haskell. Max hoped the Susie he was calling wasn't as perceptive as the author. As he dialed, he considered what role he might play this time.

"Hello." She packed a lot of living into two syllables, her throaty contralto as smooth as Johnny Walker Black easing into a tumbler.

"Susie Dunlap?" He tried for an amused, confident tone.

"Yes."

"John Wells here. For the *New York Star.*"

"John Wells." The way she said it made Max wish the name belonged to him, and he was a single newspaperman from up north. But just for an instant. Those serious gray eyes were watching. "Nice name," Susie said huskily. "Are you a nice man?"

Max guessed that John Wells was a very nice man. Sometime he'd have to ask Wells's creator, Keith Peterson. As for right now—he brushed the sweat off his upper lip—for right now, it was probably a good thing this was going to be a phone interview.

"Nicest guy I know," he said lightly.

A sultry laugh. "What can I do for you, Nice Guy?"

The white Lincoln Continental sported a Dallas Cowboys bumper sticker. The drive also held a red Mercedes coupe and a Ford pickup with a gun rack in the back window. As Annie passed the pickup, she noted muddy hunting boots, a couple of well-worn ball caps, a dirt-stained, bramble-pricked camouflage jacket, and a beat-up Styrofoam cooler. Appurtenances of a good old boy.

But there was nothing down-home about Buck and Billye Burgers' Tudor mansion. The antique brickwork, half timbering, and sharply peaked gables looked only a little odd among the live oaks and stubby palmettos. This kind of construction, dating to the 1920s when period building was in vogue, dotted every wealthy suburb in Texas. Annie would guess the Burgers' home in Dallas was a blood sister to this house. As she pressed the bell, she admired the Tudor stone arch over the front door.

When the door opened, Annie knew immediately why Laurel had decided a watchman lived on the Burger property. Though the man standing in the Burgers' doorway might be serving at this moment as a butler, he had nothing in common with those she had come to know from Christie novels and short stories—Alton in *Thirteen at Dinner,* Carson in *Endless Night,* Lanscombe in *Funerals Are Fatal,* Graves in *Poirot Investigates,* and Holmes in "The Adventure of the Christmas Pudding." Her picture of the English butler was indelibly affected by Lanscombe. (Dear Lanscombe. So *nearsighted.*) The striking difference from this man's English counterparts wasn't simply in his choice of clothing, a navy turtleneck beneath a blue blazer, and gray slacks. None of Christie's butlers resembled NFL linemen, 260 pounds of muscle with a battered face and light golden eyes as impersonal as those of a marauding tiger.

"Is either Mr. or Mrs. Burger at home?"

"Who's calling?" His high, soft voice was impersonal, too, and gave her the creeps.

"I'm their neighbor, Mrs. Darling. Please tell them I've come about a neighborhood problem."

He nodded impassively and closed the door.

Max tugged at the collar of his shirt. It wasn't hot in his office, but he could have done with a tall, cool one.

"You ever get down this way? I could show you a good time." The invitation was lazy but unmistakable.

Thank God, he'd had the wit to say he was calling from New York. He gave Annie's picture a reassuring nod. "No, but I sure wish I did. And I sure wish you'd been in town and talked to Sydney. We were hoping you could tell us if anything out of the ordinary had happened to her lately."

Susie didn't answer.

Max's hand tightened on his pen. There was something different in the quality of this silence.

"Like I said," she continued finally, "I hadn't *talked* to her. I was in the Bahamas and just got back last night." Max's immediate mental vision of Susie's activities in the Bahamas would have distressed Annie. "But she left a message on my machine Monday night." Susie's voice was unaffected now, and Max glimpsed the girl who had grown up in a small town, before she decided the world was a sexual arena and her body was her weapon. "Of course"—and it was almost as if she were speaking to herself, with a hint of impatience and irritation—"Sydney was *always* in tears over some man. So what else was new! But when she called Monday night, she was . . . terribly upset. It was different. I mean, usually she called to cry about some guy dumping her and I always told her another man would come along. See, she had this silly idea that someday, some way she was going to find the perfect man and he would love her forever. She never understood that the way she held on to guys just scared them to death. But this time, it wasn't about a guy dumping her. She was kind of hysterical. She kept saying, 'I found him in bed with her. How could he do this to me? How could he make love to *her?*' "

Max felt an instant's qualm, then realized he needn't worry. Laurel had arrived only Tuesday morning. There certainly wasn't time for— He skirted the thought and asked quickly, "Her? Do you have any idea who Sydney was talking about? Either the man or the woman?"

"No. Oh, I knew she was sleeping with somebody new. The signals were always the same. This time she went on and on about how fresh it all was until I stopped listening. She was always really coy about it at first. You can bet the guy was stressing how this was just a great, wonderful secret love between the two of them. Of course, they *never* want their wives to know. Sydney was such a fool. But I knew she'd eventually tell me who he was. She always did when the guy dumped her."

"This call was Monday night?" On his legal pad, Max sketched a double bed with intertwined question marks.

"Yes. I . . . Look, she was *so* upset. Do you suppose she found her husband in bed with somebody?"

Max tensed. So that idea had occurred to Susie, too. But he was almost certain he'd unearthed everything there was to know about Howard Cahill. And there was no hint that he was romantically involved with anyone. Until he met Laurel Tuesday morning. But that was Tuesday *morning*.

"Do you think it would have upset her that much, if she thought Howard was involved with another woman?"

"Oh, yeah." A wry laugh. "Yeah, I'm sure it would have. Like I say, I don't know what the deal was, but she was more upset than I'd ever heard her."

Max wrote on his pad: *How could he make love to her?*

Yes, Susie Dunlap had heard something different in Sydney's frenzied call.

This time Sydney wasn't being dumped; this time Sydney was being duped. Would she have been that upset at the duplicity of a lover?

He thought out loud. "You'd think she was used to being pushed aside."

Susie's voice was decisive. And sad. "A woman like her never gets used to it. Poor old Sydney. She was such a sap. I mean, she always thought she was in *love.*"

Max didn't ask what Susie thought. He knew damn well *she* never confused sex with love. He glanced once again at a familiar picture. God, how good it was when the two were one.

Unaware of Max's exposure to influences she certainly would not consider benign, Annie followed the massive, distinctly nonbutlerish back through the baronial entrance hall with its heavy carved-stone beams, dark parquet flooring, and hand-troweled stucco walls to a massive arch that opened into a magnificent drawing room bursting with old-world color, from the wine-red Aubusson carpet to the enormous blue and gold sixteenth-century Flemish wall tapestry to the ornately figured purple, cinnamon, and maroon gros-point Louis XV beechwood chairs.

Billye Burger rose from one of the chairs. "Thank you, Marshall." Her nod to the giant was dismissive. She flowed gracefully toward her guest. "Annie, it's so *good* to see you." Her speech was quintessentially Texas rich, a lilting southern undertone beneath a light, social, impervious patina. Her lips curved in an automatic smile, but shrewd blue eyes studied Annie thoughtfully. As always, her improbably blond hair was piled high on her head in an elaborate beehive. Her black and white pebble print silk dress made Annie feel like a peasant misplaced from the fields, although she'd been rather pleased with her khaki skirt and shell-pink blouse when she'd dressed that morning. The double strand of pearls at Billye's throat had the unmistakable sheen of the finest Majorca could produce as did the matching earrings. A diamond ring that glittered like a glacier in the midnight sun was set off by an ivory bracelet with a gold lion's-head inset. A matching gold pin, the lion in full stride, rode on her collar. Rubies served as eyes for the king of beasts.

"I feel so *bad* I haven't been over to see you, welcome you to our lovely retreat." Her embrace, one perfumed cheek grazing Annie's, was as light as the brush of a monarch's wing. Her comments flowed on, relentless as a river of honey, as she directed Annie to a sofa with alternating bands of rose and taupe fabric. She dropped into one of the gros-point chairs and beamed at her guest.

"So *delighted* you and Max have joined us here at Scarlet King." Billye didn't permit a frown to crease her perfect skin—Annie wondered how many times she'd resorted to plastic surgery—but her mouth pursed with distaste. "Of course, everything's so hideous now, with this dreadful crime." A sober shake of her head left the lacquered hair undisturbed. "Marshall said you wanted to see Buck and me about a neighborhood matter? Why, I bet that you and that handsome husband of yours are trying to figure out who killed Sydney. Am I right now?" Her shrewd gaze didn't match her arch tone.

Annie admired her skill. Without abandoning a scintilla of her social manner, Billye had cut through to the bone. Which prompted Annie to alter her plan. Her chattery approach to Lisa Graham wouldn't work here.

"In a way," Annie replied, with, she hoped, a convincing appearance of frankness. "Certainly, if Chief Saulter were in charge of the investigation, we wouldn't interfere. But the circuit solicitor from the mainland has taken over, and it looks like he's convinced that Howard murdered Sydney."

Her hostess fingered the shiny golden lion at her throat. "You don't think so?" Her tone was neutral at best.

Annie looked at her in surprise.

Unabashed, Billye gave the daintiest of shrugs. "Husbands do so often kill wives, you know," she drawled. "I can't *tell* you how many times Buck defended some fellow who'd had enough." Her perfect rosy lips twitched a little in amusement. "There, now, I've shocked you. A young girl like you, just married. Believe me, honey, a man may tomcat all he likes, but he won't put up with his wife in somebody else's bed for one minute. Not for a second." She smoothed her shiny blond coiffure. "At least, not in Texas."

There was more than a germ of truth in that one, Annie knew.

"So you believe Howard's guilty?" Annie asked slowly.

A delicate sigh of regret. "I don't see how anything else figures." There was honest bewilderment in the honeyed voice. "All this insinuation in the paper about Sydney slipping away to an illicit rendezvous and being killed by her lover. Why, you and I know that's nonsense." Billye shook her head slightly. "Poor Sydney. Men couldn't get away from her fast enough once they'd satisfied themselves. I mean, face it, honey, all she had was her body."

The soft-spoken words hung in the air between them like the mournful echo of faraway church bells.

Poor Sydney. Poor, poor Sydney.

But where did that leave them? If a lover didn't pen that valentine, then who hated Sydney enough to send a siren song to summon her to death? Her husband? Or had Howard followed her to the gazebo and struck her down in a jealous fury?

Annie glanced at the garlanded cupids adorning a gilt mirror frame that hung on the wall behind Billye. "Howard had put up with it for a long time, from all we've heard. But you and Buck knew them well, didn't you?" She paused, took her courage in hand, and asked, "Did Buck like Sydney?"

There were no lines on Billye's marble-perfect skin to crease in a smile, but a subtle change of musculature indicated amusement. "Why, he sure did, honey. Buck's all man. I guess you can tell that, as well as any woman. But let me tell you something, he's *my* man."

"So you're sure Buck never was involved with her?"

Billye leaned back comfortably in the regal chair; now her smile was wide. "I didn't say that, honey. But you can ask him for yourself." She looked toward the archway. "Come on in, honey. Annie and I've been worryin' over what happened to Sydney."

Buck Burger made even a Tudor archway seem small. And there were, Annie decided, no flies on Buck when it came to male pulchritude. He wasn't, by any means, her ideal (as in young and blond and well built with dark blue eyes), but Buck's skin-tight Levi's and smooth-fitting yellow cotton knit crewneck emphasized muscles and lots of them in all the right places, despite his sixty-odd years. His body was in better shape than his face. Broken blood vessels splayed his heavy cheeks with tiny rivulets of red and his brow and nose and chin were simian-blunt under thinning gray hair.

"Why, hello there, Annie. Sure good to see a neighbor. We'll have to have a little drink to celebrate." His red alligator cowboy boots glistened in a shaft of sunlight from a west window as he moved toward a sideboard. The ruby ring on his hand flashed as he picked up a diamond-bright Waterford crystal tumbler and reached toward a row of decanters. "What'll you have, sweetheart?"

Billye, with a born hostess's perception, saved her from answering. "Now Buck, I imagine Annie'd rather have tea or a spritzer."

"Tea, please." Annie flashed an appreciative smile as Billye pressed a button.

Buck's huge hand closed on a matching cut glass decanter. He poured a tumbler almost full. "Good enough. You ladies pick your own poison. As for me, I'll have some Texas tea." His chest rumbled with laughter. He held out the glass for Annie to see. "Bourbon," he amplified.

A slim, dark, uniformed maid appeared in the archway.

"Iced tea, Elena, for Mrs. Darling and me."

Buck settled heavily in the beechwood chair opposite Billye's. He propped his boots on a Queen Anne bench with a travertine inset and drank down half the glass. "Now, Billye, Annie"—he wiped his lips with the back of a hand—"it's much too pretty a day for you sweet ladies to be talking about depressing things." It was, even for Buck, an exceptionally inane comment, but Annie wasn't fooled into dismissing him as a rich buffoon. The gaze he fastened on her, as he lifted the tumbler again, was canny, pugnacious, appraising, and not the least bit stupid.

Annie started to simmer. Did they think she was an idiot? Max was always reminding her that honey captured more bees than vinegar. But sometimes she didn't give a damn. Like now.

"From what Billye says," Annie said crisply, "I gather she didn't mind that you had an affair with Sydney."

For a split instant, the hand holding the tumbler paused in mid-descent and bloodshot green eyes widened. Then another deep rumble of laughter sounded. "My, it sounds like you ladies really let down your hair."

"Did you have an affair with Sydney?" Annie pressed.

Buck finished off his drink, then glanced good-humoredly at Billye, who smiled at him approvingly. "Why, I don't want to disappoint my wife. If she said so, why I guess it's so."

The maid entered with a silver tray and huge old-fashioned glasses filled with crushed ice and tea. Slices of lemon and orange and sprigs of mint decorated the rims.

"Sugar?" Billye asked, only of course it sounded like "shugah."

Annie shook her head and damned the social proprieties. Every time she felt close to ferreting out something useful, she was offered tea. And she felt abruptly that this interlude had been expertly stage-managed.

It was as fake as any Holmes pastiche.

Only in Noel Coward comedies did husbands and wives indulge in pleasant nattering about infidelity.

Unless Billye and Buck Burger inhabited a totally different emotional plane than she and Max.

But they might.

So she didn't know what she believed. What she heard. What she saw. Or what she felt.

Was there uneasiness in Buck's apparently placid gaze? Did pain lurk behind the shrewdness in Billye's eyes?

Annie put down her tea untasted. "You didn't even care?" she asked Billye softly.

That carefully and artfully tightened new-old face showed no emotion, but the no longer young hands lying in Billye's lap, fingers laden with gold and diamonds, were rigidly immobile. Yet her voice still flowed like Texas honey. "Of course I cared about poor, dear Sydney."

It was, Annie felt confident, a willful misunderstanding.

"But you have to understand that Buck and I had nothing to do with any of it."

It was a declaration. Annie wondered if it might also be a prayer.

Annie lifted her glass again and welcomed the cold, sharp, fresh tea. It almost washed away the ugly taste in her mouth. "So neither one of you saw Sydney after the party?"

"Nope," Buck said. "Last I saw of poor old Sydney, she was smooching it up with George." He started off with a mournful headshake, but it didn't last long. A wicked light shone in his eyes and his meaty shoulders shook with suppressed laughter. "The general really knows how to stick it to a man. Jesus, what a show."

If Buck cared for Sydney, if seeing her in the arms of another man wounded him, it certainly wasn't evident.

Billye made a series of clucking noises, indicating disapproval. "Such a naughty thing to do."

"The prosecutor believes Sydney's embrace with George right in Howard's own house was the last straw. What do you think?"

The Burgers exchanged shrewd glances.

Billye turned thoughtful blue eyes on Annie. "Howard's a patient man. But every man has his limits."

"Howard was a damn fool to marry her. Even if she was a sexy bitch." Buck shoved his hands deep in his Levi pockets. "Hell, you don't *marry* women like Sydney."

"Men do sometimes," Annie said quietly, and she watched her hostess. "Howard did."

Billye's smooth, scalpel-tailored face was untouched by emotion, but those wrinkled hands clung tightly to the chair arms. Her eyes locked with Annie's and another bright smile curved her rose-red lips. "Howard was all alone. That's how *that* happened."

But plenty of married men had apparently delighted in beguiling away time with Sydney.

And Sydney was young and very lovely.

Not all the plastic surgeons, not all the lovely clothes, not all the creams and lotions and unguents can turn back the years.

Buck was at that dangerous age when a young woman's body could bring back the excitement, if not the reality, of his youth.

"Did either of you see Sydney after the party ended?"

Their denials were quick and smooth and determined.

Annie kept doggedly on. "How about later in the night? Did either of you hear anything unusual?"

"The siren," Billye said quickly. "I thought the general had had a heart attack. I see him out walking sometimes and his lips are blue. I expect he'll keel over any day now."

Buck nodded. "He's got a bad heart. Has to take a handful of pills. Insists he's okay." He sighed heavily. "Damn fool won't quit playing golf and sometimes you can't get out of a foursome with him. Rather play with a goddam rattlesnake. Got a real mean streak. Spends half the time popping nitroglycerin under his tongue. Course, if I had to take the damn blood pressure pills *he* takes, I'd be a mean shit, too. Damn doctors don't care whether you can screw, but I'd just as soon hang it all up if I couldn't get it up. There's plenty of medicines for high blood pressure besides that one. That's probably why the old buzzard's always in such a nasty humor." There was a fleeting glint of sympathy in his eyes. "I'd bet the ranch that's why he was so goddam down on Sydney. But hell, just because you can't eat the ice cream doesn't mean you ought to want to close up the ice cream store."

"You don't think it was moral disgust on the general's part?" Annie asked.

Buck looked at her blankly. She might as well have spoken in Etruscan.

Billye translated. "Annie means maybe the general was disgusted by the way Sydney slept around and wasn't hateful just because he wasn't getting any."

Buck gave an elaborate shrug. "Hell, I don't know. I'm not a head man. Who can say what's wrong with that old fart! I just wish he'd stay the hell away from the club."

Annie wasn't interested in any more speculation about the general's sex life or lack of it, although Buck's conviction that Houghton was impotent made it clear that the general surely wasn't involved in an affair with Sydney. Annie had never considered that possibility very seriously. Sydney might be loose but surely she wasn't desperate enough to be involved with a man old enough to be her grandfather.

She tried to redirect the conversation. "Okay, you heard the siren." She paused, then forced herself to continue. "Were you both in your bedroom?" She couldn't quite bring herself to ask directly if Billye and Buck shared a bed. Annie didn't have Kinky Friedman's chutzpah.

Billye was openly amused. "You can't imagine I put up with all his snufflings and snorings, do you?" Her smile widened. "You newlyweds. Just you wait. One of these years, you'll have your own suite."

Buck guffawed. "Don't think I don't get my share."

Annie felt her ears redden.

"But a man wants his own room. Besides, adds a little spice to life, goin' to a woman's room with all that satin and lace and stuff that smells good. Anyway, Billye's right next door. She called out to me when the siren sounded."

Billye nodded.

Annie fled the topic. "Did you hear anything else unusual?"

Buck hesitated, drumming his stubby fingers on the chair arm. "Well, *we* didn't hear anything else. But Marshall was on du— was up late that night. He heard something. I called the circuit solicitor, but he wasn't interested. I guess if you're hell-bent on springing Howard, you might want to talk to Marshall."

Max poked his head inside Death on Demand.

"Hi, Ingrid. Anything I should tell Annie?"

Ingrid, grinning from ear to ear, looked up from her book. Max admired the jacket, a dark brooch of five ravens lying against a bright pink chrysanthemum that rested on a dark, veiled hat. *The Widows' Club* by Dorothy Cannell.

"Tell her I'd like to turn Agatha over to the Widows' Club as a candidate for Someone To Be Removed. That cat is deranged." A thoughtful look crossed Ingrid's face. "Although, to tell the truth, if Agatha hears about the functions of the Widows' Club, *she* may apply for a special membership as a deserted offspring rather than as an ill-treated wife and Annie'd better watch out. Of course, so far as I know there's no American branch." At Max's bewildered look, she relented. "Max, it's the *funniest* book. A women's club in England whose aim is to terminate husbands for women who choose widowhood over divorce—"

"Can't wait to read it," he said politely. Honestly, he was all for women's rights, but weren't there any limits? "I gather Agatha's still unhappy."

As if on cue, Agatha stalked out from behind the True Crime shelving, outrage apparent in the glitter of her amber eyes and the horizontal level of her flattened ears.

"Agatha. Good cat. Nice cat." Max bent down and reached out.

Eyeing him warily, Agatha approached slowly, sniffed the hand, then pushed her head against it.

Max shot a triumphant look at Ingrid and began to pet the sleek, black fur.

There was the bare beginning of a grudging, tentative purr when a small ball of white fluff gamboled up the central corridor.

Agatha stiffened and glared. Her tail puffed and a venomous hiss issued from behind bared fangs.

Max, ever sensible, hastily withdrew his hand.

Dorothy L. frolicked toward him.

Agatha gave Max an "Et tu, Brute" look and fled into the American Cozy area.

Max looked up at Ingrid, who nodded unhappily.

"It's enough to break your heart," the clerk said softly.

Max nodded. Thwarted love was no laughing matter.

"Tell Annie I think I'll take Dorothy L. home with me tonight," Ingrid said. "I like to keep the bloodshed in the books."

"Okay. Everything else all right?"

"Moving at a snail's pace. The usual February day. Sold three of Dick Francis's latest and a couple of Charlotte MacLeods. Oh, and forewarn Annie that Henny's really got a bee in her bonnet this time."

• • •

Very little light seeped through the mullioned windows of the entry hall. As Annie and Buck stepped into the gloom, Marshall appeared from down the hall in response to Buck's call.

"Marshall, this little lady's interested in what happened around here late Tuesday night. Why don't you walk her down to the dock and tell her what you know."

Marshall nodded. He held the door for her, then followed her down the steps. As the oyster shells crunched beneath their feet, they walked to the side of the Tudor mansion.

The butler's voice was not only high and soft, it was without tonal variation. "You'll note the open expanse between the live oaks and the house. That provides a safe corridor. An intruder can find no cover. At night, the perimeter lights are activated."

Annie peered up at the banks of lights appropriate for a baseball park, then surveyed the immense and lovely house, its rich rose and brown hues gleaming in the late afternoon sunlight. If this wasn't an armed camp (and that was an interesting bulge beneath Marshall's blazer), it obviously came damn close. The lights, of course, weren't visible through the swath of forest that separated the properties. But the glow of light would be clear to anyone on the lagoon. She looked across the murky green water at the portions of the Houghton house visible through a mass of bougainvillea and tall, spiny ranks of Spanish bayonet. The thick shrubbery of the Houghton estate emphasized even more the barren Burger lawn. Not a single shrub dotted the thirty feet of sleek grass between the house and the thick cover of the pine forest.

"The lights are turned on every night?"

Marshall nodded curtly.

"Why?"

"Security." Her muscular guide picked up speed. She followed him past the back of the house and the elaborate patio and pool. Despite his bulk, he moved lightly and silently. About midway down the path to the lagoon, without breaking stride, he pointed. "Dock."

Annie nodded. She hurried to keep up and was glad to catch her breath when they walked out onto the small pier. Nearby, a great blue heron stalked snakes and snails and other tasty marine tidbits, placing his long graceful legs so carefully that not a ripple moved in the still water. At the sound of their footsteps, the heron's huge wings moved and it lifted gracefully away into the sunset.

Only rowboats were moored at the piers. There were no speedboats, of course. A restrictive covenant in the deed prohibited them. They wouldn't, given the size of the lagoon, have been appropriate anyway. But the lagoon was perfect for a lazy row, although Annie was leery of gracing with her presence any body of water that afforded a home to as many snakes as Scarlet King Lagoon. She wasn't even taking into account the rat snakes that delighted in climbing trees and sunning on branches, with the nasty habit of falling into passing boats. Further, there was the resident alligator. Max judged he was at least twelve feet long. Annie had no desire for any kind of close relationship with Murphy, as Max persisted in calling him. Actually, the jogging path was as close as she intended to come to the lagoon.

"Tuesday night." Marshall's light golden eyes flicked toward her, then back to the lagoon. "At twelve minutes before oh one hundred hours, I heard oars shipping water."

Oh, my God. A rowboat in the lagoon just before Sydney was murdered.

Dorcas. Dorcas Atwater! She'd been out in her rowboat toward the end of the party. What time was it then? Eleven-thirty perhaps? Dorcas could have returned. If she had and if she found Sydney in the gazebo—

"Did you see anything?" Annie demanded excitedly.

"You can't see out from a lighted area into the dark," he said curtly. "I ran to the bank and out onto the dock. By then the sound was gone."

Annie tried to visualize it, Marshall making his "circuit" and hearing the oars, the bright swath of light encircling the Burger house, the blackness of the lagoon and the forest on either side of the house. A startling revelation hit her.

"You were down here—in this yard or on the dock—at about one o'clock?"

"Affirmative."

"Could anyone have used the path without your seeing them?" Shading her eyes from the sun, a blood-red ruby riding just above the feathery green umbrella tops of the pines, she pointed at the narrow band of asphalt winding out of the pines from the direction of the Atwater house, crossing the grassy bank that belonged to the Burgers, and curving into the pines en route to the Graham's house.

"No way."

But Dorcas could have come by water, had earlier come by water.

Annie turned back to the lagoon. Shadows were lengthening as the sun began to plummet in the west. Soon, it would sink out of sight behind the tall evergreens, and Scarlet King Lagoon would be dim and cloistered. Already the air was cooling and felt much more like February than false March.

"Could you tell what part of the lagoon the boat was on?"

Marshall, too, looked out across the dark water. The Cahill gazebo was just visible through a stand of weeping willows.

"Not when I first heard it."

She picked up on that immediately. "You heard it a second time?"

"It was gone or maybe out of my hearing by the time I got down to the dock. I looked damned hard, I can tell you, but I couldn't make out any movement on the lagoon. Thing is, anything that happens out there is off limits to us. My concern is any approach to this house. The rowboat hadn't landed here. I knew that for sure. So I thought, What the hell, and started back toward the house. I was almost around a couple more circuits, when I heard the boat again. This time I took a side approach to our landing."

Annie didn't ask for a definition of a side approach, but she could imagine this tough, well-muscled man, gun in hand, moving soft-footed through the pines, ready to accost anyone docking unheralded at their pier.

"What happened?" she asked impatiently.

"Nothing. The sound faded away. I thought maybe I heard a thump, somebody walking on another pier. The lights at the end of the piers don't really illuminate them. I decided somebody was out for a midnight row. That's their business. Fine, so long as they don't come here."

"There was a scream. A few minutes after one. Did you hear that?"

It was his turn to be impatient. "Sure."

"You didn't do anything?"

Those light amber eyes were devoid of expression. "It wasn't," he said distinctly, "over here."

Someone, she wanted to say, could have been screaming for help, for life.

But that wouldn't have mattered to this man.

She went at it several different ways, but Marshall didn't have anything else to add. There had been a rowboat. Coming and going. Or maybe one rowboat going and another rowboat going. Who could say? No sight of movement. No hint of origin for the boat (or boats). And he was sure nobody had crossed the Burger grounds going from or coming to the Cahills.

"Did either Mr. or Mrs. Burger come out?"

"No way."

So the Burgers had an alibi—if Marshall could be believed.

And somebody—Dorcas Atwater?—rowed a boat on Scarlet King Lagoon—if Marshall was telling the truth.

Annie looked up at the stolid-faced butler. "You know that Mrs. Ca-hill—Sydney Cahill—was beaten to death in the Cahills' gazebo Tuesday night."

"I read about it. In the paper. That's when I told Mr. Burger about the boat."

He stood with his back to the setting sun, his face in shadow.

"Did you know Mrs. Cahill?"

Her words hung on the soft night air.

"No."

Annie wished she could see his face. Could any man have lived so near Sydney and never thought about her, never made an effort to meet her?

"I'm part of the workin' stock. I don't fool with the gentry."

Was her face that readable?

"Of course," she said quickly to hide her confusion. She thanked him then for his cooperation.

Cool golden eyes looked at her emptily from an immobile face.

Annie turned away, glad to be leaving. She headed for the path to the Atwater house. She could feel Marshall's eyes—his impersonal, alert eyes—on her back as she stepped into the clammy dimness of the shrub-choked pinewoods. She shivered.

But not from the cold.

THIRTEEN

The pale pink stucco house, aglow in the final wash of crimson from the setting sun, should have been enchanting. The white columns seemed touched by fire. Pink silk panels in the Palladian windows matched the rich hue of the stucco. Deeper pink tiles crowned the roof.

At first glance, the house delighted the eye, a confectionary design celebrating sun and marsh and pines. But, as Annie drew closer, signs of neglect spoiled the lush holiday impression.

Stubborn sprigs of grass poked up from the shell walk.

Paint peeled from the Ionic columns.

An ugly rust stain scarred the chimney.

A shutter hung askew on the second floor.

Rainwater simmered with a rich island brew of insects in a long-neglected child's plastic wading pool.

Mud streaked the front steps.

The windows were dark. Not a single light shone, upstairs or down. Dusk was falling. The rooms would be dim. Obviously, Dorcas Atwater wasn't home. Annie almost turned on her heel, then shrugged and pushed the doorbell.

Faintly, she heard a muffled peal. Another. And another.

No one came.

Frustrated, she retraced her steps. Oyster shells crunching beneath her shoes, Annie continued her puzzled survey. This place was going to seed. Was Dorcas Atwater broke? Why didn't she sell? The house was well worth half a million.

An owl hooted mournfully from the stand of pines. Annie's neck prickled. It sounded wild and forlorn, like the laughter Jane Eyre heard in the corridors of Rochester's home, like Dorcas's eerie laughter the night Sydney died. Damp earth smells wafted on the cooling evening breeze. She hesitated at the entrance to the undergrowth-choked woods. It wasn't, of course, that she was frightened.

But it was dusk and last night a woman had been bludgeoned to death not far away. And Annie was all the way across the lagoon from home.

The tiny seed of unease flowered into fear. She plunged into the woods, walking fast, then faster, finally breaking into a run. The occasional lights in the pines only made the growing dark more ominous.

She burst, breathless, into the corridor of light circling the Burger mansion and was halfway across the lawn before she noticed the Burgers' soft-voiced and soft-footed butler-watchman. He was watching her, his stance alert, his right hand slipped within his blazer.

She was well into the stretch of ill-lit path leading to the Grahams before it dawned on her that Marshall was prepared to draw the pistol that nestled in a shoulder holster.

My God.

It was a relief to reach the Grahams' property. Lights glistened in the swimming pool and cheerful oblongs of brightness marked the windows of several rooms, upstairs and down. There was neither the sense of a brilliantly delineated no-man's-land as at the Burgers nor the feeling of forlorn abandonment at the layers of darkness that swathed the Atwater grounds.

Annie slowed to a walk. Max would probably be home and she didn't want to appear disheveled and out of breath. Max. Her steps quickened once again.

Then she paused.

There was a light in the Grahams' garage apartment. Joel was home! As she started across the hummocky ground, a gunmetal-gray Mercedes roared up the drive and jolted to a stop in front of the garages.

"Damn," Annie swore softly, coming to a stop. She could scarcely ask Joel whether he had lusted after Sydney with his father present.

Graham slammed out of the car.

The front door of the garage apartment burst open, and Joel Graham ran lightly down the outside steps.

"Dad, hey Dad! I've got to talk to you about last night." His voice was husky with strain.

In the light that spilled downstairs from the open door to Joel's apartment, George Graham's face mirrored the shock that Annie felt.

Moving as quietly and quickly as she could, Annie ran lightly toward the garages to a huge pine only a few feet away from the father and son.

The smell of pine resin mixed with the fading fumes from the diesel car.

There was no trace of the island's most affable dentist in the tightly drawn features of the man beside the Mercedes. Graham looked every year of his age and more.

Joel stopped at the foot of the garage apartment stairs, hands jammed in the pockets of his jeans, his eyes averted. "Jesus, Dad. I don't know what the hell to do. Listen, last night, I . . ."

"Stow it." The words shot out like a steel door clanging down to meet concrete.

Joel's head jerked up. "Oh God, Dad—"

"Keep your mouth shut, Joel." There was no disguising the fear beneath Graham's anger. "Listen to me, that goddamned Cahill's got all the money in the world. You can bet they won't get him. But I don't intend to be the goat. So you tell the cops—if they ever ask—that you went to bed about midnight and you don't know a damned thing."

"Dad, please, we've got to talk. I—"

"Nobody left our house Tuesday night. Nobody."

"Dad—"

"Goddammit, Joel. Keep your mouth shut." Graham turned on his heel and strode away through the darkness toward the light cascading down the steps of the Victorian back porch.

Joel took a couple of steps as if to follow, then whirled to his left and broke into a stumbling run. At the jeep, he yanked open the driver's door.

"Oh, shit. Oh, shit, shit, shit."

The jeep roared to life, jolted backward, then U-turned and accelerated up the drive.

Annie ignored the flash of the message light on the phone's answering machine, and dialed Frank Saulter's number as fast as she could. No answer. Damn, he needed to know that *something* happened late Tuesday night at the Graham house. And it wouldn't do a bit of good to call Posey. He wouldn't listen. She glanced up at the clock. Almost six. Where was Max? He would surely be home soon. And no trace of Laurel.

Laurel!

She punched the Play button on her answering machine.

"Annie—if I may—rather than Mrs. Darling. I do feel that tragedy removes formal barriers. We of the Scarlet King compound must face what has happened together. This is Eileen Houghton, General Houghton's wife." The voice was smooth and controlled. She sounded extremely competent and capable. So why identify herself as the general's wife? Wasn't her own identity enough? Did she perhaps feel that Eileen Houghton had no clout, no reality, except as a wife? "I know that you and your husband have had some experience in matters of this sort. I'm hoping that you will feel, as the general and I do, that the mere idea of suspecting Howard Cahill of murder is totally and patently absurd. Surely the police can't continue to hold him! If you would be so kind as to return my call at your convenience, the general and I would appreciate it. The number is 555-1314. Thank you."

Annie scratched the number on a pad.

A bleep. The second message: "One bloody nose—Dorothy L.'s; one bloody hand—mine; one renegade cat—Agatha; two broken mugs (courtesy of Agatha)—*The Footprints on the Ceiling* by Clayton Rawson and *Murder Against the Grain* by Emma Lathen; one terrified customer —identity unknown—who fled when a streak of black fur—Agatha— tore down the center aisle, flew up on top of the Thriller section, and knocked down four books."

Irritation sharpened Ingrid's voice. "Some of our best books: *The Great Impersonation* by E. Phillips Oppenheim, *Brass Target* by Frederick Nolan, *The Day of the Jackal* by Frederick Forsyth and *The Tamarind Seed* by Evelyn Anthony. Dented the Oppenheim. Anyway, I'm closing early. Henny assures me that Agatha won't really kill Dorothy L., but I'm not convinced. I'm taking Dorothy L. home to spend the night. Only thing to do."

Hope flickered in Annie's heart. Was there a solution to the Great Impasse (or the advent of a new cat on an old cat's turf)? Beneath Eileen Houghton's number, Annie wrote: DOROTHY L., INGRID, NEW HOME???

She was reaching for the phone to return the call from the general's wife when the front door opened.

"Where's the prettiest girl in the world?"

Annie began to smile.

Max was home.

"It's nighttime," Max said serenely. "Time for all good workers to rest from their labors."

Annie popped to her feet. "Max, listen, maybe I ought to try and catch the chief at home—"

Max reached up and gently drew her back to her seat. "Dear love, Frank is probably making clam chowder right now." He glanced at the green ceramic wall clock (could they possibly have too *much* green in the garden room?). "No, to be more accurate, Frank has finished his clam chowder and is now in front of his VCR watching the fourth game in last fall's World Series."

Annie glared. That was right down on a level with subliminal advertising. Max *knew* how much she enjoyed watching last summer's Cubs games on their VCR. Well, he might think he was subtle, but she wasn't to be deflected from her duty.

Even if the next tape in her collection was that wonderful June 5 game when they trounced the Mets 15 to 2. If that wasn't a giddy moment for Cub fans!

"Max, we can't just do *nothing* tonight!"

He smiled. "Of course we can. In the morning, we can report what you overheard to Frank. And, if you think about it, Annie, it isn't much to go on. Certainly it isn't proof that George Graham had anything to do with the murder, though it does indicate he knows something. As for Laurel, she's quite safe—and won't be here tonight."

Honestly, he'd go to any lengths to suborn her from duty.

However, she *had* worked hard at it all day. And she'd come up with a lot. But she hadn't even looked at Max's bios of the suspects. She should get right into those. And she needed to keep an eye out for Joel's return. Talking to the teenager and to his father topped her list.

Max delicately massaged her tight shoulders. "Tired minds do not work well, sweetie." A pause. Then, as if an afterthought, he added, "The special at the club tonight is beef Wellington."

A sentry crow cawed an urgent alert—raccoon, danger, raccoon!—and the air was abruptly filled with shrieking, tar-black birds rising in a whir of gleaming wings. The grayish, ring-tailed predator stood upright in the early morning shadows at the edge of the pinewoods and lifted his Lone Ranger–masked face to watch the receding flock. Then he turned and eyed Annie and Max at their breakfast table.

"Go home, fella," Max advised. "Time to tuck in for a nap."

Annie had heard many of the wonderful South Carolina raccoon stories: the agile animals' ability to manipulate even the most sophisticated garbage can cover, their enjoyment of television (could it really be true coons changed channels if bored?), the ease with which their clever black fingers unlatched doors and opened refrigerators. Jar tops posed no problem for them either. In her book *Nature Watch,* Charleston reporter Lynne Langley tells of one raccoon who showed up when a certain piece of classical music was played and departed for the woods when it ended. The Hilton Head Island Packet carried a story about a coon who learned how to enter a house and always headed straight for the bedroom where Godiva chocolate was kept on the nightstand (Annie's kind of house, Annie's kind of raccoon).

Their dark-eyed, shaggy visitor completed a bold, measuring, thoughtful survey, dropped to all fours, and stepped toward them. It looked like she and Max were going to have an unwelcome guest for breakfast. But after a last, lingering appraisal, he turned and trotted back into the pines.

And that reminded Annie of Valentine's Day morning when another unwelcome guest, Sydney Cahill, had shattered their early morning idyll by the pool. And that, of course, revived the Calvinist imps in Annie's mind that tried hard to keep her from having *too* much fun. Last night, she had succumbed to Max's importunings that enough was enough and it was time to relax, that they would work even more effectively if they took the evening off. He'd stressed that it was just the two of them (not, of course, that he was happy with Laurel's detention on the mainland, but after all, she'd brought it on herself), and he'd finally resorted to an out-and-out bribe, beef Wellington at the country club. Annie was too mellow when they came home to even think about investigations. (She was always mellow after imbibing the club's triple chocolate delight, which included three kinds of rum, crème de cacao, whipped cream, Hershey syrup, butterscotch ice cream, and semisweet chocolate bits.) Max was quite correct in pointing out that although it was much too late to pursue their investigation, it was quite the right time for other, more sensual pursuits.

(The little Calvinist imps frowned darkly. What had happened to her commitment to duty?) Annie wriggled uncomfortably. Of course, she'd *tried* to talk to both Dorcas Atwater and Joel Graham yesterday evening. It wasn't her fault that Dorcas hadn't been home or that Joel had stormed off in his jeep. But she did have pangs of guilt over her failure to read Max's bios last night. And she shouldn't have acquiesced in Max's acceptance of Laurel's detention. (Here the imps totted up high scores on the selfishness range.) It was an incredible avoidance of familial duty to leave Laurel jailed on the mainland. Of course, Max said lazily, there was no real sweat. No appeals court would uphold the magistrate's decision not to grant bail for Laurel. Frankly, they'd have to grant bail even if Posey charged both Howard and Laurel with murder. Obviously neither could be considered a threat to society and therefore their due process was being violated. But Max insisted they let Laurel stew for a while. Do her good. And surely Cahill's lawyers were busy right this minute.

As the sun peeked over the umbrella tops of the pines, lacing the night shadows with fingers of gold, it was time and past time to get to work. She looked sternly at her handsome husband and had a moment's difficulty in keeping to her resolve. Honestly, an unshaven Max in rumpled blue-and-white-striped shorts had a definite appeal. Their eyes met and the unmistakable message in his threatened to sweep away her resolve, but first things first. (The Calvinist imps gave a sigh of relief. But remained alert.)

"Max, we have to get Laurel out of jail!"

The sun-drenched Maserati, windows shut, provided Max with a snug cocoon as the ferry chugged slowly across Port Royal Sound. He sprawled comfortably against the dark red leather and drowsily watched the mainland grow near. He wasn't altogether convinced Annie was right in arguing that all possible measures must be taken to free Laurel. But it was a beautiful morning to be on the ferry, and it would be fun to lock horns with Posey. A frown touched Max's face. If he could find Jed McClanahan . . .

The Calvinist imps thoroughly approved of jogging. An aid to self-discipline and good digestive habits. Besides, it gave Annie a good excuse to circle the lagoon. The silky air in the night-cooled pines ruffled her hair, caressed her skin. The pale February sunlight poked into the shadowed woods. As she came to the clearing behind the Graham house, she slowed. A flock of tree swallows glided gracefully toward a massed clump of bayberry. The white-bellied birds with the blue-green backs and wings discussed their morning search in a high, liquid chatter that sounded just like a room full of women conversing as fast as possible. Annie was still smiling when she spotted Joel's jeep in the shadows near the garage. Lights streamed from the garage apartment windows. Of course, he was up early to get ready for school. With only a single uneasy glance toward the main house, Annie veered toward the garage apartment. Hurrying up the steps, she knocked softly on the door.

"Just a sec." A gruff, sleepy voice. The door swung open. "Yeah?" His longish blond hair was plastered wetly on his head and water still glistened on his stocky shoulders. The towel wrapped around his midriff revealed a muscled chest, flat stomach, and well-built legs. His heavy-lidded, brown eyes widened in surprise, then he smiled in satisfaction. "Oh, yeah." His voice came alive. "You lookin' for fun?" His full lips curled into a sensuous half smile.

It hadn't occurred to Annie that he would so completely misconstrue her appearance. Admittedly her nylon jogging shorts were short indeed and, enjoying the cool air, she wore only a T-shirt. Joel's lascivious, up-and-down appraisal made her mad.

As always, she spoke before she thought. "Down, Sonny."

"With you? That would be neat."

The towel rode lower on his hips.

"Look, Joel, I'm a married woman and—"

"Who isn't? I *like* married women. And they like me. Why don't you come on in and I'll—"

"I know one married woman who didn't seem to buy your program."

"No way," he said huskily. "I know how to make them happy. And I'll do the same for you." He reached out for her arm.

Annie took a step back. "Then why did Sydney Cahill jerk away when she realized you were her partner at the Valentine ball?"

The hot light in his eyes died, replaced by wariness. His hand fell. "No big deal," he said quickly. "I guess she thought I was somebody else."

"She seemed upset."

"Who says so?"

"I saw her pull free, run away from you."

He thought about it, then shrugged his muscular shoulders. "Maybe she needed to go to the john," he said insolently.

"Did you meet her at the gazebo?"

"Hell, no. I didn't see her after the party."

Oddly, she believed him, which made the undertone of worry in his voice just that much more interesting.

"What *did* you see when you were out late after the party?"

Joel tensed. "Who says I saw anything?"

"I know you did."

For an instant, he was young and vulnerable, his eyes bewildered, his lips half parted. "Jesus, it's all crazy. I didn't see a goddamned thing. That's what's so crazy." He was talking to himself, her presence unimportant. "That's what gets me. I didn't *see* anything. But the hell of it is, I don't know where the hell everybody was." His eyes focused on her and sharpened into a mean and spiteful gaze. "But I don't have to tell you a goddam thing. So you can haul ass back to the police chief and tell him I don't know anything."

"The chief? I'm not here for him," Annie objected.

"The hell you're not. Everybody knows you're a mystery nut." The phone rang. He whirled and stared at it warily, then shot another hostile glance at Annie. "See you later," and he slammed the door.

The peal of the telephone broke off.

Annie tried to eavesdrop, but the apartment was well built. She heard nothing more than an indistinguishable mumble.

She jogged on around the lagoon (the imps would be satisfied with no less) and wondered just how irritated Frank Saulter was going to be with her.

• • •

Annie consciously squared her shoulders. "Now, Frank, that's not fair. I didn't warn him about anything. His dad'd already told him to keep his mouth shut."

"For God's sake, why'd you go see him this morning? Why didn't you call me first?"

Annie preferred not to admit that she was a creature of impulse. (The imps shook their heads in dismay at such dissembling.) "I'm calling now. And tell me the truth—if I'd called you earlier, would you have hurried out here to talk to him?" She picked up a pencil and in a few strokes sketched heavy-lidded eyes and a sensuous mouth in a frowning face topped by a brush of wet blond hair.

Silence.

"Frank?"

An exasperated sigh. "I guess not. Posey's closed the investigation. Says we have plenty to lodge a first-degree murder charge against Cahill."

"Closed it!"

"Annie, Cahill's had it. We found that mace. God, what a weapon. Spiked, for Christ's sake!"

She remembered all too vividly: the round metal ball, the wickedly sharp prongs, the age-smoothed, easy-to-grip handle. What recourse did Sydney have against a weapon like that? And what kind of hatred had propelled the hand that slammed those spikes into a woman's face?

Should she tell Saulter about Carleton and his claim that he'd found the weapon, thrown it into the lagoon? But that wouldn't help Howard.

"There's no proof at all that Howard took that thing to the gazebo," she insisted.

"Nope. But it's his jacket that's drenched with blood. That's for certain. And that's not all. If the murderer sent that valentine to Sydney, it's proof of premeditation. Right?"

"Right," she agreed cautiously.

In the still of the night,
Our hearts can take flight.

How thrilled Sydney must have been. How eagerly she must have run down the oyster-shell path toward the gazebo, escaping from Howard's anger, running to the enveloping arms of a lover.

A homemade valentine.

Who made it?

"Yesterday afternoon we searched the Cahill house and everything in it. We hit pay dirt on the second floor. We found crumpled pieces and scraps of red construction paper, the newspapers used to cut out the letters for the words. Hell, we even found the glue. And the lab tests make it positive. The valentine was made with his stuff."

Annie drew scissors, dripping with blood. "Where'd you find it?"

"Shoved down into one of those big blue Chinese vases."

Annie remembered them. She drew a huge vase, decorated with a frowning dragon. "Anybody at the party could have brought the scraps and hidden them in the vase."

"Sure," Frank agreed. "But so could Cahill."

"When's Posey going to arraign him?"

"Later today, probably."

"Frank, what about Laurel?"

A long hesitation. Then, wearily, "I'm not sure. The accessory charge will still stand. At the very least."

"That's ridiculous," she snapped, "and you know it." But Annie knew this was a world rife with injustice. What if Posey charged Laurel with murder? That was a far cry from an accessory charge. What would be the effect of a capital criminal charge on a sensitive nature such as Laurel's? She suppressed the cynical snort from her subconscious and the traitorous supposition that Laurel would enjoy the experience to the hilt. "So you're telling me you aren't going to even talk to Joel? Or his dad? Or anyone?"

"All right, Annie." The chief's voice was somber. "I'll stick my neck out. After all, nobody's been charged yet. I'll talk to the Grahams, but I want you to cool it."

This time she was silent.

"Annie"—he sounded genuinely worried—"if you keep poking at a wasp's nest, you're going to get stung."

The valentine scraps nagged at Annie. She had a short, unpleasant phone call with Carleton Cahill—"Hell, how should I know whether there's usually any red construction paper here!"—but she obtained the name of the housekeeper and was connected through to her.

"Mrs. Gaffney?"

"Yes'm."

Annie introduced herself as a new neighbor and stressed her conviction that, of course, Mr. Cahill was innocent of the dreadful crime.

Mrs. Gaffney relaxed. "I tell you, Mrs. Darling, they never *was* a nicer man than Mr. Howard and he would never have hurt Mrs. Sydney. No, ma'am."

Red construction paper?

"I sure don't think so. Not that I've ever seen anywhere. No, ma'am. And if those *police* found anything like that in this house, they done put it here. I tell you, I dusts inside and out. Any house I cleans is *clean.*"

As for the day of the party, "Mrs. Sydney, she was *so* excited. She loved parties. But I didn't see anything like a valentine. Not in her room or anywhere. And I went home at five, like usual, 'cause the caterers, they took care of everything for the party. But you can ask Reba."

"Reba?"

"Reba Mason, Mrs. Sydney's maid."

It took Mrs. Gaffney a little while but she found Reba's telephone number.

Annie dialed immediately, but there was no answer.

A temporary setback—she'd catch Reba this evening. Annie was raring to go. This vigorous plunge into detecting invigorated her. She hurtled into work, determined to wrest any helpful bits of information about the suspects from the stack of bios Max had left behind. She counted them. Twelve! Max had certainly worked hard yesterday afternoon, accomplishing a prodigious amount of research. (The Calvinist imps sighed at the tiny glisten of jealousy in Annie's eyes and her unworthy thought that surely *Max* hadn't outworked her!) No matter. She was ready to take on the world and that included Circuit Solicitor Bryce Willard Posey. She felt as tenacious as Cyril Hare's Inspector Mallet. Perhaps, with brilliant insight and rapier-like thought, she could be as successful as Alan Hunter's Chief Superintendent George Gently at coming into lives at a moment of crisis and bringing about a resolution. (The Calvinist imps conferred concernedly about bigheadedness.)

She placed a full thermos of Colombian coffee beside the plate of peanut butter cookies. So she had enthusiasms. It was unkind of Max to say that she fastened on a new favorite taste like a hungry squid. Comfortably settled, she resisted the impulse to start with two cookies (the imps congratulated themselves) and picked up the first folder.

HOWARD CAHILL—b. September 3, 1930, Shreveport, La. Father, Ed, owned dry goods warehouse. Family financially secure until Depression when business failed. When Cahill was 6, father committed suicide. Mother, Beatrice, worked as a seamstress to take care of Howard and his younger sister, Marie. Finished high school 1948, took job in local shipyard. At 21, assistant foreman. Worked night shift and started college. Took six years. Also supported mother whose eyesight was failing. Business degree 1957. Joined Farrell Shipbuilding. Rest, as they say, is history. Married Chelsea Farrell, owner's daughter, 1960, promoted to vice president; four years later took over as president. By 1970, Farrell Corp. had absorbed half dozen smaller shipbuilding firms and shipping lines, culminating with takeover of Med-Pacifico. Amassed fortune conservatively estimated $47 million. He and wife bought cottage on Broward's Rock when first married. Holidayed all over world, but always came to Broward's Rock twice yearly. Moved full-time to island 1973; built Scarlet King mansion 1974.

Henry Farrell, Chelsea's father, had nothing but praise for Howard. "Finest son-in-law a man could ever have had. Chelsea was happy every day of her marriage. And Howard's the finest businessman it was ever my pleasure to know. A hard man in a deal, but honest and fair. He may have made enemies from succeeding where others failed, but he never made an enemy from bad faith." Farrell is incensed at any suggestion that Cahill could have murdered his second wife. "Look, between the two of us, it was a damn unwise marriage. A pretty girl, but no substance. But Howard—it just about killed him when Chelsea died. So he made a mistake. But Howard never broke his word, never welshed on a contract in his life. He wouldn't start now. You can take my word for it."

Cahill rarely drinks. Keeps fit by jogging three 9-minute miles four times weekly. Plays tennis twice weekly. Has exceptionally strong overhead smash (Doubles partner: "I've seen a ball go 30 feet straight up"). Ambidextrous; switches racket from right hand to left, in effect playing two forehands. Health excellent. No history high blood pressure or heart disease. Considered remote figure by employees; no intimate friends. However, well liked by those who know him socially. No one can recall seeing Cahill angry. Always controlled, temperate, and reasonable.

His doubles partner, Sam Cohen, said absurd to suspect Cahill of wife's murder. "Look, this is a decent man. So damn decent, in fact, he didn't dump Sydney. I think he felt sorry for her. It was an infatuation thing. You have to understand that on a short-term basis Sydney was irresistible. Thing is, Howard's the marrying kind, and by the time he came to his senses, it was too late. But he was too loyal ever to talk about her, although he couldn't have helped knowing what was going on."

Cahill sued three years ago by former employee, Robert Milton, who was fired for allegedly tipping off competitor to Med-Pacifico's strategy in a takeover battle. Milton claimed Cahill blacklisted him in shipping industry. Cahill defended notifying major shipping companies of Milton's betrayal to competitor on basis that Milton treated his employer treacherously and other companies had right to know full employment history. Jury decided in favor of Cahill.

In the margin, Max had scrawled: *Not a man to trifle with.*

And if he would go to these lengths when an employee broke faith, what would he do about a faithless wife?

Annie placed the report to one side. On her scratch pad, she wrote:

Cahill's not accustomed to losing. What happens to people who never show anger? But he was openly angry with Sydney, shortly before she died. How upset must he have been to lose his customary control?

Annie poured a cup of coffee and reached for a cookie. (The imps wrung their hands, but they couldn't expect to win them all.) Max's report didn't, of course, contain the results of Annie's conversation with Carleton, and her conclusion that Cahill was refusing to cooperate with Posey because the magnate was protecting his son. But that could be an elaborate double bluff.

Her hand flew as she recorded her queries: *Would Cahill use his own son as a smoke screen? Is Cahill truly concerned about his son? Or is he a desperate murderer who wants everyone to think he's nobly protecting Carleton?*

What about Carleton? she thought. Could he possibly be bitter enough at his father's remarriage to kill the woman he saw as a usurper? She shuffled through the reports.

CARLETON CAHILL—b. 1962. Only child. Artistic, emotional, hot tempered, selfish. Scoutmaster: "not a good camper." Excelled in art, mediocre in other subjects. "Bright, but lazy" recalls high school counselor. Usually involved with one or more women. Marriage when just out of college ended in divorce less than two years later. Played competitive tennis both at Broward's Rock Preparatory School and in college; never made the top rankings. BFA art, Emory; MFA, University of Louisiana; working on PhD, University of Georgia. Presently teaching in suburban Detroit prep school. Lives in luxury condominium; expensive lifestyle. Receives trust income from mother's estate. Rumored to be involved with wife of local attorney. Ex-wife says spoiled rotten. Headmaster describes work as satisfactory, says Cahill not dedicated teacher. Cahill jogs sporadically; accomplished sailor.

Annie sipped at her coffee. So Carleton wasn't quite the wimp she'd taken him for, but he was certainly no prize.

On her sheet, she wrote: *Why did Carleton give the jacket to Laurel? Was he really afraid the police would find it? Or did he want the police to find it?*

The next report was on Sydney. She picked it up eagerly. She needed to know all about Sydney. As Poirot always pointed out, the character of the victim was all-important because in that particular life were sown the seeds of death.

SYDNEY WHEELER CAHILL—b. 1955, Branson, Mo. Four years old when parents, John and Claudine Wheeler, divorced. Father left town; no further contact with Claudine or Sydney. Claudine manicurist local barbershop, sang country music on weekends at local bar. Entered Sydney in beauty contest when she was six. Sydney won first place. By time Sydney graduated from high school, she'd won seven beauty contests. Super athlete; played basketball, softball, tennis in high school. Claudine died from cancer spring of Sydney's senior year. Sydney won tennis scholarship to local junior college. Attended one year. Quit school to marry a boy she'd dated in high school, Dick Rivers. Rivers deserted her 1976. Assistant tennis coach Branson resort 1974–80. Engaged twice but each time fiancé ended relationship. Came to Broward's Rock 1980; children's tennis coach Island Hills Country Club. (Carleton Cahill on country club team; knew her as did Howard and Chelsea Cahill.)

Starting six months after Chelsea's death from cancer in 1983, Howard Cahill played tennis obsessively. Married Sydney 1985, apparently unaware of her reputation as the favorite after-dinner indulgence of the club's male members. List of men she knew intimately lengthy. Friend, Susie Dunlap: "Sydney was always in search of love. With every new guy, she was sure true love had entered her life. Each time, the man broke it off, and she grieved until a new one came along." Hairdresser Maggie French: "Sydney didn't know how to keep her mouth shut. I mean, I heard about every man she ever slept with and what he thought about his wife and the club and the motions in front of the Town Council and any other damn thing he let drop, but she never meant any harm. Think of what could have happened if she'd had it in for people? Still, a guy had to face it, a tumble with Sydney would be hot news around town pretty soon. I guess old Howard didn't know because he was a close-mouthed sort and people must not have opened up to him. But people who liked gossip, I tell you, they loved Sydney."

A few people who knew Sydney genuinely liked her. The tennis pro: "She was sweet, always remembering everybody's birthday." The manager of the tennis store: "Sydney was always willing to help out. If she didn't have a clinic scheduled or a lesson, she'd offer to work behind the counter if we needed an extra hand." The president of the bridge club to which Sydney belonged: "Not a very good player, really. She never could keep track of the cards, and, of course, it drove some of our members mad to have to play with her. But she was fun to be around; she always knew the latest about everyone."

An appended list contained the membership of the bridge group. Annie scanned the names. She underlined three: Lisa Graham, Billye Burger, and Eileen Houghton.

She grinned. Did Max actually think one woman might murder another over bridge?

Her smile fled as she read the final paragraph:

Private services for Sydney tentatively scheduled Thursday afternoon Hourihan Funeral Home, contingent upon Howard's release from custody. Body to be transported to Branson, Mo., for burial next to mother, Claudine.

Annie drew a coffin and a truck. So Sydney was going home. Because Broward's Rock had never been home here, had it? Annie felt confident there was a plot in the Broward's Rock cemetery for the Cahills, but no room in the family plot for Sydney. Somehow, that seemed the unkindest cut of all.

The telephone rang. Annie jumped up and moved eagerly toward it, suddenly hungry for the sound of a living voice.

Max scowled and slammed shut the sticky phone book. He pulled out his handkerchief and scrubbed his fingers. His nose wrinkled. It couldn't have smelled worse if the phone booth had been the site of a six-day indoor athletic contest such as the one described by Peter Lovesey in *Wobble To Death*. Max glowered at the phone. Where the hell was Jed McClanahan staying? Max had checked all the hotels. McClanahan wasn't registered. Darn it, Laurel never should have hired the blustering, whiskey-fond trial lawyer. But Max was stymied. Laurel had hired McClanahan so no one else could represent her as long as she retained him. Max's scowl intensified. Serve her right if she had to spend a month in jail. He shoved open the folding door, then paused on the threshold. Dammit, Annie would go from Shapiro–mournful eyes to Bertha Cook–furious if he didn't get Laurel out of jail. With an exasperated sigh, he stepped back into the stuffy booth, reopened the tattered phone book and flipped again to the yellow pages, this time to Clubs.

"If you keep digging, you can come up with the dirt. Even if it's years old." Henny's voice was triumphant. "Just like James Willop."

Annie's eyes narrowed like Agatha's sighting Dorothy L. She didn't say a word.

"Dig, dig, dig. Persistence pays off. That's the hallmark of any outstanding reporter."

"Enough is enough, Henny."

"Why, Annie." Injured innocence oozed from the beautifully modulated response.

Dammit, Henny could pack more meaning into two words than most people could manage in several paragraphs.

"I mean, I can't read every new book that comes out!"

"Not even the Edgar winners?"

Annie scrambled through a welter of titles. But James Willop still didn't ring any bells. Of course, it would be another first novel.

Might as well get it over with. "I give up."

Carolina Skeletons by David Stout. First rate."

"I would imagine so," Annie said politely. "They don't give Edgars for less."

"Anyway"—Henny's voice dropped conspiratorially—"I've been digging and guess what? Dorcas Atwater hated Sydney like poison!"

It may not have shown great character, but Annie couldn't resist. "So what else is new?" (The imps agreed they really had their work cut out for them.)

"You know?" It was fair to say that Henny's tone was deflated.

"Oh yeah. I've known that for a while." Annie did resist insinuating it was common knowledge on the island. (The imps weren't impressed.)

"Oh, well. And, uh, the reason?"

It was Annie's turn to be brief. "Don't know."

"Don't know?"

"No."

"Well," with an entirely different inflection. "You certainly haven't made much progress if you don't know *why* they hated each other."

"I'm working on it, and I expect to get the facts very soon," Annie said blandly.

"I'll bet I can find out," Henny challenged. "I've got friends who know all the gossip on Broward's Rock. I'll get after it. And I want to find out where that valentine came from."

"The police found remnants of the material it was made from hidden on the second floor of the Cahill house yesterday afternoon."

An irritated sniff. "You've discovered quite a bit," Henny admitted reluctantly.

Annie took pity. "I talked to the chief a while ago. He told me. But I haven't found out whether anyone saw Sydney with it that evening. Maybe you could check with her maid."

"I'd already thought of that." Henny hadn't totally lost her spirit. "I'm trying to track Reba down right now."

Annie held her breath. Would there be yet another reference to a first novel in Henny's farewell?

"I'll give you a ring after I talk to her," Henny promised.

Annie relaxed. Perhaps Henny'd realized the joke had gone far enough. It was scarcely sportsmanlike to continue rubbing it in that

Annie was so far behind Henny in reading the latest crop of new writers.

"Great. We'll put our heads together." Annie felt a warm glow of camaraderie. It was damn nice of Henny to go all out for the investigation. "Max and I certainly appreciate your efforts to help Laurel out of this mess."

"And you didn't even hold a twelve-gauge to the back of my head," Henny drawled in a deep voice. "Course, that particular case, I guess I should've had my brains examined."

Annie's hand tightened on the receiver. Her fingers itched for that talented larynx. She made no response at all. Had Henny no shame?

Apparently not. In high good humor, the island's most disgustingly well-read mystery fan confided, "A Joe Hannibal mystery. *The Burning Season* by Wayne D. Dundee. A hell of a good read. Starts in a cemetery. The gal with the shotgun has a bad mouth and a good heart."

And the connection was broken.

Annie grinned and settled down again with the bios. She thumbed through the stack until she found the one she sought.

DORCAS MAXINE FRENCH ATWATER—b. 1933, Clearwater, Fla. Miss Clearwater 1951. Graduated local business college 1952. Secretary two years to bank president. Moved New Orleans 1954, worked downtown bank. Active in church activities, women's circle, Sunday school. In 1956 married bank president, Theodore Wilburn Atwater, widower, superintendent Calvary Baptist Church Sunday school program. Atwater native Memphis. First wife, Alma, died car wreck 1954. Two children that marriage, Harold and Joan. Two children by Dorcas, Jimmy and Sue Lee. Atwater retired 1984; he and Dorcas moved to Broward's Rock, house in Scarlet King compound. Atwater died 1987, heart attack. After Atwater's death, Dorcas withdrew from social activities. President Broward's Rock Bridge Society said she'd never much liked Dorcas, but she was okay until Ted died. "My God, from one minute to the next, you never know what she's going to do! Scream at you one minute, sob the next. Grief's all very well and good, but this is outside the norm. And she decided everybody was making fun of her behind her back! For heaven's sake, you know how women are at bridge! They talk faster than they deal—unless they're fanatics. But we play bridge for fun, so there's a lot of kidding around. Dorcas only came twice after the funeral. Too bad. She was a good player." Pastor local church: "We've tried and tried to persuade Dorcas to come back to us. The church is the place for unhappy souls. But she—"

The phone rang.

Annie creased the corner of the page to mark her place. (This maddened Max. What, he demanded, were bookmarks for?)

"Hello."

"Annie, I'm really worried about Agatha."

Annie felt a sharp pang of guilt. She hadn't even *thought* about Death on Demand or its feline occupants this morning. Of course, she knew Ingrid would be there, coping. Still, she should have called. "Oh, Ingrid, is Agatha still unhappy?"

"Unhappy? She's about as cheerful as Chick Graham in *The Man With My Face*. Similar trauma in a way. There he is, not a care in the world, and he goes home to find a man who looks just like him claiming that *he's* the real Chick Graham. Annie, Agatha's lips are trembling and she's growled so hard she's hoarse."

"Ingrid, I'll be right there."

FOURTEEN

The beach on a February morning—even one that promised uncommonly warm weather—was little populated. Joggers, of course. Max considered jogging an excessive activity, right on a par with overworking or overeating. He espoused moderation in all things. (Almost all things —afternoon delight, on the other hand . . .) But as far as sweat-producing exercise was concerned, he was convinced an amble along the strand was quite enough. Shading his eyes, he surveyed with a jaundiced eye and an inward sigh the jiggling bodies that passed by. What a waste of energy. And surely the waitress at the Good Times Bar and Grill was wrong in suggesting that Jed McClanahan—Max's eyes widened. By God, who would believe it!

McClanahan, his back to the beach, stood ankle-deep in the gently surging water, arms crossed behind him, white duck pants rolled up to the knees. His balding head gleamed in the sunlight.

The air temperature might be deceptively warm, but Max knew the water was damn cold. He hoped McClanahan's toes were turning blue.

"Hey Jed! Jed!"

The diminutive trial lawyer slowly turned.

Max tried to interpret the expression on McClanahan's wizened, red-veined face. It looked like a cross between bemusement and idiocy.

McClanahan's thin lips cupped in a gentle smile; his red-rimmed, watery blue eyes shone with fellowship. "Max, come join me in a moment's meditation."

Max's scarcely-contained irritation with Laurel for hiring the whis-pery-voiced, grandstanding old windbag boiled over.

"Meditation, hell! We need to get to the courthouse before they call the docket and see if we can get Laurel out on bail!"

The South's gift to the trial bar responded with a pious look tinged with condescension and splashed to shore. "My dear fellow, we will go at once. I can see that you are in dire need of counseling by your *remarkable* mother. As she pointed out to me, and I have taken it to heart—I'm writing poetry, now—we must always remember the wis-dom of Saint Fulgentius of Ruspe: 'He who walks in love neither can go astray nor be afraid.' "

"Oh God," Max moaned.

McClanahan looked heavenward in dismay. "As Saint Francis Xavier so aptly remarked, 'How many souls are led astray from the path of glory simply because of their indifference.' "

"Come down, Agatha. Lovely girl. Dearest cat in the whole wide world."

Agatha's amber eyes were pinpoints of fury.

"Come on, love." Annie held up a bowl filled with fresh mackerel. "You're the only cat here, the only cat in the whole world."

Agreeable Dorothy L. had thought the cat carrier quite interesting and was still purring when Annie put the cushion-lined wooden carrier in the front seat of the car. (Maybe she should have named her Nancy P. after the charming first president of Sisters in Crime. Annie didn't think the original Dorothy L. would have shown this much good hu-mor.)

"Your store," Annie crooned. "All yours, sweetheart."

Agatha stood. And launched herself toward a nearby table.

This would have been quite acceptable except that she had been resting on a line of collectible books standing on end atop the Rare Books section.

Former President Johnson's domino effect was illustrated in spades, or books. Six rare books (first editions, mint) tumbled down: *The Fools in Town Are on Our Side* by Ross Thomas, *The Blunderer* by Patricia Highsmith, *The Woman Chaser* by Charles Willeford, *The Lolly-Ma-donna War* by Sue Grafton, *The Deadly Truth* by Helen McCloy, *The Ghostway* by Tony Hillerman.

Annie could have sworn the whiskered face sported a diabolic grin.

By the time the court session was over, Max's nerves were strung like a steel guitar. The agony of watching McClanahan posture ("Your Honor, it is my sincere pleasure and bona-fide delight to appear this morning in one of the greatest courts in the great State of South Carolina in defense of a noble lady whose Con-sti-tu-tion-al rights are in jeopardy") was almost more than a reasonable man could bear.

Even worse—Max sank down in his seat and tried to look as if he had no connection with McClanahan at all—was when the gnomish little lawyer stood on tiptoe to peer earnestly up at the judge. "Your Honor, my client—and she is the finest lady that it's ever been my pleasure to represent—has shared with me a precept which will edify all of the honorable ladies and gentlemen of the bar of the great State of South Carolina, and I would like to close by sharing with you this lovely lady's admonishment. She told me—and I extend this to everyone herein— that we should all ponder thoughtfully Teilhard de Chardin's wonderful advice that "we make our way to heaven by doing the work of the world.' "

The judge stared, gimlet-eyed, at the little attorney, cleared his throat, and mumbled, "Proceed, counselor."

The interminable—to Max—session finally ended in victory, the judge granting bail both to Laurel and to Howard. Now all Max had to do was go to the jail, pick up his mother, and return to Broward's Rock. Restored to good humor at the prospect of soon being free of the feisty little lawyer, Max clapped him on the shoulder as they walked out of the courtroom. Max even managed to sound fairly sincere in his congratulations. "Great job, Jed. Well, you can go back to the beach—"

"The beach?" McClanahan looked around in alarm at the clusters of dark-suited attorneys thronging the halls. "What would the world's greatest trial lawyer do at the beach?" He beamed at everyone in general. "Hello there, Curtis. Richmond. Harry. Selina Bea. Joe Bob. Winston. Carrie Ann. Great to be back in this courthouse. Some of my grandest battles have been here." A whispery laugh. "Right against some of you very ladies and gentlemen. Gather round, I want all of you to meet Max Darling, the son of one of my best clients."

Max's plan to scoot from the courthouse to the jailhouse in record time went down in a welter of southern hospitality.

Annie put the cat carrier down in the middle of the kitchen and opened it.

Dorothy L. immediately popped out, purring, and frolicked into the sun room. Annie spread out an *Island Gazette* and opened a can of tuna. "Now, don't think this is going to be standard fare. I just haven't stocked up here with cat food. And you might as well count on being a house cat. There's an alligator out in that pond who thinks cats are hors d'oeuvres."

Would Dorothy L.'s disappearance appease Agatha? Or was her sleek black feline friend irretrievably estranged?

Annie glanced at the clock. After eleven. No wonder she was so hungry. But first she must see about her messages. Not, of course, that she was a slave to curiosity. But it might be important. Maybe her mail-order ticket had won the Illinois lottery. En route to the phone, she stopped in the downstairs bath to splash rubbing alcohol on her latest wound from Agatha, a two-inch scratch on the back of her right hand.

The first message was from Eileen Houghton. Annie clapped a hand to her head. Of course, she should have called the woman first thing this morning. But Eileen Houghton was so confident of her social eminence, it apparently hadn't occurred to her that she'd been ignored.

"So sorry neither the general nor I were at home this morning to receive your call. I'm at the hospital for a board meeting and this is the general's morning to have his checkup. I did talk to Howard Cahill's son and Howard is still being detained. The general and I are appalled at the obvious miscarriage of justice that is occurring. Although I hesitate to interfere in the lives of others, I feel that I *must* reveal information which may affect the investigation. I have been unable to contact Chief Saulter or the circuit solicitor, so I will hope to utilize your good offices. Please meet me at two this afternoon at our pier."

The second message was from Henny and it lacked her usual pizzazz. "Haven't found Reba yet. It's her day off. Her mother thinks she went fishing. But I'll find her."

Henny rang off without a reference to a first mystery. Annie hated to take pleasure in others' discomfiture but— (The imps turned and, arms entwined, shoulders drooping, drifted sadly into the nether world inhabited by good intentions.)

The third message was from her normally unflappable husband. Max's usually mellow tone was absent. He sounded, in fact, both irritated, disgruntled, and a shade worried. "Annie, I'm at the office, waiting to hear the latest lab reports. Give me a ring as soon as you can."

Annie promptly dialed Confidential Commissions, and Barbie put her right through.

Max went straight to the point. "Where's Laurel?"

Since he had left the island bright and early to spring his mother from the county jail, the question and its accusatory tone seemed a bit unreasonable to Annie.

"How should I know? Did you get her out of jail?"

A burdened sigh. "Yes, finally."

As Max described his morning, Annie stifled her giggle. She really did enjoy being married.

There was a long silence after Max concluded his report. Annie, truly, could think of nothing to say.

Max didn't seem to notice, apparently still engrossed in his own thoughts. Finally, he asked plaintively, "Annie, do you suppose by work of the world, she meant going to jail?"

Annie was glad she didn't have to face him and answer. Some questions are far better left in rhetorical limbo. Especially if they concerned Laurel. She made a noncommittal noise.

"Anyway," he continued wearily, "it went okay in court. The judge agreed that not granting bail to Laurel and Howard was absurd. Posey immediately amended the charges to murder and conspiracy to commit murder, but the judge granted bail anyway. Said the accused were respectable members of the community, and the likelihood of their jumping bail was nil."

Annie wisely didn't share her thought that the judge obviously didn't know Laurel.

"Thing is, McClanahan ran into a bunch of old cronies—I mean, they never told me in law school there were lawyers like *these*—anyway, by the time I finally shook free of the mob and got over to the jail, Laurel had already left. Now, dammit, Annie, don't you think she could have waited for me? She should have known I was coming!" An outraged snort. "She *did* know I was coming. She left a message for me." He breathed heavily.

"Max, perhaps if you used your mantra . . ."

Laurel had chosen a lovely mantra for Max when she was in the midst of her psychic studies.

"Annie, that is not funny."

She realized she might have gone too far. Instantly sympathetic, she cooed, "Laurel's message?"

"Annie, if you see Laurel, corner her until she explains. Here, listen to this note she left for me: 'Dearest Max. And Annie, of course. So *sweet* of you to think of me. I've used this quiet period to direct an appeal to wonderful Saint Jude, the Saint of Those in Desperate Straits, the Saint of the Impossible. As you know, Saint Jude is *always* willing to help, but he *does* expect us to take charge of our own lives.' " Max heaved a worried sigh. "Annie, what the hell do you suppose she's up to?"

For once, the trite rejoinder suited: "The good Lord only knows," Annie murmured.

Liverwurst had *such* a delicious tang. (Dorothy L. obviously agreed; she clambered atop the tiger-pine breakfast table three times before Annie surrendered and put a slice in her bowl.) Time was when health fiends *urged* consumption of organ meats as a source of all-important iron. Annie was not a fairweather friend. This anticholesterol craze was obviously out of control. She tucked in another sliver of Vidalia onion, finished the sandwich, and nobly resisted the impulse to fix a second. However, a delicious lunch deserved a cup of excellent coffee. She brewed several cups of Irish Creme, washed the dishes and settled at the table with her coffee and the stack of bios. She picked up Dorcas Atwater's and skimmed to the end:

> The church is the place for unhappy souls. But she says she can't bear to have people looking at her. Frankly, she needs a psychotherapist, but she became almost hysterical when I broached it during a visit and since then she's never answered the door when I call.
>
> Atwater's children and stepchildren refuse to visit because her erratic behavior frightens the grandchildren. Sue Lee Atwater Danforth said tearfully, "I just don't know what to do about Mother. She won't talk to any of us. And whenever we mention Dad, it's dreadful. She just goes to pieces."

Annie picked up the next bio. Oh yes, that charming fellow, the general, with his ashen face, icy gaze, and arrogant demeanor.

> LT. GEN. (RET.) COLVILLE SINCLAIR HOUGHTON—b. 1923, Prescott, Ariz. Oldest son wealthy ranching family, which traces ownership to Spanish land grants. West Point graduate 1934. Second lieutenant under command Gen. George S. Patton, Jr. Full colonel at 33, multi decorations for European campaign World War II, including Bronze Star, Silver Oak Leaf. Promoted brigadier general at 42. Served in Korea, wounded Heartbreak Hill. Completed career in Pentagon as lieutenant general. Ret. 1978 Ft. Lauderdale, Fla. Still extensive family holdings in Arizona. General reputed to have an income excess $200,000 yearly aside from retirement benefits. In 1938, married Lucille Bernard, daughter Lt. Gen. Milton Bernard, met at Ft. Leavenworth while attending Command and General Staff College. Two sons, Robert, 1963 graduate of West Point, killed as captain Vietnam, and Anthony, who committed suicide 1979.

Annie drew her breath in sharply. One son dead in the war, one son dead by his own hand. No wonder the general was such an embittered man.

She read on:

> Anthony involved in peace movement after Robert's death. Jailed during riots at 1968 Democratic Convention in Chicago. Excelled as student, completing doctorate in physics at Berkeley. Taught at several well-known colleges, but Anthony's drug use, begun during

60s, debilitated him. Fired from last academic post. Anthony sought drug treatment but had no medical insurance and didn't have the $12,000 it costs for 28 days of treatment at most facilities. Public treatment center had six-month waiting list. Anthony contacted his father and asked for help. General said no. Anthony checked into local hotel, found dead of self-inflicted gunshot wound. Widow Susan Houghton said, "The money wouldn't have meant anything to the general, but it was the difference between life and death for Anthony. He needed treatment. He needed it immediately. His father might as well have loaded the gun Anthony used. I called the general to tell him about the funeral and he wouldn't even come to the phone. His second wife said, 'The general declines to accept this call. As far as he is concerned, he had only one son, Robert.' "

Dorothy L. jumped into Annie's lap. Annie scooped up the kitten and pressed the soft ball of fluff to her cheek and felt the warmth of the little creature and the rapid flutter of her heartbeat. Life—vulnerable, irreplaceable.

And the general, unforgiving and heartless.

Annie gave Dorothy L. a kiss and dropped her gently to the floor.

The general, of course, has no need to worry about payment for his hospital stays, enjoying full military pension. Used private fortune, however, to avoid stays in VA hospitals. Health began to deteriorate several years ago. Now on heavy-dose medications. Suffers from hypertension, heart disease, moderate emphysema, arthritis, gout. Has had two moderate heart attacks, undergone triple bypass. During convalesence from latter met second wife. The former Eileen Berry, physical therapist. Married 1977 and bought present home in Scarlet King compound.

Annie slapped down the general's bio. With a quiver of distaste, she searched through her stack.

EILEEN MORGAN BERRY HOUGHTON—b. 1948 Pensacola, Fla. Graduate Florida State. Physical therapist seven years; quit to marry Johnnie Berry, stock car racer, killed Florida May Day rally 1977. Berry previously married, father of three. No children second marriage. Berry good-looking, stocky, coal-black hair, quite a ladies' man until married Eileen. She always toured with him; marriage apparently happy. Couple enjoyed white-water rafting, scuba diving, spelunking. After his death, Eileen returned to work and that's how she met general. Quit work again at second marriage. Expert bridge player. Physical fitness enthusiast, attending aer-

obics classes three times a week. According to Kris Thompson at
Figure Fair, Eileen good enough to be leader and certainly good
enough to be in advanced class. "I keep telling her she should come
to the six o'clock session. I mean, those are people who can do. But
she just shakes her head. Once she said something about her husband preferring for her to exercise with women. She said, 'The
general has such old-fashioned views.' I thought she ought to tell
the old jerk to stuff it, but she's really into this Madame General
thing."

Annie knew about that six o'clock coed class. Bodies of steel. She
liked exercise, too, but there was a limit. So Eileen Houghton was on
that level. How wearisome to be saddled with an unpleasant, old husband.

The rest of the report listed Eileen's club memberships. A lot of
them, including bridge. The president of the Audubon Society said,
with a just detectable note of disdain, "Mrs. Houghton seems to be
quite aware of her status as the general's wife. Unfortunately, it hasn't
occurred to her that this is a resort community, not an army post."

The phone rang.

Annie reached for it. "Hello."

"Annie, has Laurel shown up *yet?*"

"Not yet, honey. Why?"

"We definitely need to keep a leash on her. It's looking blacker for
Cahill every minute, and who knows what she may try to do to help
him. No wonder Posey filed the murder charge! I just got a copy of the
lab report. The blood on Cahill's jacket has definitely been identified as
Sydney's. Plus they found his fingerprints on the mace."

Annie recalled Laurel's message, the Saint of Those in Desperate
Straits. She had a feeling that Laurel did indeed know all about that lab
report—and who knew what else?

But, of course, the duty of a wife is to reassure her husband in times
of difficulty. "Oh, Max, everything will be all right. You know Laurel."

She realized, when she hung up, that her answer could scarcely have
consoled her worried husband. Oh well, there were sure to be marital
failures as well as successes.

Annie was settling again at her desk, reaching for another bio, when a
disquieting thought struck. Was Laurel even now at the home of a man
who had been accused of first-degree murder?

Surely not.

Surely even Laurel had the good sense not to make a bad situation
worse. Annie could imagine Posey at the trial, glowering at a winsome
Laurel on the witness stand: "Mrs. Roethke, on the night of Sydney
Cahill's murder—the night that beautiful young woman was viciously

and sadistically battered to death—did you enter the gardens of the Cahill mansion with the express purpose of visiting—and this was after midnight—with Sydney Cahill's husband, Howard? Answer yes or no, Mrs. Roethke, yes or no."

Annie stifled a sigh and popped back to her feet.

Annie hesitated when she reached the Cahill drive. A black limousine was parked near the front steps. She almost turned back. Then the frightful thought occurred: What if Laurel went to the funeral with Howard? Shoulders squared, Annie marched past the limousine and up the steps.

A mournful-faced middle-aged woman in a dark, rustling dress opened the door.

"Hello. I'm a next-door neighbor, Mrs. Darling, and I need to speak briefly with Mr. Cahill. Would you—"

"Why, yes, ma'am. You step in here right now." Her voice dropped conspiratorially. "I'm Mrs. Gaffney and we talked earlier today and I know all about you and that nice husband of yours and I know you're doin' all you can to help Mr. Howard. You just wait right here and I'll go see if he can talk to you." Her shoes scraped on the stone floor as she turned away.

The entryway, with only the lights in the wall sconces burning, had an uncannily funereal air. Annie didn't look toward the suit of armor. She didn't want to remember the mace.

But she did.

The heavy metal head studded with inch-long prongs; the smooth wooden handle worn shiny by years of touch.

"If you'll—"

Annie jumped convulsively.

"Mrs. Darling, I'm so sorry. I didn't mean to scare you to death." Mrs. Gaffney's face drooped even more. "Oh my, I don't blame you a bit. This is a scary place now. Everywhere I look, it seems to me I can see Mrs. Sydney, and her pretty face is all streaked with tears. And poor Mr. Howard. Only a few minutes now and he has to go to the service. Just him, it's going to be. And I think that's a cryin' shame, too. Nobody else there to mourn for Mrs. Sydney. But you come with me. He'll see you before he goes."

Once again, Annie was in the library of the Cahill mansion, but this time she faced Howard instead of his son.

He stood in front of the desk, his face remote. "Hello, Annie. Mrs Gaffney said you needed to see me." His olive skin had a grayish cast. He looked unkempt, his chin marked by a red cut where he'd shaved that morning, his dark hair ill combed, his suit jacket and trousers wrinkled. He didn't ask her to sit down.

Annie went straight to the point. "Where's Laurel?"

He wasted no words either. "I'm not a damn fool, Annie."

"She's not here?"

"No, definitely not," he said crisply. His blunt-featured face mirrored impatience.

Annie couldn't refrain from a sigh of relief.

For just an instant, Howard's face softened. "You're right, of course. She wanted to come." He looked inquiringly at Annie. "She never counts the cost, does she?"

"Not when she cares."

"I wish—" The brightness seeped from his face, leaving it once again weary and depressed. His voice was again cool when he continued. "Don't worry. I won't permit Laurel to place herself in any worse situation than she already faces. I made that clear to her this morning."

Annie's immediate thought was that Howard Cahill had a very imperfect understanding of Laurel. Howard wouldn't "permit" Laurel to do something? Oh, he had a lot to learn.

Howard began to walk toward Annie, and she knew she was on her way out.

"It's very good of you to come on her behalf," he was saying, with finality. "I hope someday the circumstances will be different."

Annie knew she was treading on dangerous ground, but she spoke up anyway. "You could easily change the circumstances."

He stopped, looked at her warily. "Oh?"

"Tell the police the truth. About Carleton."

His dark eyes bore into hers. "What about Carleton?"

"Have you talked to him?" she asked impatiently.

The lines in his face deepened. "Yes."

"Didn't he tell you what happened that night?"

"I have no comment at all to make about that night. Nor will Carleton. Ever." The words were harsh, clipped, final, and Howard's dark eyes glittered with fear.

Annie was shaken.

Howard Cahill was a man struggling with terror. He was deathly afraid that Carleton was the murderer.

Wasn't he?

The cookie jar held only five more peanut butter cookies. Annie was starving, her adrenaline still pumping from her encounter with Howard Cahill. What a mess. And what could she do about it?

She ate the cookies in a rush but forced herself to leave two. It was hell to face breakfast without a peanut butter cookie.

But the little spurt of good feeling engendered by the cookies did nothing to alleviate the turmoil in her mind.

Howard, fearing for his son.

And Carleton, after his talk with his father, without doubt even more afraid that his father committed the murder.

Annie sat down at her table and poured another cup of coffee. Did this mean she could with no question cross both from her list of suspects?

Not on your life.

Either could be guilty and running a double bluff. Annie sighed and looked at the bios. Surely somewhere in all of this information lay the key to Sydney's death. She glanced at the clock. Almost two. She wanted to finish the bios before her meeting with Eileen Houghton. And surely Laurel would arrive soon. Annie would insist upon a frank, serious, realistic discussion of the present situation.

Sure. And the alligator in Scarlet King Lagoon wanted a tutu to celebrate May Day.

Annie grabbed the next bio.

LEROY WILLISTON (BUCK) BURGER—b. 1925, Del Rio, Texas. Joined USMC 1942. Lied about age. Served South Pacific. In landing party Iwo Jima. Purple Heart. Mustered out sergeant first class. BA Texas A&M, 1949. LLB Baylor University, 1952. Order of the Coif. Assistant DA, Dallas, 1952–57, DA 1957–63. Established Burger and Associates 1963. Handled both criminal and million-dollar divorce cases. Involved in numerous well-known controversies. Reputed to be man to hire when it didn't look like there was any way out but jail. Hard-nosed trial lawyer. Gave no quarter, asked none. Phenomenal 89 percent success rate. Licensed to carry a gun for self-protection. Involved in shoot-out San Marcos court house 1972 with divorce client's husband. Burger wounded right leg, shot assailant dead. "Drilled him right between the eyes," a deputy said admiringly. Enjoys flamboyant life style. Owns five-acre estate in Dallas, peacocks and llamas on lawns, hunting lodge down in hill country, ski lodge in Taos, house on Broward's Rock. Poker player, rides, hunts, fishes, scuba dives. He and his wife, Billye, have five children, all grown and married, and nine grandchildren. Although Buck has reputation as womanizer, has been married to Billye for almost 37 years. In own fashion, devoted family man, often flying in whole clan for holidays. All three sons avid sportsmen, often join father in fall for deer hunting.

Annie was willing to bet those were boisterous outings.
She picked up the next sheet.

BILLYE JO KURTH BURGER—b. 1932, Abilene, Texas. Well-to-do rancher's daughter, apple of his eye. Billye shopped in Dallas at Neiman-Marcus high school days on. At Baylor, fraternity queen, yearbook beauty. Young men courted her from first day on campus but moment she met Buck Burger, future decided. Married end her freshman year. Billye glories in femininity, but, reflecting ranch background, excellent horsewoman, first-class shot. In her thirties she took up tennis, still plays twice a week. An intense competitor. As one of her opponents said, "Why, Billye'd rather *die* than lose. I've seen her come back and win when she's down five games. Playin' on clay on a *July* afternoon!"

Annie felt an instant kinship. It was something Max would never comprehend, that do-all-or-die attitude of the committed tennis player. Why Max wouldn't even *play* tennis on a July afternoon, pointing out, he thought quite reasonably, that it was *hot*.

She placed Billye's bio atop Buck's. Max's research confirmed Annie's judgment; the Burgers were imperious, aggressive, and tough as a West Texas boot.

And Sydney's killer had to be tough as they come.

Which brought her to the only live-in employee in the compound, the Burgers' houseman-watchdog.

JIM TOM MARSHALL—b. Amarillo, Texas, 1946. Joined army at 18. Two tours Vietnam. Discharged sergeant first class 1970. Won division heavyweight wrestling title twice. Worked for Acme Security Dallas 1970–72. Hired as watchman/bodyguard by Buck Burger 1972. Belongs local bodybuilding club. Never married. Lt. Col. Richard Gonzales: "Born soldier. A crime he had to get out of the service. I don't give a damn what a man does on his own time when he can soldier like that." Walt Melton, owner Acme Security: "Tough son of a bitch. Light on his feet. Mix it up with anybody." When asked about sexual preference, Melton asked, "You think anybody's gonna get on Jim Tom's case? Man, he's six foot two in his socks. So he likes guys. I didn't give a damn and neither did Buck. You want to feel safe, you're lucky to find somebody like Jim Tom. Buck wanted the best bodyguard in the business; he got him." Was Jim Tom the kind of gay who hated women? "Oh, hell no. He's no nut. He doesn't care about women any way at all."

No wonder Marshall had been immune to Sydney's charms. But Annie wasn't quite ready to dismiss the bodyguard from her list of suspects. Just how far would he go, how much dirty work would he do for his employer? Would he lie to protect Buck Burger?

She glanced at the clock. Just time before her appointment with Madame General to finish up with the Graham bios.

GEORGE BRUCE GRAHAM—b. 1943, Reston, Va. Second son career government official. BS Washington and Lee, DDS University of Virginia. Track and field athlete in college. Served three years U.S. Army, Ft. Dix, N.J., captain, medical corps. Married Kathleen Murray 1969. One son, Joel, b. 1971. Established practice on Broward's Rock 1971. Active United Fund Drive, Chamber of Commerce, Red Cross, Men's Dinner Club, Broward's Rock Runners Club. Divorced from Kathleen 1984. Joel in mother's custody but returned to island as high school junior after mother's remarriage to engineer based in Norway. Married Lisa Wetherby 1985. No children. Was involved with Sydney before she married Howard. Embrace in alcove at party suggests continued involvement.

The next two bios were shorter.

LISA WETHERBY GRAHAM—b. Columbia, S.C., 1957. Youngest of four daughters. BA University of South Carolina. Worked summers as waitress on Broward's Rock. Joined Binton and Associates Public Relations after graduation. Member Broward's Rock Runners Club. Consistently places in top ten her age group in 10K races. Ranked tennis player. Married George B. Graham 1985. No children.

JOEL MURRAY GRAHAM—b. 1971, Broward's Rock. Senior Broward's Rock High School. Moderate discipline problem. Suspended one week forging doctor's excuse for unexcused absence. C average. Three tickets for speeding in last year. Not active in school sports, but committed mountain climber. Skilled at rappelling. Enjoys scuba diving.

Annie spread the sheets out on the table, glanced at the clock—she needed to hurry—and scrawled, as fast as she could, the questions that had to be answered.

1. HOWARD CAHILL—Beneath his mask of self-control, how did he really feel about Sydney's infidelities?

2. CARLETON CAHILL—Was he angry enough at his father's remarriage—which he saw as a betrayal of his mother—to murder Sydney and attempt to place the blame on his father?

3. SYDNEY CAHILL—Was Sydney a voracious destroyer of mar-

riages or was she a sadly romantic woman seeking a love that she never found?

4. DORCAS ATWATER—What turned her from an unremarkable island matron to a distraught, apparently neurotic recluse? Why did she quarrel with Sydney?

5. GEN. COLVILLE HOUGHTON—For health reasons, he obviously wasn't involved with Sydney, but from his comment the night of the murder—"People stay in their own beds, follow the rules, world'd work damn sight better"—he was well aware of Sydney's proclivities. Just how offensive did he find her?

6. EILEEN HOUGHTON—The general's wife. No overt connection with Sydney so no—

Annie's pencil stopped, scoring the sheet. For Pete's sake! Eileen Houghton was trying her damnedest to get involved. Why? How had she put it? "The general and I are appalled at the obvious miscarriage of justice which is occurring." Why should she be so exercised over Howard Cahill and whether he was in jail? Maybe the answer to that was blindingly simple. Maybe Howard, who had swept Laurel off her feet, was equally attractive to another middle-aged woman. This one with an old, unpleasant husband. Annie wrote: *Does Eileen have a secret passion for Howard? Did she want to see him single, hoping that she too would be widowed before long? Does she envision going from the General's Wife to the Wife of the Chairman of the Board?*

"Maybe, maybe, maybe," Annie said aloud. Dorothy L. took that as an invitation and leaped into her lap. Annie scratched her behind the ears. Suddenly that two o'clock appointment with the general's wife looked enticing indeed. She checked the time and hurried on to the next question.

7. BUCK BURGER—Buck strayed off the preserve, no doubt about it, but he valued his family. Obviously, Billye kept him on a loose leash. Had her patience run out? Was Sydney planning, in a crazy romantic fashion, to make some kind of public announcement of another Great Love—and did Buck veto the plan?

8. BILLYE BURGER—Conversely, had Billye finally had enough of Buck's women? Was Sydney the last straw? Or had Buck, in a midlife crisis, broken the pattern and served notice he intended to dump Billye for Sydney?

9. JIM TOM MARSHALL—A very tough fellow. How much would he do for Buck Burger?

10. GEORGE GRAHAM—A tomcatter, on his own admission. But a man who didn't like the even tenor of his life disturbed. Had Sydney refused to leave him alone? Was he afraid he might lose Lisa?

His insistence to his son that no one had left their home the night of the murder indicated pretty clearly that someone surely had. Was it George? Or was it Lisa?

11. LISA GRAHAM—She knew George was susceptible to other women. After all, he'd fallen for her when married to Kathleen. Was she afraid Sydney might steal him from her?

12. JOEL GRAHAM—What did he mean when he said, ". . . I don't know where the hell everybody was!" He'd tried to tell his father about "last night," the night Sydney was murdered, but George refused to listen. Joel was worried before he talked to his father and even more worried afterward. But he insisted that he hadn't seen anything. So what could he possibly know about the murder?

Annie shook her head in frustration and circled Joel's name with question marks. The teenager obviously intended to do as his father ordered and keep quiet. Maybe the only way to find out the truth was to confront George Graham.

She gathered up the bios and her list of questions, put them in a neat stack, and jumped to her feet. Time to talk to the General's Wife.

FIFTEEN

Annie reached the Houghtons' dock first. The lagoon looked like pea soup under the unseasonably warm sun. The sawgrass along the shore rippled in the springlike breeze. A pileated woodpecker—Annie's friend from Wednesday morning?—drummed cheerfully against a gum tree. Annie walked out on the pier and the row of sunning cooter turtles on a fallen red maple limb flopped into the green-scummed water one after the other as neatly as if choreographed. Half submerged near the bank was an old blackish log—then Annie saw the wide, flat snout and two obsidian eyes watching her intently. She stepped back a pace. "Honey," she called, "it's yours, all yours."

The toasty feel of the sun against her skin reminded her that summer was just a dream away. The wind-rustled grass, the soft liquid call of Carolina doves, and the erratic splash-splashes in the water evoked the coming lazy, hazy days of summer, when Annie could sit in the shade of an umbrella and read the latest books—except when she was busy at Death on Demand, ordering, shelving, and selling. But this scene was hypnotic, a siren song that threatened to lure her away from the world.

That was why the residents of Scarlet King had bought homes here, of course.

She walked to the end of the pier, shaded her eyes, and surveyed the pine-rimmed shore. There was the Cahill pier and a glimpse of the gazebo. The next house, of course, was her own. At the end of their pier, Max's cheerful yellow raft moved languidly on its line. Annie could see only a portion of the house. The rest was screened by the pinewoods that separated their place from the Cahills'. But this vantage point afforded an excellent view of the Grahams' garages, Joel's apartment, the pool cabana, and the gingerbread top of the Victorian mansion. The Burgers' imposing Tudor house appeared fortresslike on their cleared, bare-bones grounds, which looked desolate amid the thick undergrowth and pinewoods of the other properties. The nearest house, as the jackdaw flew, was that of Dorcas Atwater, on the other side of the fourteenth green from the Houghtons'.

Annie's eyes strained. It was hard to see into that undergrowth-choked backyard. Brief flashes of light glittered beneath the canopy of a weeping willow. Was it the sparkle of sunlight reflecting off glass? Annie strained to see.

"An excellent view." Her voice was smooth, almost oily.

Annie turned to face Eileen Houghton, who looked every inch a general's wife this afternoon in a Cambridge wool gabardine suit and blue patterned blouse with an ivory background. She was rather formally dressed for a meeting on a pier, but, of course, she'd been to a hospital board meeting that morning. In the soft glow of the sunlight, her round face had a healthy glow beneath the sleek gray-blond coronet braid. She looked younger than her age, except for the grim set of her lips, which emphasized the deep lines on either side of her mouth. "I wanted you to see for yourself," she continued in that unctuous voice. "The distances across the water are very short indeed."

Annie again faced the lagoon. Eileen Houghton stepped up beside her. The faintly peachlike scent of her perfume contrasted with the nutrient-rich odor of the water. She shaded her eyes. "It's been just over two years." A musing tone. "Dorcas Atwater has brooded for two years over Ted's death. Everyone can tell you how her personality has changed. She is obviously unbalanced. When Sydney was killed, it should have occurred to me at once. The night Sydney died was the anniversary of Ted's death. But"—her stocky shoulders moved in an impatient shrug—"I assumed the police would do their duty. Instead, they focused at once on Howard—"

Annie looked at her sharply. Did she say his name with a lover's care? No. There was not even a flicker of emotion on the stolid, healthy face turned toward Annie.

"—which is completely ridiculous. In fact, the police haven't even talked to all of us and when I call, some underling asks me to leave a message and it's much too delicate for that. I must speak to someone in authority." Her pale blue eyes gazed at Annie without especial warmth. "You seem to have entree somehow to the investigation, so I am going to tell you about Ted Atwater. When the police know, they will surely see that the solution to Sydney's murder is quite obvious." A wasp zoomed close to her cheek. Eileen brushed it away. "Two years ago, Sydney rang my bell late one evening. She was hysterical. Fortunately, the general was out, attending a meeting of the Retired Officers' Association. He is on the board, of course. Howard Cahill was out of town. Sydney was shaking and sobbing, almost incoherent, begging me to help. She thought I'd been a nurse. I went with her. Ted Atwater was dead in her bed. Obviously a myocardial infarction. Unfortunately, it had occurred during coitus. Which was readily apparent. I agreed to help Sydney. I don't quite know why. But I did." Her voice held an echo of self-surprise. "We rolled him in a sheet and managed to get him downstairs and into his rowboat. I dropped his clothes and shoes in, too. We removed the sheet. Sydney was no help. She kept wringing her hands and wailing and asking what we were going to do. I told her to go take a bath and go to bed. I walked back home, got our rowboat, rowed to the Cahills', attached Ted's boat to mine and began to row across the lagoon. I had intended, upon nearing the Atwater property, to overturn his boat. It might then look as though he'd gone out on the pond, suffered a heart attack, and fallen into the water. Of course, it was awkward that he had on no trousers or shorts, just an undershirt, but heart attack patients sometimes feel their clothes are constricting them." Another shrug. "It was surely better than being found in Sydney's bed. And I thought the water—well, anyway, that's what I intended. But the towline broke or slipped loose. I rowed about, trying to find the boat, but it was a very dark night and I had no flashlight. Then the light came on at the end of the Atwater pier and Dorcas was out there calling for him. The Burger lights were on, of course, as they always are. Buck heard Dorcas calling and he yelled to ask if she needed help. She said yes. So I had no choice. I couldn't look for Ted's boat any longer. I rowed home." Annie could imagine those muscular arms, the oars slipping in and out of the water with calm regularity.

Eileen smoothed an invisible wrinkle from her skirt. "I suppose Dorcas insisted on knowing the results of the autopsy. And autopsies are so complete. Then the police returned to her the blue sapphire earring that had snagged in his undershirt. A rather distinctive earring. A circular antique silver setting. Dorcas recognized it, of course. And then she knew." She gazed thoughtfully across the water at the uncontrolled growth in the Atwater grounds. "Interesting, the reaction of some personalities to stress."

She said it in the same even tone she might discuss an unusual bridge hand.

Annie felt chilled, despite the silky warmth of the sunlight. "You want me to tell the police?"

Eileen's light blond brows knitted. "I suppose they will want to talk to me. It's just a little awkward. The general doesn't know, you see."

"Will he be upset?" Annie asked gingerly.

Was there the beginnings of amusement in those light blue eyes?

"About the circumstances? Oh, nothing surprises him. He would think it was all very irregular. But he would approve of my effort to shield Dorcas. He has very strong feelings about the sanctity of the home." She glanced toward the Cahill property. "It would certainly confirm his opinion of Sydney."

"He didn't think much of her, did he?"

Eileen Houghton was no fool. She looked at Annie quite candidly. "Not much at all. Thought she was a whore. But from my understanding of the force involved in the attack, I am quite certain the general was not involved. He would not have been physically capable of such an attack. With his heart condition . . ."

The implication was unnerving. Eileen Houghton's appraisal saw the general as physically—but not mentally or emotionally—incapable of brutality against Sydney.

No wonder Annie felt cold. It was obvious the general's wife looked at everyone with a cool and objective eye.

Now those coldly dissecting eyes fastened on Annie. "You must tell the police as soon as possible. Right now. It sickens me to think of Howard, locked in a cell for no reason."

"Oh, he's out of jail," Annie said reassuringly.

That surprised Eileen. She blinked and for an instant her face was totally expressionless. "He has been freed?"

"On bail," Annie clarified. "He's charged with murder"—again an emotion Annie couldn't read touched those pale eyes—"but he's definitely free on bail."

"I drove by his house a few minutes ago. He usually leaves his car in the turnaround. I didn't see it." Eileen didn't quite say it accusingly, but she was by no means convinced.

"I don't know where his car is," Annie replied. "But I talked to him just a little while ago. There was a limousine there, and Howard was getting ready to leave for Sydney's services."

Annie remembered one of those hundreds of facts she'd absorbed from the bios. Private services. Who would be there to mourn?

"Eileen! Eileen!"

Eileen and Annie looked toward the shore.

The general stood by an obelisk sundial beside their patio.

Eileen lifted her hand in acknowledgment and started for shore. "Coming, Colville." She didn't noticeably hurry, but she moved briskly, her footsteps echoing from the wooden planks of the pier. After a moment's hesitation, Annie followed.

The general remained in place, a gnarled hand clasped to his cane. He wore brown slacks, a white shirt, a tweed sports coat, but his attire looked as military as any uniform. Perhaps it was because he stood and awaited them so rigidly, his shoulders back, his head lifted imperiously.

As they came close, Annie realized he was staring at her fixedly, his dark liverish eyes unwavering, his downturned mouth a tight line between his sunken cheeks.

"Jezebel," he trumpeted at Annie.

Eileen's colorless eyebrows rose for an instant, then her face was as bland as cream stucco. "Colville, Mrs. Darling is just leaving. You know that she's involved with trying to help Howard. You'll be glad to hear Howard's been released from jail." She turned toward Annie with an empty social smile. "Thank you so much for coming over. It's time now for the general to rest, but we'll be—"

The ugly blue pulse in Houghton's right temple throbbed. "Bitches. All the young bitches." He stooped toward Annie, eyes blazing. "Don't think you can sneak around and not be found out. Walk four miles around the pond. Every morning. Saw you this morning, young woman. Shameless. Going to that boy's room—he without a stitch of clothes and you with the bare legs of a harlot."

Eileen's head jerked toward Annie.

Annie was so shocked that she stared at the general open-mouthed.

"Fornicating with a boy. Sickening. Leading him to evil."

"General Houghton, I know you aren't well, but you would be better advised to ask before you jump to—"

The old man's chest heaved with his anger and his words rolled over hers. "Graham ought to horsewhip that young pup—and that's what your husband ought to do to you! Lash those bare legs till you'd cover them forever."

Annie exploded. "And maybe your wife ought to wash your mouth out with soap, General. I doubt if she could clean up your filthy mind. I wanted to talk to Joel Graham before he left for school—and he'd just stepped out of the shower. But he did have on a towel, General. Next time when you eavesdrop try to get a little closer. Or maybe you could get a seeing eye dog to help you out. As for Joel Graham, that kid's about as obnoxious in his way as you are in yours. But I *know* that he knows something about Sydney's murder—and I'm going to find out what it is!"

She whirled and stalked off, leaving a shocked silence behind her.

She had reached the tennis court at the Cahills' when she began to

shake with delayed reaction. That nasty old man. That creep. That—
she stumbled to a stop remembering the hatred and fury in his eyes—
that murderer?

Then she heard, finally piercing her anger, a plaintive cry.

"Annie? Anniiieeee?"

Voices carry beautifully in the humid air of Broward's Rock, even
husky, soft voices like Laurel's.

Thank heaven, Laurel was finally home—and *not* with Howard. Annie broke into a trot.

The husky call came again. Annie picked up speed, although it was
hard to run in leather shoes. Laurel didn't sound like she was in trouble,
but, with everything that had happened, Annie wasn't taking any
chances. Besides, she had her orders: collar Laurel and find out what
she was up to.

Annie tore along the asphalt path. She hardly spared a glance at the
gazebo. Would she ever see it—ever—without an instantaneous hideous
recall of Sydney, crumpled on the steps?

Tendrils of Spanish moss fell victim to her breakneck speed. Frantic
rustlings in the undergrowth signaled the rapid redeployment of startled raccoons, squirrels, cotton rats, and marsh rabbits. Her right foot
stubbed on a pinecone, kicking it into a pile of leaves. A chuck-will's-
widow, the nocturnal bird that sieves insects from the air during its low-
level flights, rose sluggishly, rudely awakened.

When Annie burst out of the green tunnel onto their patio, she was
too breathless to gasp in amazement, but she couldn't help exclaiming,
"Laurel, what are you *doing?*"

If Posey could see Max's mother now, there would be no doubt in the
circuit solicitor's mind that he was dealing with a loony.

Laurel's pith helmet tilted at a rakish angle because of the saucy
ponytail that peeked from beneath the back rim. However, despite the
severity of her khaki blouse and slacks (Banana Republic safari special?),
Laurel, as always, exuded femininity. Only the pale pink of the scarf at
her throat and the deep rose of her knapsack reflected her usual exqui-
site taste.

She beamed at Annie, her dark blue eyes aglow with fervor.

"Contemplation, my dear, that was the way of so many of the saints.
They withdrew from society, seeking the solitude of caves or desert.
Their names are legion, from Saint Acepsimas to the Blessed Hugolino
Zefferini." A tiny frown. "It's too bad the water level is so high here. No
caves at all. And, of course, the desert is *such* a distance. But a determined mind can circumvent all such geographic deficiencies. I shall
retreat to the center of Scarlet King Lagoon." She gestured at her knapsack. "Of course, the *modern* approach is to eschew deprivation. I heartily concur, don't you, Annie?"

"Uh—"

"I find that I think best when the body is nurtured." Another tiny frown. "Your refrigerator is somewhat of a challenge. I'm sure"—a reassuring smile—"that it is only because of the recent move. I know, when you have a moment free from murder and mayhem, you will sally forth and return with a plethora of fruit. I do so enjoy mangoes and kiwi. Such *cheerful* fruits. But one must accept what one finds, though I would never have expected such a concentration of"—a delicate pause —"calorie-laden edibles: chocolate chip banana loaf, chocolate truffles, chocolate crispy cookies, chocolate chip sour cream cake." Laurel's head tilted sideways in gentle inquiry. The pith helmet began to slip. Laurel righted it with an elegantly manicured hand, the shell-pink polish rosy in the sunlight. "Surely, my dear, an overabundance from the cacao plant? But do not be concerned. Ever self-reliant—as all the dear saints encourage—I surveyed the possibilities and have put together a supply of appropriate foods for my retreat." She pointed proudly. "Strawberry yogurt, lemon-flavored seltzer, carrots, cantaloupe, and pepitas."

None of it sounded familiar to Annie, but she didn't keep track of Max's grocery purchases. To each his own. She looked down and noted the minicooler, but her glance locked on Laurel's footwear. Desert boots?

Laurel lifted one foot, which still managed to look disgustingly dainty, and wriggled it. "So appropriate for sojourns in the wilds."

Annie checked the lagoon, simmering in the toasty sunlight. Lime green algae, produced by the unseasonable heat, drifted sluggishly. The lagoon did indeed look springlike, creeping marsh pennywort and canna lilies abounding. But it did not resemble Annie's vision of the wilds.

Annie smiled hugely. "A splendid idea, Laurel," she said heartily. "Meditation is just the thing." Though she doubted that the Desert Fathers or any of the other reclusive saints would consider Laurel's topic suitable. But no matter. What safer spot could exist? Laurel in midlagoon aboard a rowboat sounded dandy to Annie. She bent to pick up her mother-in-law's rose knapsack.

A muffled ring sounded.

In a half crouch, Annie froze and stared at the knapsack. Some kind of bomb?

Another muffled peal.

Laurel swooped to the knapsack, unzipped the top, and lifted out a mobile phone. "Hello." Her husky voice exuded good cheer and happy expectation. "Oh, Henny. How are you, my dear?" Attention, then a vigorous headshake, setting the ponytail in motion and the pith helmet adrift. A slim hand patiently righted it. "One must always have the proper perspective," she said gently. "I am taking the *long* view. I find it quite inconceivable that poor, irritable Mr. Posey—one sometimes is forced to wonder if he suffers from intestinal maladies—so typical of those with protuberant stomachs—too much food *confuses* the digestive tract—will persist in his unjust accusations. And the judge—such a *forceful* man—agreed ever so strongly with dear Mr. McClanahan that it was quite unjust to deny bail to Howard and to me. Of course, even I will admit that dear Howard is being difficult. I told him it was quite absurd, his present posture, he suspecting Carleton and Carleton suspecting him. I told him that he should go home and have a good *talk* with Carleton, though I very much fear that his normal good judgment is impaired. Parents are always so fearful for their children." She nodded emphatically; the pith helmet dropped over her right ear. Shell-pink nails flashed as she put it back in place. "And *I* intend to meditate upon our future course." She listened for a moment, then a genuinely affectionate smile touched her classic features. "Why, yes, she's here. She just came." Laurel handed the receiver to Annie.

Annie took the phone and braced herself. She wasn't disappointed.

"The thing about it is, it's a job. You don't have to take a lot of crap." A world-weary voice. "And I'll take on almost anything. If I feel like it."

"Another private investigator."

"Right. And I don't like crooked races."

Annie almost asked how she'd like a crooked nose, but she couldn't resist trying to recall PIs who were into horses. A Dick Francis book? But his heroes weren't private eyes. Did anybody else do horses?

"Horses," she muttered.

Laurel, who was rummaging in her knapsack, looked up inquiringly.

"A big hint," Henny offered in her own voice, thick with satisfaction. "Louisville, Kentucky."

"Oh, dammit," Annie said irritably. "I give up. Another first novel?"

Laurel made a sympathetic moue and fished out a pair of binoculars.

Annie gritted her teeth. How maddening to be the object of Laurel's pity! As her mother-in-law arched one perfect blond brow in inquiry, Annie tried to move her lips into a smile, but knew she probably looked as sincere as Sergeant Barbara Havers when she was assigned to work with Inspector Thomas Lynley. Annie's smile improved. By golly, there *was* a first novel she had read, Elizabeth George's *A Great Deliverance.* Her smile fled. She couldn't figure out any way to work it into the conversation.

"So unsporting of you, Annie, to give up so quickly. *The Last Private Eye* by John Birkett. Michael Rhineheart, PI. A very good read."

"Thank you, Henny." She was proud of her polite tone. "When I have time for fictional murders, I'll keep it in mind." Inspiration struck. "Right now, I'm concentrating on the job. Just like Sergeant Havers."

"Touché," Henny retorted, goodhumoredly. "Best book of the year. Listen, Annie, I've found out about the valentine. Of course, a few points about the valentine are obvious. Anyone with any investigative abilities can figure out *when* Sydney received it and *how*." Henny waited expectantly.

Annie recalled her conversation with Ingrid the day before. Annie wasn't above regurgitating what she'd learned from the source, one of those talents honed so sharply in college. "Obviously," she replied smugly, "from the content and from Sydney's presence at the gazebo, she received it Tuesday."

A deflated pause. "Oh. Well. Glad you figured it out, too."

Annie knew she should be ashamed to accept equal credit. After all, it was Henny who'd reported this deduction to Ingrid, who had, in turn, passed it along to Annie. But Arthur Abdel Simpson, the protagonist of Eric Ambler's *The Light of Day*, was a con man, a petty thief, an inept police spy, and one of Annie's favorites in all of mystery fiction. Obviously, there was no hope for her character.

"Do you know *how* Sydney got it?" the bookstore's greatest reader asked grumpily.

Time to restore Henny's good humor. "No. But I'll bet you've found out."

Laurel, too polite, of course, to evince impatience, turned her profile to Annie, displaying her exquisitely fine bone structure, and gazed at the lagoon. Meditatively.

Henny made no effort to disguise her satisfaction. "I hit pay dirt with Sydney's maid, Reba. She's savvy. Young, pretty, working for the Cahills while she goes to school at night. Going to be a nurse. She said Sydney was boring, but nice. Never thought about anything but men, clothes, men, jewelry, men, makeup, men—but you get the point. Anyway, Reba stayed late Tuesday to help Sydney dress and see about any last-minute things for the party. One of the caterer's men brought the note to Reba about six, said he'd found it on the patio on a table. He was supposed to be setting the tables up for drinks and snacks."

Six P.M. on Tuesday.

"Six o'clock! Henny, you realize what that means?"

"Of course. It's another indication that the murderer must be a resident of Scarlet King. Unless," and her tone dismissed it, "one of the caterer's employees put it there. Reba ran over the list of workers and said so far as she knew not a single one had ever had any contact with Sydney, other than in a service capacity. And Reba's sharp. Just in case we're wrong, I called the caterer's and offered a hundred-dollar reward to anyone who can give me information about the valentine."

Six o'clock. Two hours before the gate was opened for the party guests. The deadly little circle around the Scarlet King compound had just grown tighter.

Annie admired Laurel's contemplative pose. Right on a par with *The*

Thinker and a lot more graceful. "What did Sydney say when Reba gave it to her?"

Henny's voice was suddenly crisp and unforgiving, just like Miss Marple's when she unmasked the murderer in *What Mrs. McGillicuddy Saw.* "Sydney was as excited as a child, thrilled to death." A pause that bristled with anger. "She grabbed Reba and they did a waltz step around the room. Sydney said it was one of the loveliest days of her life, to have a secret admirer on Valentine's Day. She chattered about it the whole rest of the time she was dressing, thinking out loud as to who it might be. No new names, though."

"Oh, Henny."

"Yes. Cruel sport, Annie. I'm not prepared to like this murderer." Henny cleared her throat. "Reba swears by Howard Cahill, said he is the kindest, most thoughtful man. Said he didn't have much to do with Sydney, but he was always polite to her."

That, of course, would be preferable to outright ugliness. But what cold comfort on a winter's night.

"Anyway, why would Howard hand-place the damn thing on a table on his own patio?" Henny asked impatiently. "He's supposed to be a corporate genius. You'd think he would have put it in the mail to imply the sender was barred from the compound."

"Double bluff?" Annie suggested.

"Hmm, maybe. Well, I'd like to hook him up to Bihn's lie detector—if it wouldn't blow all the fuses." There was a subtly Oriental lilt now to a calm, unhurried voice. "That would show Bihn that I admire his skill in police science and am willing to consider modern inventions." There was the faintest stress upon "consider."

"Henny, isn't enough enough?"

"You don't recognize it?"

"It's been a busy year." She tried to keep the whine out of her voice.

"Certainly, Annie. But you will enjoy Superintendent Bamsan Kiet. The protagonist in *Pigeon Blood* by Gary Alexander. Truly delightful. Such a shame you missed it. And the sequel's already out. *Unfunny Money.*"

Annie decided to distract Henny. "Howard's out of jail."

"Hmm." A thoughtful pause. "What's Laurel up to?"

Annie smiled at her mother-in-law, who smiled meditatively in return. "She's going to go out in the middle of the lagoon and meditate."

"Hmm. I suppose that's safe enough."

Annie felt a prickle of concern. "Why shouldn't it be?" she asked sharply.

"I don't know," Henny said slowly. "I just have bad vibes. I think somebody really nasty is at work. Really nasty. Take care of Laurel, Annie." She spoke with such grave intensity that Annie's prickle turned into a chill of foreboding. As the line went dead, Annie looked sternly at her mother-in-law.

"Laurel, are you planning something I should know about?"

The glow of innocence emanating from her mother-in-law would have done justice to Marian Carstairs' children in *Home Sweet Homicide.* "Annie, I give you my word, I am simply putting myself in the hands of Saint Jude. And *that* shall be that." A beatific smile.

Shouldering her knapsack, Laurel started down the path to the lagoon. She only paused long enough to trill, "Oh, Annie dear, perhaps you should check the answering machine. Such an *intriguing* message from Chief Saulter."

SIXTEEN

As Annie hurried into the garden room, she tried to dismiss her uneasiness about Laurel. After all, what mischief could her mother-in-law get into in the middle of a lagoon? It was, in fact, an inspired spot for her. Meditation might be good for Laurel. Open her mind to new vistas. Annie suppressed a shudder. God knew, the vistas Laurel perceived were challenging enough. They scarcely needed for her to improve her reach.

"Loony tunes," Annie muttered, heading for the bamboo table and the answering machine. But at least Dear Old Desert Boots was now safely in the middle of the lagoon, whatever she might be contemplating. Annie glanced at the clock. Almost five. The good news was that Max would soon be home. The bad news was that her mind churned with facts, suppositions, and uncertainties. She felt no nearer a solution to Sydney's murder than when she had begun the day, eager to sink her teeth into the bios. Surely somewhere in the mass of information she'd processed, there lay the clue that once perceived would lead unerringly to the murderer. Just like the locket in *Caught Dead in Philadelphia.* What she needed was time to analyze, correlate, and interpret. Instead, she'd been buffeted with surprise after surprise. Now there was Laurel's somewhat enigmatic farewell. What could be intriguing about a message from Frank Saulter?

Annie punched the Play button on her answering machine.

"Uh. This's Frank Saulter. About half past three Thursday afternoon. Uh. Listen, Annie, Posey's madder'n a coon dog after a skunk bath. Judge reamed him out, wanted to know if Posey didn't understand grounds for bail. Anyway, Max's mom and Cahill are on the loose. But if they step out of line, Posey'll clap 'em back in jail faster'n Charles Paris can down a drink."

Annie smiled. Simon Brett was one of Saulter's favorite authors. Saulter always stocked up on the latest books from Death on Demand when he went fishing.

"Uh." A lengthy pause, emphasized by the whirring of the tape. "Thing is, Posey's got another string to his bow. Eyewitness says"—he cleared his throat—"says Sydney was all over Max Tuesday morning on your patio. Course"—now his words raced—"witness says you were there, too. Said you looked mad as a hornet. Now, maybe you ought to give me a ring about this."

Annie yanked up the receiver, then paused and took several deep breaths. All right, all right. She was going to keep her cool. No way was she going to lose it. Calm, cool, collected, a woman far above petty jealousy in regard to her husband, even when provoked by licentious witches.

Max frowned at the busy signal. He replaced the receiver, and leaned back in the luxurious embrace of his red leather chair. "At least," he said plaintively to Annie's picture, "you are finally home." He quirked a blond brow. "I don't suppose," he addressed her serious, *responsible* gaze, "that I can lure you out to the club two nights in a row? After all, I *did* spring Laurel today, which entailed spending entirely too many hours in the company of the greatest trial lawyer in South Carolina. Something I would only do for my mother. Now look, Annie"—he offered his most charming and persuasive smile—"everything's okay for now. Right? Laurel's out of jail. Howard's out of jail. Posey's on the mainland." A frown replaced his smile. "Laurel." Max sat bolt upright. "Annie, I feel it in my bones. Laurel's up to something!" He grabbed for the receiver.

"Yeah, Annie. 'Preciate your calling back."

Annie tried to keep her voice neutral. "How's ev—"

Just as the chief launched into speech. "You try—"

A silence.

Saulter cleared his throat.

Annie, proud of her hard-won control, opted for a lateral approach. "Anything happening, Chief?"

"Posey's sweating."

"Does he think he made a mistake, charging Howard?" She picked up a pen and sketched a pig mopping its snout.

"Naw. Posey's sure he's guilty as hell. But he's afraid of Howard's influence. A lot of calls are coming in. Howard's got friends in high places." A pause. "So does Max's mom. Would you believe the Archbishop of Canterbury?"

Annie would.

"Sheesh. Posey kept calling him 'Your Eminence.' "

"Wrong church. And only for cardinals."

"Whatever. Posey's nervous. He knows his case is circumstantial. I mean Harry K. Thaw, they had him dead to rights. This one's more like the Cullen case in Fort Worth. But Posey's got the physical evidence, Cahill's jacket with his wife's blood on it, the mace with his fingerprints."

Annie drew a mace, the prongs dripping blood. "It's Howard's mace, so why shouldn't it have his fingerprints on it?" she asked reasonably.

"Oh, sure. Defense counsel can make arguments. Then there's his alibi. Posey thinks it's a put-up job, but he's afraid of the effect Laurel might have on a jury."

"God knows," Annie said simply.

"Right." Saulter sighed unhappily. "So maybe you and Max better get prepared."

"Max and I? Why?" She didn't intend to make it easy for him.

"Uh, Tuesday morning." His voice faded away in embarrassment.

Annie could imagine Saulter's ears. She drew a hound with drooping ears, fished around in the telephone table, found a red pencil, and added color.

"Somebody—uh—saw it all."

So far as she knew, she and Max had been unobserved, enjoying their morning together on the patio until Sydney arrived in her almost sheer negligee and honed in on Max like a Sidewinder missile. "So who told you?" She tried to keep her voice smooth, but it twanged like barbed wire.

"Can't reveal the name of a witness."

Obviously, his source had to be a resident of Scarlet King. And she would find out. She hadn't spent her youth devouring mystery fiction from Anthony Abbot's *About the Murder of the Clergyman's Witness* (pen name of Fulton Oursler, who is much better remembered for having written *The Greatest Story Ever Told)* to Dornford Yates's *Blind Corner* (a jolly novel typical of British upper-class reading between the wars) to be stymied in this quest. But there was no reason to fuss at Frank. He was male and did have this pukka-sahib mentality about not violating confidences. But she would find out.

"Oh, well," she said carelessly, "it doesn't really matter."

Saulter heaved a sigh of relief. "Sure glad you understand, Annie."

"No problem." Any woman would have seen through the false geniality in her voice.

"Great. I kind of thought this might make you kind of mad."

"Mad. Why should I be mad? It didn't amount to anything anyway." Only Max and Agatha knew better and, thank God, considering their present relationship, Agatha hadn't yet progressed from growls to speech. As for Max, he'd been pretending nothing had happened since the episode occurred. "I suppose I *did* look a little grouchy. I'm not a morning person." That, at least, was the truth. "It wasn't Sydney's silly behavior that irritated me, it was being interrupted on my own patio with my own husband in time that belonged to us. It was outrageous." Annie took a deep breath and reminded herself that she mustn't speak with such an edge in her voice. Dulcet, that was the ticket. She inserted a soft laugh. "You can imagine, Frank, how it would bug you to have someone drop in unexpectedly at breakfast."

Saulter spit it out in a rush because, obviously, he hated having to say it.

"The witness said she was in her nightgown and she sat on Max's lap."

"So *difficult* to be accurate when spying," Annie trilled, then realized with a pang of horror that she sounded just like Laurel. Was it *catching*? But Frank's words were evoking Tuesday morning in her mind and she lost it.

"Listen, Frank, Sydney was a slut who made passes at anything in pants!" Annie knew she shouldn't lose her temper, but my God, she'd hardly ever been madder in her life! "And you can tell Posey for me that no female will ever get her slimy paws on Max. Not while I have a single breath left in my body. That bitch! Sashaying over to my house, *ignoring* me, talking to Max, and batting her eyelashes like Theda Bara with palsy! Then turning to go and taking a little stumble, right into Max's lap. I mean, it was disgusting!"

She tried to catch her breath.

Saulter sighed.

"I mean, actually, I felt sorry for the poor thing," Annie said stiffly.

The chief's sudden bout of coughing sounded suspiciously like suppressed laughter. "Yeah. Sure. I mean, obviously, nothing to it. Thing is, though, Annie, you might want to phrase it a little different when you talk to Posey."

"Talk to Posey?"

"Yeah. He's been on the phone with—with the witness. He's coming over to the island tomorrow morning. To finish up his investigation."

"No sweat," Annie snapped, slamming down the receiver.

Which was dumb. Frank couldn't help it that one of her neighbors wanted to make her a laughingstock—or maybe send her to prison.

Annie stalked into the kitchen and riffled through her papers on the breakfast room table. She found the map of Scarlet King Lagoon and the surrounding properties.

Annie saw it in a glance. Their patio couldn't be observed from the Cahill, Houghton, Burger, or Graham properties. And it hadn't been the general on his morning perambulation because he had passed by more than a half-hour after Sydney finally left.

But straight across the lagoon was the Atwater house.

"Dorcas Atwater." Annie said it aloud. For some reason, a vision of Agatha flashed into her mind, Agatha with her eyes blazing, emitting a growl that rivaled the Daytona 500.

Max frowned as the message came on. "We are unable to answer the phone right now." He almost hung up, then caught the start of a new message. "Max, I'll be back in a few minutes. Going to talk to Dorcas Atwater. Listen, Laurel's okay." Max tensed. "She's out in the middle of the lagoon. Meditating. See you in a little while."

Meditating? It *sounded* innocuous. Actually, it sounded delightful. Laurel in the middle of the lagoon.

Max replaced the receiver, straightened his desk blotter, and began to hum. Time to go home. Annie would be there soon. And tonight the special at the club was mulled-down shrimp served piping hot over grits, a low-country specialty, a mixture of cooked bacon, onions, brown sauce, and shrimp. Annie loved it!

As the sun dropped behind the pines, the temperature rapidly chilled and Annie was reminded that it was still February. She shivered and wished she'd grabbed a sweater. As she hurried along the darkening path, a fetterbush quivered and a black snake flashed deeper into the undergrowth. Annie bolted ahead. She knew it was harmless, but there was something in her that didn't like a snake. Her pace redoubled when a little ground skink darted across the path. She burst out of the woodlands onto the Atwater grounds just as a water turkey flapped past.

The house huddled in darkness as it had the evening before.

Annie's eyes adjusted to the deep dusk, and she could discern the pitch of the roof, the darker masses of azalea bushes, the ghostly grayness of the pier.

A red dot glimmered for an instant among the shifting shadows in a grove of willows. A faint sour smell of cigarette smoke drifted on the light night breeze. Annie recalled the flashes of brightness that afternoon as she and Eileen surveyed the lagoon. Binoculars, no doubt.

Dorcas was there. Hidden in the shadows. Spying. Morning and night. And telling tales.

When she wasn't paddling about the lagoon in the dark reaches of the night.

"Mrs. Atwater." Annie's voice rang out angrily. Oyster shells crackled beneath her feet as she strode up the path.

The cigarette glowed brightly, subsided.

The mournful cry of a loon wavered in the chill night air.

The cigarette flared again and then a bright brief arc traced its path into the water.

Annie's neck prickled, but she kept on going. When she reached the willows, she could discern a figure slumped in a deck chair behind a screen of trailing branches.

"Mrs. Atwater, you were spying on us Tuesday morning. I don't like being spied on."

"I wasn't watching you. I don't care about you." A simple statement of fact, utterly convincing. "I was watching the slut."

Annie didn't need to ask who Dorcas meant.

A heavy sigh. A thin hand fumbled wearily in the pocket of the terrycloth robe. Dorcas put a cigarette in her mouth, fumbled again. A click. In the flash of the lighter, lank hair framed dull eyes, flaccid cheeks, the downturned gash of a mouth.

"She's dead." There was the faintest hint of satisfaction in the toneless voice.

"And you're glad, aren't you? Did you kill Sydney? Did you row back across the lagoon that night and find her in the gazebo and beat her to death?"

The cigarette glowed. Dorcas inhaled deeply, blew out the sour cloud of smoke. "I could have, couldn't I?" A little high giggle began, then trailed away. "But I never thought about her being dead. I always thought about her surrounded by males, ready to pounce. That's what men are. Animals. Hanging around women like her. She was—" Vile words spilled out in an ever increasing tempo, her voice hoarsening. "She went after every man. Every one of them. She killed my husband." She peered up at Annie. "You never knew Ted, did you? He was— I always thought he was wonderful. But he wasn't, was he? Everybody laughs, you know, about Ted. It isn't funny. It was ugly. So ugly. Ted died and it didn't matter to her. She just kept on going, every man she could find. Old, young, it didn't matter to her. Not if they could screw. She would have had your man, too. You don't need to think she wouldn't."

Annie didn't bother to answer that. Her trust in Max would only underscore Dorcas's betrayal. Instead, she demanded, "Why did you tell the police about Tuesday morning? Are you afraid they may start to wonder about you? And what you were doing on the lake the night Sydney was killed?"

"The police." Her voice crackled with hatred. "I hate the police. They thought it was funny, too. The way Ted died. I'd never talk to the police. I don't have to tell them what I did that night. I'll never tell them what I did. I'll never tell the police anything."

Annie's neck prickled again. Because she believed Dorcas Atwater. So who had told Saulter about Sydney coming on their patio Tuesday morning?

Dorcas giggled again, a high, snuffling noise. "I was watching her. And you. And I watched the general watch you. He sneaks around in the mornings, looking in windows, don't need to tell *me* he doesn't. Goes to bed early. I know. I watch everyone. But he has night blindness. That's what the general has. Night blindness. Silly old fool. He'd go after women, too, if he could. So it serves him right. Silly old night-blind fool. Just a nasty old man. But all men are nasty, that's what's true. Ted, too. Ted." And the giggles splintered into sobs.

Annie could have gone the other way around to go home, gone past the Houghton house, told the general she knew what he'd done.

But she didn't.

She was, she realized soberly, as she hurried across the bright white no-man's-land at the Burgers, more than a little afraid of the general.

Max cupped his hands and bellowed into the darkness. "Laurel, Laurel!"

The unmistakable husky voice flowed back across the water. "Max dear, I hear quite well. How are you this evening?"

"Fine, sweetheart." He peered into the impenetrable darkness. A thick cloud cover. No moon. Black water. "Listen, aren't you going to come in for dinner? Annie and I are getting ready to go to the club. Mulled-down shrimp."

Max smiled at Annie, who nodded abstractedly. Annie looked a little peaked. She must be overdoing. She'd barreled out of the woods like a bat out of hell. Certainly, they should make it a point to relax this evening. Perhaps they shouldn't even discuss the crime. After all, everything was under control right now. He'd spotted Howard's car in the turnaround as he passed the Cahill mansion, so he was safely home. And Laurel meditating in the middle of the pond suited Max just fine. Dampish, but so nicely removed.

"So thoughtful of you dear children to remember me. But I'm just in the *midst* of my meditations. And I'm drafting quite a lengthy petition to Saint Jude."

Annie made gestures.

"A food cooler?" Max whispered.

"Full," Annie retorted, succinctly.

"One cannot be concerned with base appetites at such a moment," Laurel caroled.

Annie avoided looking at Max. She scooped up a pinecone and tossed it from hand to hand.

"Very dedicated of you, Mother."

Annie's left eyebrow lifted sardonically.

"We'll check with you when we get back," Max called reassuringly.

Annie waited until they were in the midst of dessert—Max had cheese and crackers and Annie a French pastry with shaved chocolate on top—before she told him about Saulter's call and her confrontation with Dorcas Atwater.

She shivered. "Max, she's really spooky. And—and scary. And terribly sad. The night of the party was the second anniversary of her husband's death. Don't you know how awful that must have been, to look across the water and see all the lights and hear the music? Oh Max, I can see her bashing Sydney, bashing and bashing and bashing. But," she added fairly, "it wasn't Dorcas who told the police. It was the general. Max, he snoops!" And she described the general's window-watching activities, as related by Dorcas.

"The jerk," Max said crisply, putting down his knife. His normally equable face—Annie did enjoy those dark blue eyes, that clean-cut chin, those lips—looked stern. "What's with this trespassing? I won't have the foul-minded old lecher prowling around my property first thing in the morning."

"Foul-minded is right," she retorted, and she told him of the general's interpretation of her call on Joel Graham.

Max progressed from stern to outraged in an impressive matter of seconds. Then he paused. "In a towel?"

"Yep. And ready to drop it at the first hint of sociability on my part. Joel likes married women."

As she said it, she and Max forgot dessert, forgot the general, forgot their vow to relax.

They both spoke at once.

"Married women!" she cried.

"Sydney!" Max exclaimed.

They looked up at the dark windows of Joel Graham's garage apartment.

"You don't suppose he's already asleep?" Annie asked.

Max snorted at that and ran up the outside steps to knock at the door.

They gave up finally because there was no telling when Joel would return. Obviously, he had no real supervision.

"We can catch him in the morning before school," Annie said reassuringly, as they walked quietly through the dark tunnel of the pinewoods toward home.

The path curved. In the light of Max's flash, a gray fox, a marsh rabbit clamped in its jaws, paused for an instant, then bolted into the undergrowth.

"Oh my gosh," Annie cried, grabbing Max's arm.

"Not a good evening to be a marsh rabbit," Max observed.

As they walked up to their patio, a cheerful and welcoming oasis of light in the darkness of the night, Annie said determinedly, "We need to be just like that gray fox. He's a stalker, creeping up on his prey, then pouncing. That's exactly what we need to do."

Of course, it is never easy to get underway with any project. So many things to do.

A last check on Laurel.

"Ma, are you *sure* you want to stay out there all night?"

"Oh, quite sure."

"Isn't it uncomfortable?" Max persisted.

"My dear, comfort is in the eye of the beholder. When one thinks about dear Saint Osith! Marauders attacked her monastery and cut off her head! Why, I can't complain about a few earwigs."

"Of course not," Annie agreed heartily.

A delicate pause. "Of course, my sojourn might be even more effective if you and Annie should care to join me."

Blue eyes and gray exchanged horrified glances.

"We wouldn't dream of it, Laurel," Annie called. "In no way do we feel that our powers of meditation are on a level with yours. Why, Max and I might even interfere with your meditation." Annie felt a bit muddled. Was it something like radio waves?

Max was even more emphatic. "Some are called and some are not."

Annie murmured, "And when you're hot, you're—" She broke off at Max's chiding glance.

Laurel's husky voice exhorted, *"Do* give some thought to our great Saint Peter, my dears."

Annie was reluctant to ask, but she was a dutiful daughter-in-law. "Why Saint Peter, Laurel?"

"He always encourages us to persevere despite our inadequacies. Good night. God bless."

Then Dorothy L. was insistent. Annie put down a second serving of Braised Beef Tips. "You're too little to eat this much. You're going to be all stomach. Believe me, you'll never make your way in this world if you are all stomach."

Dorothy L. merely ate faster and purred harder.

And it took time to collect their papers and arrange themselves comfortably in the garden room. Max seemed to think it was better for them to share the wicker chaise longue. Annie popped up once to put TV trays on either side, a second time to get each of them a fresh notepad and a pen, a third time to pour cups of chocolate raspberry decaffeinated coffee, a fourth time to prevent Dorothy L. from chewing on the leaves of a poinsettia. Were they really poisonous? She dropped the kitten into Max's lap.

Max, of course, watched Annie fondly, with that nice eagerness that presaged amatory frolics.

Annie said sternly, "Max, we have to work. You don't want Laurel to go on trial, do you?"

A mischievous grin. "The circuit courts of South Carolina would never be the same."

Annie settled beside him, but underscored her commitment to duty by removing his hand from her thigh and placing it on Dorothy L., who purred like a motorbike going downhill.

Max draped his arm around Annie's shoulders.

Annie removed it and tucked a pen in his hand.

"Okay," Max said agreeably. He poised a pen over his pad. "What's first? Motives? Alibis?"

Annie gazed thoughtfully at the fresh notepad. "We need to start over."

Max sighed. "Start over? It's only Thursday night, yet I feel like I've spent my life with these people. I know more about them than I ever wanted to know. Howard Cahill won a welterweight championship as an amateur boxer. Sydney Cahill won a couple of thousand at bingo at the club and she spent it all hiring a private detective to try and trace her father. No luck."

Annie twisted to look at him in surprise.

"I did not spend today twiddling my thumbs," he said with great dignity. "After I got Laurel out of jail, I kept digging."

Annie shuffled through the bios, found those for Howard and Sydney and added the new information.

She looked at him expectantly.

"Joel Graham. Some young guy answering to his description's been renting a room at the Sleepy Glade Motel on Highway 278 every Monday afternoon. Lisa has a housecleaning crew in on Mondays."

So the garage apartment wasn't available.

Annie wrote down SYDNEY and wreathed the name with question marks.

"The general is a man of very regular habits. Up at five A.M., oatmeal and orange juice for breakfast, walks four miles, spends an hour or so in his study, lunch, afternoon golf, an early dinner, to bed at nine P.M. A little surprising that your scream woke him Tuesday night as he has some hearing loss, plus he takes a sleeping pill every night."

"It was a hell of a yell," Annie said with some pride.

"Eileen Houghton was watching a late movie in her bedroom and didn't hear anything. The movie ended and she started downstairs for a glass of milk. That's when she realized the general's light was on. She hurried into his room, afraid he had been taken ill, and was startled not to find him anywhere. She was just coming outside to search for him when he arrived with the group of witnesses."

"Wonder why he didn't tell her?" Annie asked.

"He said her door was closed and he assumed she was asleep. Saw no need to disturb her. Besides, he was certain the scream had come from next door. Thought he ought to hurry."

"Did he tell you all this?"

"Actually, Barb tackled him. Told him she was police lieutenant Sigrid Harald."

Annie grinned. But obviously Barb had not gone on to explain that Lieutenant Harald, Margaret Maron's protagonist, was with the NYPD.

Max continued, "Recently, Buck Burger threatened to cut off the money when his son, Buddy, moved out on his wife and shacked up with a girlfriend."

"What happened?"

"Buddy decided to come home. He's still seeing the other woman, but circumspectly."

"Ah, those Burger men," Annie said dryly.

"As for Billye, if she's ever strayed off the reservation, nobody knows about it."

"Did you see Buck and Sydney together Tuesday night?" Annie asked. "I did, and I had the feeling he'd done some feeling there before."

"That would be no surprise," Max agreed.

"You know," Annie mused, "it would help a lot if we knew when the mace was taken from the stand in the front hall. Did you find out anything on that?"

"No luck there," Max admitted. "Some people think they saw it during the party, others swear it was gone. So who knows?"

"It makes a big difference. If it was in place at the end of the party, after all the guests left, it looks a lot worse for Howard."

Max disagreed. "No way, honey Look at it. Laurel was with Howard after Sydney ran down the path and Carleton rushed off toward the tennis courts. If Howard killed Sydney, then he was taking advantage of Laurel's appearance to set up a kind of alibi. After he left her, he would have had to run like hell to get to the gazebo so the mace would have had to be already hidden there. Certainly there wouldn't have been time for him to return to the house, get it, then go to the gazebo."

Annie poised her pen over her pad. "Max, that's brilliant."

"Of course," he said modestly.

"Not the bit about Howard. We all know that. No, I mean you've put your finger on the critical point. Who had the best opportunity to kill Sydney? Come on, let's work it out and rank everybody in order."

"What order?"

Annie was patient. "The most likely to the least likely in terms of opportunity."

There were a few interruptions. A pause for more coffee. An interlude with Dorothy L., who had to be dissuaded from climbing the macramé plant holder in the kitchen. A frantic search by Annie for the peanut butter. (She could face—temporarily—being out of peanut butter cookies, but she had to have some sustenance to tide her over.)

But finally they finished and exchanged lists.

ANNIE'S LIST

1. Carleton Cahill. He was closer to the gazebo than anyone. Howard saw him running toward the house, clutching a bloody jacket.

2. Howard Cahill. He could, of course, have reached the gazebo in time if he ran—and if Sydney took a walk before reaching the gazebo.

3. The general. If he committed the murder, he could have heard Annie yell and decided to arrive on the scene, playing good neighbor to the rescue. There was absolutely no proof at all that he was in bed and came from his house.

4. Dorcas Atwater. She could easily have paddled across the lagoon after the party ended. But how could she have obtained the mace? Could she have slipped unseen through the gardens earlier? Sure! She could have just finished putting the mace in the gazebo when she accosted Annie on the pier.

5. Eileen Houghton. On the spot, of course, but tricky to see how she could have done it and gotten back to the house before the general came out. However, she could have seen him leaving the house and hidden in the shadows until he passed.

6. George Graham. If he did it, he must have just missed being seen by Laurel. But it was certainly possible.

7. Ditto Lisa Graham.

8. Ditto Joel Graham.

9. The Burgers. Their bodyguard said they didn't leave the house, but either of them could have timed his circle of the property and slipped by. Also likely to have run into Laurel.

Max's list had a drawing of the lagoon and enough X's and O's and arrows to pass for a football coach's blackboard.

MAX'S LIST

1. Howard Cahill
2. Carleton Cahill
3. Dorcas Atwater
4. The general
5. The general's wife
6. The three Grahams
7. The Burgers

The grandfather clock chimed eleven and the glazed gleam in Max's eyes was replaced by a warmer glow.

Annie would have worked longer.

But sometimes Max had such good ideas.

Max slept, of course, the sleep of a man well satisfied with his day and its close.

Annie tossed and turned.

The timing.

More to it than just the spread of moments between Sydney's departure for the gazebo and her discovery by Annie (and previously by Carleton, if he could be believed).

Why Tuesday night?

Because Valentine's Day gave a good excuse for that enticing missive?

Or was there some other reason?

Annie sat bolt upright, her heart pounding.

That splash. That splash that sounded so near. Laurel out on the lagoon.

Annie rolled out of bed and ran for the stairs. At the garden-room door to the patio, her hands fumbled with the lock. Hurry, hurry, hurry. Behind her, she faintly heard Max's sleepy call, "Annie? Annie?" The urgent, desperate, overwhelming sense of something wrong propelled her out into the night.

A single lamp at the far end of their pool glowed golden in the impenetrable darkness.

"Laurel?" Annie heard the sob in her voice, felt the thickness in her throat.

Something awful.

Certainty pervaded her.

She was almost past the pool, racing toward the lagoon, when she saw the crumbled mortar at the corner near the lamp. Three-foot-high porcelain vases sat on low, tiled platforms at either end of the pool. In season, they would hold a profusion of marigolds.

Skidding to a stop, Annie stared at the bereft platform. The vase? Where—

Relief pumped through her. She moved swiftly to the deep end. That splash! Certainly the vase toppling into the pool would be enough to wake her. Her heart still thudding irregularly, Annie peered over the side into the greenish depths, the waters faintly illuminated by the occasional underwater lights spaced every few feet.

"Oh, no," she cried aloud, not wanting to see, not wanting to believe.

Khaki. Oh God, khaki! And wavering tendrils of blond hair.

SEVENTEEN

The water was cold, so cold. Down, down, down. Her hands grappled against sodden cloth, pulled. Oh God, too heavy! She couldn't— Her lungs were bursting.

A splash drummed against her ears, and the water quivered against her. Helping hands. Together, she and Max pulled, hauled, burst up to the surface, Annie gasping for breath. Water slapped into her mouth. She choked, and a scarlet thread of pain laced her chest.

"Hold steady," Max yelled, and he was up and over the side, pulling their deadweight burden onto the tiles. Then he reached down and lifted Annie out of the water, held her tight until her choking subsided.

Her shoulders still shaking, she stared down at the inert form.

Khaki and limp blond hair, darkened by the water.

"Oh God, Max. It's Joel!"

Never again in this lifetime did Annie want to see the kind of anguish that transformed George Graham's face, destroying forever her image of the smooth, self-satisfied, prideful dentist and leaving in its place a shattered figure, with empty, tortured eyes.

He clung to his dead son's hand and cried, over and over and over again, "Joel." Lisa stood rigidly beside the grieving father and the dead son, hands thrust deep into the pockets of her robe, her face flattened with shock.

Chief Saulter knelt beside him for a long time. "Go home for now, Dr. Graham. Please, go home for now."

Everyone was there, of course, roused by the siren, drawn to tragedy and held there by the unspoken knowledge that once again a resident of Scarlet King had killed. They knew. It was clear in the abrupt, sidelong glances, in the way they stood, tense and wary.

Howard Cahill turned to his son. "God, I can't believe this." Howard's face held an unaccustomed look of bewilderment and uncertainty.

Carleton didn't answer. His eyes moved from one person to another.

Laurel stood quietly by Howard, her face sad in repose.

Buck Burger, barechested and barefoot in his Levi's, glowered at Saulter. Finally, he erupted. "Goddammit, Chief, there's a madman running loose on this island. I want complete police protection. How the hell did something like this happen?"

Saulter ignored him.

George Graham was on his feet now. The dentist looked shrunken. He finally turned, at Saulter's continued urging, and began to walk toward his home, his steps shambling. Lisa followed. But she didn't touch him. Her hands were still thrust deep in her pockets, her shoulders rigid.

Buck moved restively, still glowering at Saulter. Billye put a quieting hand on his arm. No matter the hour or circumstance, Billye's unruffled blond hair glistened a pale silver in the light of the lamp. She wore a well-fitting negligee that emphasized her voluptuous figure. Her face was pale and strained. And alert.

Once again a pistol butt poked from the pocket of the general's tattersall robe. His gaunt chin sunk against his chest, he stared coldly at Joel's body. With his balding head and iron-gray mustache, he looked like an ancient and dangerous bird of prey.

As Saulter turned to face the watching residents, General Houghton rasped, "Better ask *Mrs.* Darling why that young man was here—in the middle of the night."

Beside him, Eileen Houghton tensed. She raised a hand, as if to intervene, then let it fall and remained silent. Her face was smooth and expressionless, but her breathing was quick and shallow.

Dorcas Atwater provided the ugly finale. Thin, pale lips stretched wide in her bony face, and she began to laugh, little snickering hiccups of laughter. "Scarlet King Lagoon. A nasty green murky place, that's what it is. Who knows what goes on in the depths of the water—or on the shore. Wouldn't you all like to know?" She turned and lurched a step or two toward Saulter, then began to walk with mincing dignity, her unbelted chenille bathrobe dragging the ground. "Wouldn't you all like to know!"

Dorcas Atwater was royally drunk.

Some sleep, yes, but not enough, troubled sleep that left Annie tired and drained. She poured more coffee for Max and for herself.

"Shouldn't we take some breakfast out to Laurel?"

Despite their pleas, Laurel had insisted upon returning to her boat.

"My vigil is not yet at an end," she informed them with great dignity.

It was, surely, safe enough now. Saulter posted an all-night guard to patrol the circumference of the lagoon. And every security light in the compound glittered until long after daybreak.

Max shook his head. "Let's leave her out there, as long as she'll stay. It gives me cold chills to think of Laurel wandering around this compound. Maybe Buck's right. Maybe there's a homicidal maniac loose. Why would anybody kill Sydney, then Joel? It doesn't make sense."

Annie took another sip of the always strengthening coffee. "What if our guess is right and Joel was involved with Sydney?"

Max shrugged. "In effect, so what? You think somebody killed Sydney because she was cheating on him, then killed Joel because he was the guy?"

"No," Annie said simply. She didn't have to explain. It was Sydney's tragedy that no one had ever cared enough, not enough to really love her, surely not enough to hate her.

But if nobody loved her or hated her enough to kill her, then why—

The phone rang.

"Hello." Annie knew her voice sounded tired and more than a little tense. What next? her mind wondered. What next?

"Dreadful, isn't it," Henny said soberly. "Have you heard about Howard?"

Annie's heart lurched. She had reached the point when any horror seemed possible. "Oh my God, what?"

"Back in jail. Charged with murdering Joel Graham."

Had she and Max been wrong, all the way? And Laurel, too, of course. Was it that simple—or that profound? Had Howard Cahill loved his young wife and suffered tortures over her infidelities? Had a liaison with a man younger than his son driven him to murder?

Henny was still talking. ". . . autopsy report. Broken neck. They think he must have been sitting on that low wall that runs behind your pool. Somebody came up behind him, dropped a dog leash over his head and yanked. Hard. There's a big bruise on Joel's back. The murderer jammed him in the back with his knee when he pulled on the leash. It was quick. But Joel must have lurched as it happened and knocked over the vase that sat there. It's at the bottom of the pool."

"But why Howard?"

"Oh. The leash. It hung in his garage. An old one. Belonged to a spaniel that his wife had. First wife." A thoughtful pause. "Carleton identified it."

Annie glanced out of the bedroom window. She looked quickly past the pool. She didn't like to think about the pool. Of course, rationally, the site had nothing to do with Joel's death. Then again—she paused mid-way in the fastening of an earring—why their pool? An attempt to turn suspicion toward them? But the leash was such a giveaway. Surely Cahill must have known it could be traced. Or had he assumed that no one would connect it to him? Would anyone have done so, had it not been for Carleton?

Her gaze scanned the lagoon.

Where was Max's yellow rubber raft?

Where was Laurel?

Annie glanced toward the half-open bathroom door. Usually Max sang in the shower, a clear tenor. Annie loved to hear him sing, though she made it a point not to say so. Max was quite well pleased enough with himself and his talents. But this morning there was only the splatter of water against the shower tile. Not a morning for singing. She'd better not wait. She finished dressing in a flash and hurried for the stairs.

As she neared the landing, she could hear the scrape of furniture being moved. Hurrying on downstairs, she found Laurel trying to shift an immense wicker couch, which was much heavier than it looked.

Laurel smiled brightly at her. "Over against the wall, Annie, that's a dear."

Annie looked at the wall. Her eyes widened. Where was the tea cart? And the three planters? And the bric-a-brac stand? Her gaze swung around the room. Why was the Ping-Pong table folded? And the pool table shoved against the far wall? Where had Laurel found all these chairs, now ranged in neat rows? They looked suspiciously like the chairs from Death on Demand.

Henny poked her head into the garden room. "I can't find anything that looks like a lectern? I could run— Oh hi, Annie, we're getting everything ready. Listen, I don't even care that you beat me to it God knows, this has to end."

"Ready?"

To say that she had not an inkling was totally accurate. She looked from Henny to her mother-in-law.

Laurel—surely those were fresh khakis—beamed impartially upon them. She clasped her hands, a pose that showed off the luster of her pale pink nails to advantage.

"Dear Saint Jude," Laurel said. "He made it so clear. Of course, I didn't want to distract you, so Henny and I are taking care of everything. I made the calls. Mobile phones are such a convenience. The minute I knew, I started dialing. Henny borrowed the chief's pickup to bring the chairs. Oh, Ingrid says Agatha is *much* happier since Dorothy L. disappeared. Not, of course, that she has disappeared." Dorothy L. raced through the garden room, a streak of white fluff. Laurel smiled. "But in *Agatha's* mind, I'm sure. In any event, I am determined that the mundane arrangements shall not be a burden to you. You must continue to bend every iota of concentration to the task at hand. But you need not worry. I am certain of our course. Such a *remarkable* demonstration of divine guidance." Dark blue eyes glistened with amazement. "Exactly eleven anhingas!"

"Anhingas? Eleven anhingas?" Annie demanded wildly.

"This morning. Such glorious creatures. So *big*. I understand a wingspan of almost *eight feet*. And this morning, eleven of them. Then one broke off and dived, oh so close to the raft, and Annie, she looked just *like* you."

Annie pictured the familiar snakebird or water turkey, with the long sharp beak, glossy black body, and elongated tail. *"She* looked like *me?"* Annie asked faintly.

"Oh, it was a female, no doubt about it. Beige head and neck, rather than black. And, my sweet, it was *you*. So *serious*. So *intent*. So *single-minded,* diving right into the water, spearing the quarry. Why, I understood at once. Eleven o'clock. And you."

The doorbell rang.

Henny moved toward the front hall.

Annie looked at the clock in horror.

Two minutes until eleven.

Dorcas Atwater was the first to arrive. Her hair was combed, but it hung straight and lusterless. Makeup only emphasized her pallor and couldn't hide the dark smudges beneath her bloodshot blue eyes. In the morning light, the ravages of alcohol and sleeplessness were unmistakable in her puffy face. Her pale blue cotton blouse was fresh but unironed, the seersucker skirt wrinkled. As she came into the garden room with Henny, her eyes darted from Annie to Laurel. One eye quivered with a nervous tic.

"I don't see why you called me to come. I heard on the radio that they arrested Howard."

"Howard had nothing to do with Joel's death." Laurel spoke confidently.

Annie glared at her. So nice she knew that. Annie didn't *know* a damned thing. How was she going to stop this, get rid of all these people?

Dorcas pushed back a lank strand of graying hair. "It's all Howard's fault. For bringing Sydney here. If he hadn't brought her here, everything would have been different."

Laurel came forward. "Now, Dorcas, you must stop brooding about the past. You must stop being so angry. Come, you can sit over here," and she led the gaunt woman past Annie. "After all, dear Saint Philip Neri cautioned those who followed him not to be forever dwelling on their sins. He said they must leave a little something for the angels. And when you think of it, surely we should not dwell on the sins of others. *Especially* not on the sins of those whom we have loved, such as your Ted." She settled Dorcas in the second row of chairs. With a little pat on her shoulder, she said, "Do give it some thought, my dear." A kindly smile. "And as Saint Teresa of Avila once wrote a sick prioress, 'For the love of God get well. Eat enough and do not be alone or think too much.' "

Dorcas stared blankly after her.

Annie could sympathize. Though surely Saint Teresa's advice was sound. However, it was likely a strained perception of Saint Philip Neri's advice at one remove. On the other hand— Annie shook her head irritably. She couldn't afford to be deflected.

Max appeared in the archway from the hall just as the doorbell rang again. As always, her heart thrummed. He was such a grown-up Joe Hardy, short blond hair, regular features, an excellent build. His hair still damp from the shower, he looked inquiringly at his mother.

"Do move that piece for me, love," she asked.

Annie darted toward him as he obediently realigned the couch against the empty space along the wall.

"Max," she hissed, "Laurel's done it this time. She's called everybody to come and hear the solution to the murders. Apparently even Posey's going to show up, with Howard."

He bent closer to her. "Who did it?" he whispered. "And how does Laurel know?"

"Max"—it was a muted wail—"*she* doesn't know *anything*. She thinks Saint Jude will direct me at the proper moment, and I will reveal all."

"Oh." Max beamed at her and damned if he didn't look just like his mother. "Why, honey, how could I have less faith in you than Laurel does!"

• • •

Posey was sweating. Annie could have turned up their air conditioning, but she was only glad that someone else was miserable, too. The portly circuit solicitor moved restively in the chair next to Howard Cahill. Posey's six-foot-three-inch bulk dwarfed the chair. In a powder blue suit that strained across his paunch, Posey looked as impressive as a gunny sack. Cahill's navy blue knit shirt and gray cord slacks fit him sleekly. The businessman looked trim, athletic, and in command, despite his obvious status as a prisoner. Carleton slumped beside his father, his long artistic hands tightly twined, his untidy blondish hair dangling over his somber eyes. Chief Saulter was at the end of the row, chin in hand, with a quizzical look.

George Graham sat on the couch. His red-rimmed eyes gazed dully at the floor. His wife held one slack hand tightly in both of her own. Lisa watched Laurel with an unwavering stare.

Laurel was in full spate.

"So difficult for all of us. I feel that in times such as these we should remember the words of dear Saint Bernard. 'In any great trouble, in any strong temptation, call upon your guardian angel, who is your guide and your helper, in any difficulty and in any time of need.' "

Posey glowered. "Look, Mrs. Roethke, I don't intend to sit around here for much longer, wasting the taxpayers' money."

Laurel waggled an admonitory finger at him. "Now Mr. Posey, you know what Saint Thomas à Kempis warned: 'Man proposes, but God disposes.' "

Annie pressed her fingers to her temples. In a moment, Laurel would turn to her and expect in all good faith for Annie to trumpet aloud the name of the murderer.

Laurel nodded firmly at Posey, whose face was turning an unhealthy purple. "As I said," she continued, "this has been a most difficult period for everyone here at Scarlet King. Sydney's life touched all of our lives. For good or ill."

It was suddenly very quiet. Sudden tears glistened in Howard's eyes.

"Her death forced the authorities to focus on her relationship with everyone in this room. And to wonder just what might drive each of us to murder. They wondered if I, because I felt such an immediate kinship with her husband, might have been tempted to remove her. But, of course, anyone who knows me is aware that I much prefer a *civilized* approach to marital rearrangements." A sweet smile.

Annie wondered sourly how the saints would evaluate that attitude.

"The police soon recognized that Sydney was not a faithful wife and so they suspected Howard. Moreover, he refused to make a statement about his whereabouts during the critical moments." Laurel leaned forward and confided gently to her listeners. "So silly of him to suspect his son. But everyone knew Carleton hated his stepmother. And when

Howard saw him running up the garden path from the gazebo, his face twisted with anxiety and panic, and clutching a bloody jacket, what could Howard think?"

"Goddammit . . ." Carleton exploded, his eyes wild.

"He had the jacket?" Posey demanded, lunging to his feet. Frowning ferociously, the prosecutor thundered at Carleton. "Listen here, young man, if—"

"Mr. Posey, please sit down." Laurel waited, bending a stern though pleasant look at him. Annie loved it when Posey sank back into his seat. "And do be patient. If you can." Once again addressing her listeners as a group, she said, "Carleton *found* Sydney dead. When he saw the mace and the jacket, which he recognized as his father's, he panicked. He threw the mace into the pond and ran to the house to hide the jacket."

"By God," Posey exploded, "interfering with the evidence at the scene of—"

Laurel sailed on. "But they were not the only persons abroad in the night. I, myself, was on the premises, to view the roses. As everyone knows, Howard walked me home. He wouldn't have had time to reach the gazebo *before* Sydney, so it's obvious that he isn't guilty. The murderer was within the dark gazebo and attacked Sydney as she walked up the steps. Carleton is innocent because the murderer used Howard's jacket to incriminate him, but Carleton tried to hide it."

Annie was more impressed by Laurel's logic than she would ever be willing to admit.

Posey's face furrowed in laborious thought.

General Houghton rasped, "Absolutely impermissible behavior," and glared at Carleton.

"General Houghton, you were out Tuesday night, too," Laurel observed.

"No secret to that. Responded to a woman's cry. Duty to do so."

"You are quite a believer in duty, aren't you, General? You didn't like Sydney. You thought her behavior was—"

"Disgusting!" A faint red flush touched his sallow cadaverous cheeks. "Women like that deserve what they get."

"Women who are sexually promiscuous, General?" Laurel looked at him inquisitively.

Houghton ducked his head apologetically toward Howard, but persisted stubbornly. "Sorry to dwell on it. But the truth's the truth."

Howard ignored him.

"Others were abroad, too," Laurel continued. She stared at George Graham. He pulled his hand free from Lisa's and hid his eyes for a long moment. Finally, his hand dropped and he looked at Laurel.

"I've gone over it and over it in my mind," George said, "but I still don't understand. Joel tried to tell me something about Tuesday night. I thought he meant he had seen me take the path toward the Darlings. Yeah, I did." His voice was flat and uninflected. "Lisa locked me out and I thought, screw it, I'll go see Sydney. I guess I was a little bit drunk and I remembered thinking she had something going at the gazebo and maybe I'd get in on it. When I got past the Darlings' house, I heard somebody on the path and I didn't want anybody to see me, so I turned around and went home. That's all there was to it. But I knew the police would make it a big deal."

"I asked Joel," Annie offered. "He said he didn't *see* anybody. Then he said, 'I don't know where everybody was.' "

Her words hung in the air. Slowly everyone looked at Lisa.

Including George.

Her chin rose defiantly. "Oh now, wait a minute. Not me, ladies and gentlemen. I had nothing to do with any of it. I told George if he wanted to screw that bitch to go right ahead, and I went into the bedroom and locked the door. And I stayed there all night!"

Annie was surprised to hear her own voice. She hadn't intended to take part. But just like Pam North, she couldn't keep quiet. This was Laurel's show and she fully intended to let Laurel stew in the juice of her creating. But— "Billye and Buck Burger don't share a bedroom. Their bodyguard swears they didn't leave the house that night, either of them. But they could have. And somebody was out on the lagoon in a boat."

Billye gripped her husband's arm.

Doggedly, Annie added, "Buck likes ladies. Sydney had a new love. A wonderful new love she'd found . . ."

Annie stumbled to a stop.

A new love. A *fresh* love.

Oh Lord, of course. It was so obvious. Sydney's lyrical descriptions to her friend, Susie, about this wonderful new and fresh love. And Joel liked married women.

Laurel took up the slack. Her voice was gentle. "Now Dorcas, it's time for you to tell what you know."

Annie looked at that puffy, tortured face.

Dorcas wandered about the lagoon at night, unable to sleep. She was up early in the mornings, too, so she knew about the general's surveillance of his neighbors.

But Dorcas said he was a night-blind old fool.

New love.

A boat crossing the lagoon after midnight on Tuesday.

Married women.

"I can't believe he'd go to bed with *her*," Sydney had wailed to the unresponsive answering machine of her friend.

Laurel still prodded Dorcas. "What did you see the night of the murder?"

Dorcas huddled in her chair and shook her head belligerently. "I hated her, I tell you. She got what she deserved!" She stared at the floor, refusing to look at Laurel.

"Did Joel?" Laurel asked.

"I don't blame her," Dorcas mumbled. "Oh God, women are hungry, too."

Annie saw the sudden comprehension in Henny's eyes.

"Oh," breathed Annie softly.

Laurel nodded in satisfaction and gestured toward her. "And now Annie is going to give us the identity of the murderer."

The funny thing was, Annie knew!

So many bits and pieces:

Sydney's never-ending search for love.

Sydney's penchant for long and intimate conversations.

Sydney's artless prattle to each new love about her old love.

Sydney's distraught message on her friend Susie's answering machine when Sydney found her new love in bed with somebody else.

A message on Monday night.

What Sydney knew, the world would soon know.

Sydney was killed on Tuesday night.

The valentine because the killer knew her weakness.

The gazebo late at night because it was remote from the house.

Annie stood and joined Laurel behind the card table which Henny had set up in lieu of a lectern.

"Everyone needs love," Annie said quietly. "No one more so than Sydney. She looked for love with every man she met. Old or young. Joel"—Annie ached at the pain in George's eyes—"Joel was young and hungry for experience and a long way from truly loving anyone. But Sydney, as always, clothed this encounter, as she did them all, with romance. So she was devastated when she found Joel in bed with some-one else."

George Graham hunched forward, watching Annie.

"Joel told me he liked married women. Women," she repeated. "So he was involved with another married woman. Who could it be?" She looked from one to another and listed them, one by one.

"Lisa Graham. Billye Burger. Dorcas Atwater. Eileen Houghton."

Lisa Graham's dark curls quivered as she shook her head once, sharply.

Billye Burger's smooth face remained unwrinkled and impervious, a tribute to the surgeon's skill, but her large blue eyes sought her husband's and her rosebud lips curved in a perfect O as she mouthed, "No."

Dorcas Atwater hunched in her chair, her face slack. Her dull eyes never left Annie's face.

Eileen Houghton slowly stood. "I won't stay here and be insulted." She looked every inch a general's wife, as usual. Just as if she were on her way to a tea in a white cotton and linen sweater with hand-embroidered roses and a cotton dirndl skirt with a tea rose pattern.

Annie looked at the four women. "One of you became involved with Joel, using him as he was using you. A fair trade, perhaps. Sex for pleasure. No commitment made, none needed. The two of you shared a liking for danger, for chance taking. But Monday afternoon Sydney broke in on the two of you. If Sydney, for all her promiscuity, had been sophisticated, if Sydney had not always believed in love, it wouldn't have mattered. Oh, perhaps a sting to pride. But nothing more.

"But that wasn't Sydney."

Annie's eyes locked with those of the killer.

"You knew Sydney would talk. Her tongue was as loose as her morals. She always talked. To her hairdresser. Everyone knew of her affairs. And if *your* husband found out—"

George Graham gave a deep animal grunt of rage and pain and hurtled from the couch, fists doubled. "You killed Joel! You killed Joel!"

It took Max and Saulter both to stop him, push him back to the couch and down.

The killer stood, twin spots of red in her smooth cheeks the only sign of strain.

"I deny any involvement." Her blue eyes glittered. "You can spin every fantasy you like. But you don't have any proof."

"It has to be you," Annie said confidently. "You were having fun, the kind of fun you had with your first husband. You pushed the limits, didn't you, Joel even coming to your house late at night, to your bedroom. Dorcas knew, that's why she said your husband was night blind. Joel must have come Tuesday night—but you weren't there. When he asked where you were, I'll bet you admitted being out, but you claimed to have seen his father on the path. This kept him quiet for the moment, but you knew he might talk to his father at any time. So he had to die. You decided that almost at once, but you waited until Howard Cahill was back home and could be blamed. You knew that if it ever came out that you'd been involved with Joel, it would spell the end of a marriage you wanted for prestige, even though you had a husband who couldn't—"

The general stood. In his hand was the stubby black Colt .45.

EIGHTEEN

"Come, Eileen!" The general was an old man. But he was a dangerous old man. Not a person in that room doubted his determination or his lethal capability. The pistol pointed unwaveringly at Laurel.

Eileen Houghton lifted a hand in appeal. "Colville, there's no proof—"

"Quiet." He'd barked orders for a lifetime. He would be obeyed.

Eileen eyed him warily, but she said nothing more.

Saulter took a single careful step forward.

The gun swung toward him. "Stop."

Saulter stopped.

"You." The general waggled the gun at Laurel. "You'll come with us. Eileen, see that she does."

Max tensed, leaned forward.

Houghton eyed him coldly. "I never miss. The gun is pointed at your mother. If anyone moves, she dies."

Eileen gave him yet another uncertain look, then, moving with the lithe grace of a tigress, gripped Laurel's elbow. Laurel didn't resist and didn't even look concerned. It took only a moment for Eileen to shepherd Laurel to the garden room door and out onto the patio.

The general backed slowly to the door, the gun rock-steady in his hand. "If you wish to see Mrs. Roethke alive again, do not follow. She is a hostage. The purpose of a hostage is to provide security. When we reach our objective, Mrs. Roethke will be released."

He stepped through the door and slammed it shut.

Max bounded across the floor, hand outstretched.

Chief Saulter's chair clattered to the floor as he tore after Max, catching him at the door. "God knows it's hard, but we have to—"

Posey peered through a window. "They're almost out of sight now. Saulter, you go through the woods. I'll follow down to the lagoon."

But by the time the door opened, Max in the lead, there was the crack of a shot.

And then a second.

"So much anger," Laurel said sadly when her breathless rescuers reached the shore of the lagoon.

The general's first shot had caught Eileen Houghton squarely in the forehead, knocking her backward, killing her instantly.

The second shot he aimed, with deadly efficiency, into his temple.

NINETEEN

Annie couldn't quite reach the hook over the front door of Death on Demand which supported the line of valentines. The stepladder quivered as she almost overbalanced. "Darn," she muttered. Clambering down, she moved the ladder closer to the door and remounted the steps. This time she managed easily, and the valentines fluttered as she lifted down the line.

Agatha stood on her hind legs, one paw stretched up, entranced by this lovely and unexpected addition to her entertainment schedule. She caught a valentine in her teeth and let Annie pull her all the way down the center aisle to the coffee area.

Setting up the ladder by the back wall, it only took an instant to retrieve that end of the line.

Agatha was happily attacking the clump of line and valentines when Annie scooped her up and pressed her face against her sleek black feline's warm silky fur. Agatha scrambled a little and draped herself over Annie's left shoulder.

"Hey, chum, it's great to be friends again."

Admittedly, Agatha didn't purr like a motorboat in a frenzy. And she lacked Dorothy L.'s other endearing trait of throwing herself down on her back and looking up at the attendant human with an adoring gaze.

Agatha was too dignified to act in such a manner.

But Agatha was once again queen of her kingdom, undisputed monarch of Death on Demand. Annie was glad. It was no fun to be around a cat with a broken heart. Dorothy L. was quite at home in the garden room. Had, in fact, chosen a particular chair warmed by the winter sun as her very own. Finally, happiness reigned again at Death on Demand.

The front door opened. Annie looked up to see Henny approaching. Actually, she was stalking down the center aisle in high dudgeon.

So, not quite everybody at Death on Demand was happy.

Henny planted herself solidly in front of Annie, her fox-sharp nose quivering with outrage "Do I understand that you accepted the solution to the February watercolors over the telephone!"

"Not exactly. Now look, Henny, Laurel—"

The most prodigious reader of mysteries in the Low Country exploded. "Discrimination! No question about it Would you let me participate in the January contest through the mail? No. Said the contestants had to be here in person to participate. Calling on the telephone is not and never will be and in no manner can be considered to be the equivalent of being personally on the premises." Henny delivered this diatribe in stentorian tones.

Annie admired her impeccable diction. She tried to say so. "Really good speaking—"

"I won't be fobbed off with puerile compliments. I want you to know, Annie, that I consider myself defrauded." She whirled around and pointed to the watercolors in order. "Tommy and Tuppence in *The Secret Adversary* by Agatha Christie, Lord Peter Wimsey and Harriet Vane in *Have His Carcase* by Dorothy L. Sayers, Nick and Nora Charles in *The Thin Man* by Dashiell Hammett, Pam and Jerry North in *The Norths Meet Murder* by Frances and Richard Lockridge, and Sarah Kelling and Max Bittersohn in *The Bilbao Looking Glass* by Charlotte MacLeod." She swung back to face Annie. "Am I correct?"

"Yes. Yes, you are. But Henny, Laurel beat you to it." Annie held up a hand to forestall another outburst. "And not by phone. Ingrid had that a little wrong. Laurel dropped by. She saw the watercolors and left a note for me."

"Left a note here?" Henny demanded suspiciously.

"I'll show you," Annie offered peaceably. She led the way up the central aisle to the cash desk and retrieved a note on lavender-scented paper from the middle drawer and handed it to Henny.

Henny studied the list suspiciously. "Christie. Sayers. Hammett. Lockridge. MacLeod." A sigh. "All present and correct. Well, sorry I fussed so. But I thought Ingrid said Laurel had telephoned—"

"Oh, she did. She called later. From the airport in Atlanta."

"Atlanta. Where's she going?"

Annie couldn't quite decide how to phrase it. But, after all, Max's mother was a single woman of the world. At the moment. Still, it was perhaps a tad unconventional. To say the least. Oh well, nothing for it but to answer.

"She and Howard. A little trip. To Paris." She recalled Laurel's husky voice. "You understand, my sweet. I must help him put the past behind. I do think I'm very good at that sort of thing. And Paris, of course. So good for lovers. Young and old." Annie hadn't pursued the topic.

"Paris! Bully for Laurel." Henny grinned wickedly. "May she have a saintly good time."

Carolyn G. Hart is the winner of both an Agatha and an Anthony for *Something Wicked*, the third in the Annie Laurance Darling mystery series, and the Macavity for *A Little Class on Murder*, the fifth in the series. *Deadly Valentine* is her sixth novel to feature Annie and her third mystery for The Crime Club. Hart and her husband, Phil, live in Oklahoma City, where she enjoys mysteries, tennis, cats, and plotting the further adventures of Annie and Max.